I0688157

Edmund Quincy

The Haunted Adjutant, and Other Stories

Edmund Quincy

The Haunted Adjutant, and Other Stories

ISBN/EAN: 9783744748315

Printed in Europe, USA, Canada, Australia, Japan

Cover: Foto ©Andreas Hilbeck / pixelio.de

More available books at **www.hansebooks.com**

Edmund Quincy

THE

HAUNTED ADJUTANT

And Other Stories

By EDMUND QUINCY

EDITED BY HIS SON, EDMUND QUINCY

BOSTON

TICKNOR AND COMPANY

1885

Copyright, 1885,
BY EDMUND QUINCY.

All rights reserved.

University Press:
JOHN WILSON AND SON, CAMBRIDGE.

CONTENTS.

AN OCTOGENARY FIFTY YEARS SINCE.

1

AN OCTOGENARY

FIFTY YEARS SINCE.

CHAPTER I.

"A gentleman he was of the old time,
    One of those relics of the golden past
    That stand among the things of modern times
    Like column-shafts taken from ruins hoar,
    Yet perfect in themselves, to grace the halls
    Of our secluded mansions."

VICTORINE, A MS. DRAMA.

IT is now something more than fifty years ago that I was an undergraduate at Harvard College. My home was in a remote part of New England, which in those days before railroads were imagined, and before even stage-coaches were introduced, was practically as far distant as the most remote of the last batch of new States is at the present day. My intercourse with my family was necessarily confined to two or three short visits during the course of my college life, — one of which I accomplished on foot, — and to a straggling letter, which now and then came lagging along in the saddle-bags of the mail-carrier, and which by a wonderful coincidence, scarcely less remarkable than the consentaneous decease of Adams and Jefferson, sometimes fell into the hands of its lawful proprietor. Whatever may be the sins of the gentleman who now presides as tutelary genius over the mail-bags of the nation at Washington, I believe that no one who remembers the way in which the epistolary intercourse of the country was managed half a century ago, would care to exchange the system of which he is the head for the good old plan which encumbered the days of the Confederation. I truly believe that the ingenuous youth who are relegated by their anxious sires to the universities of the petty princes of Germany to learn how to act the part of Republican citizens, and who often return, spectacles for men and angels, wiser than their masters, with beard and hair streaming more meteor-like than theirs, and transcending even the transcendentalism of the newest school of philosophy, in short, as Tacitus says, *Germanis ipsis Germanior*, — I say I truly believe that these rising hopes of our country are more liable to be regularly and easily interrupted in their more important pursuits by the arrival of long-drawn-out epistles, full of the exploded doctrines of the New England school of philosophy and religion, though three thousand miles removed, than I was at a distance of little more than a hundred and fifty.

Be these things as they may, whenever one of these loitering missives did arrive, it was sure to contain, among much excellent advice and sound instruction, an injunction to take the earliest opportunity of visiting old Colonel Wyborne, a distant relative of the family, and one to whom my father was under serious obligations for good services done him before the Revolutionary war compelled him to retire from Boston. Like a foolish boy as I was, I postponed complying with this repeated injunction from year to year. I felt a natural awkwardness about going near twenty miles to see an old gentleman, of whom I knew nothing with certainty, except that he lived in the most complete seclusion, and whose reputation for eccentricity, much exaggerated by common report, made me rather nervous about my reception. I much preferred spending my holidays in the congenial society of my dear old aunt Champion, and begrudged the monstrous piece that a visit twenty miles off would cut out of the longest of my available vacations. But at last my continued negligence drew down upon me a severer rebuke than I had yet received, when I was on my summer's visit during my junior year, and I was laid under the parental command (in those days the highest earthly authority) to devote the ensuing Thanksgiving holidays to a visit to this venerated relative. Upon my return to college I made it my earliest business to write an apologetic letter, excusing my long delays, and asking his permission to pay my respects to him during the Thanksgiving week. In due course of time I received a cordial affirmative, couched in the most courteous and condescending language, disclaiming any right on his part to expect such a sacrifice of time and pleasure on mine, but at the same time giving me full credit for my readiness to make it, and expressing the warmest pleasure at the idea of seeing once more in his solitude the son of his old and valued friends. The elegance and urbanity of his letter, as well as its spirit and fire, prepossessed me strongly in favor of the venerable writer; and though I could not but be conscious that I did not deserve all the commendations that he bestowed upon me, yet I resolved that my conduct should be such in future, that he should have no reason to think them misplaced. My curiosity was now awakened with regard to his character and history, and I lost no time in endeavoring to learn what I could respecting them from the kind oracle to whom I have before alluded.

On the very next Saturday I found myself sitting opposite my excellent aunt Champion, separated from her, as she sat in her high-backed arm-chair, only by the small mahogany table from which the cloth was just withdrawn by the faithful Dinah, revealing its polished surface and carved edges; and which reflected in its rosy depths the images of the aspiring decanter, rising with a graceful swell from its firm base to its tapering neck, filled with the rich vintage of the most fortunate of " the islands of the blest;" and decorated, as were the wineglasses, — perfect cones, resting securely on their apices upon the tall stems, — with a galaxy of stars, and festoons of ribbons with fluttering bows. The beams of the afternoon's sun, struggling through the leaves of the garden trees, shone aslant, with a pleasant autumnal glow, upon the carpet just behind her chair. My good aunt, when she filled her glass, and half in jest and half in earnest, gave her invariable toast, "THE KING" (a political heresy which the sterling excellence of her wine went far to palliate), looked like some dame of a former age, who had burst her cerements, and returned to upper air to reveal some ancestral secret to her youthful descendant. Having duly drained my glass in honor of his Britannic Majesty (for my excellent relative, orthodox in all points, abhorred heel-taps), and incontinently replenished it, I held up the brimming beaker to the light, and admiring the rich hue of the liquid ruby,—glowing with a richness and depth of tint which might have put to shame any cathedral-window in the world,—I sighed, and, betwixt game and earnest, said, "Ah, my dear aunt, we must make the most of this good wine, for it is now hard to find. The confounded Revolution has demolished half the cellars in the country."

"It is so indeed!" the good lady responded. "It was but last week that I dined with Governor Hancock, and I assure you the wine was scarcely drinkable. Indeed, his Excellency apologized for it by saying that his cellar had gone to the Devil during the war, and that he was but just getting it to rights again. As for his wine having gone to the Devil, I could easily account for that, for the biggest part of it had gone down the gullets of the Sons of Liberty. But that he should have been so besotted with party madness as to have neglected to keep up the well-earned fame of his cellar, is amazing — he who was acknowledged to have the best in the Province! I could almost pardon his treason sooner than this abominable folly," she said, and consoled herself with an emphatic pinch of snuff.

"It is, indeed," replied I, "a sad defect in his character. It was not so in the good old times of the royal governors."

"Bless you, my dear boy! no, indeed! that it was not," rejoined my good aunt. "Why, the cellars of the old Province House were a perfect history of the Colony: they were the very archives of good-fellowship. The old gray-headed negro butler who was transmitted from one governor to another for many years, had a history for every pipe and bin; and many a good story could he tell of the merry times of Burnet and Pownal. Ah! they were sad fellows, and had a set of roystering blades about them. All this, you understand, however, was under the rose; and their revels were so managed as to give as little offence as possible to their righteous subjects. It was pretty well understood, however, that, like old Noll, they were more given to seeking the corkscrew than the Lord."

"Our gentlemen, too," said I, "have lost much of the spirit which honorably distinguished their fathers, who would have submitted to a reproach on the fair fame of their ancestors as on that of their cellars. These confounded politics have distracted their attention from matters of real importance."

" True enough, true enough!" rejoined Mrs. Champion. " And there you have another blessed consequence of this glorious Revolution! What can you expect of men who make a boast of despising their claim to an honorable descent? They deserve to drink bad wine for the rest of their days. Cellar pride cannot long outlive family pride." She ceased and sighed.

A short pause ensued, which I profitably filled up by sipping the genial juice with the reverence which the thought that it was the last of a generous stock was fitted to inspire. My dear aunt sat silent, tapping her snuff-box with her fruit-knife, and evidently absorbed in sad meditation on the degeneracy of the times, and on the change which had stolen over the little world in which she lived, and tinged with a more sombre hue the evening of her days.

Willing to divert her mind from this melancholy abstraction, I reverted to the subject immediately before us, and, throwing an air of sympathy and interest into my manner, I inquired, —

" Pray, my dear aunt, what may be the history of this good wine?"

" This wine," she replied, starting from her revery, " this wine is the Quebec wine, so called from the circumstance of its having arrived in harbor on the same day on which the news of Wolfe's victory was received. My husband immediately christened it with the name of that glorious battle, and always, as long as he lived, nursed the infant liquor with peculiar care. One pipe of it, I remember, he forthwith, on the very day, despatched to John Wyborne at Sanfield."

"What!" interrupted I, "old Colonel Wyborne ? He is the very person I wanted to ask you about; and this is certainly a pleasant introduction to my inquiries. Pray, aunt, what manner of man was he ? For I am going to spend the next Thanksgiving holidays with him."

"John Wyborne ! He is a nobleman of God's own creation, a man of ten thousand. I have known him from his boyhood, and have never known a man on whose mind and body Nature had more plainly stamped GENTLEMAN. However, I have not seen him for these twenty years; for, since I laid down my carriage on your uncle's death, I have never been to see him, and it is more than twice that number of years since he was in Boston; so that it is not unlikely that time may have made some inroads on his outer man. But I will answer for the freshness of his mind and his heart."

"I think you may safely do that, my dear aunt," I replied, "for I have proof of it under his own hand and seal;" saying which, I produced his letter to me, and by my aunt's request read it to her, she having mislaid her spectacles. Her eyes glistened as I proceeded; for the characteristic animation and point

and high-breeding of the letter, evidently awoke recollections and feelings which had long slept, and
carried her back to the days when they were both
young and hopeful and happy. When I had done,
and restored the epistle to my pocketbook, after a
moment's musing she said, —

"Ah! that is like him: that is like John Wyborne. What a man was lost to the world when he
forsook it! That was the only mistake he ever
made — except, indeed, his taking the wrong side in
the late Rebellion."

"I have heard," said I, "that he is the least in the
world of a humorist, though no one seems to know
much about him. Do you know what induced him
to give up the world and retire to Sanfield in the
prime of his life?"

"Oh, yes!" she replied. "I know all about his
history. But as to his being a humorist in the usual
acceptation of the word, I do not believe a word of it.
I have sometimes thought that a distinction should
be made in that order of nature between the bad
humorists (by far the larger division) and the good
humorists. The first are a set of selfish, peevish
wretches, the torment of their wives and servants,
and the annoyance of their neighbors; who think
that the reputation of oddity which they have cultivated will cover and excuse the multitude of their
vexatious though petty iniquities. The second class
is composed of men of the finest natures and gen-
tlest dispositions, whom some unlucky crook in their

lot has put a little out of conceit with the world and its ways, and who, withdrawing from the beaten paths of life, pursue by themselves what seems to them the chief good of existence, indifferent to the wonder and contempt of those who are in hot chase of the more generally recognized objects of human pursuit, and in whose heart it is not easy to conceive of any other motives of human action. This sort of men, however, are most fastidiously careful never to permit their oddities to chill the kindliness of their hearts, and to interfere with the comforts of others : they ride their hobbies with so careful a rein, that they never run against or unhorse any of their neighbors whom they meet prancing on theirs on the King's Highway. A humorist in this sense it cannot be denied John Wyborne is."

"But what was the disturbing cause," I inquired, "which made him shoot from his sphere ? Was he crossed in love, or ambition, or business ? Or what might it have been ? "

"Why, he can hardly be properly said to have been crossed in either," replied my aunt ; "and yet it was certainly disappointment that drove him into seclusion. But it is a long story — too long to be told now : we will reserve it for some of our winter evenings."

"But pray, my dear aunt," I remonstrated, "give me a skeleton of his history and character, if you have not time to dissect them scientifically " (I was at this time dipping into medical and anatomical books), "for I may not see you again before I pay my visit ; and I should be sorry to venture into such a curious country without some sort of a map for my direction."

"Well, well," good-naturedly rejoined my aunt, "you were always a spoiled child, and, never having been refused anything you thought proper to ask for, I suppose that is a good reason for your not being denied anything now. So fill your glass and mine, and we will drink the good Colonel's health." Which having been duly performed, my aunt proceeded : " John Wyborne's father was a merchant in the golden days of the town (commercially speaking, I mean), when it had a free trade to all parts of the world, and no man asked of any New England ship whence it came or whither it went. In that world, before colonial policy or custom-house officers, old Mr. Wyborne flourished, and made a princely fortune, for those days, or, indeed, subsequent times ; for he left at his death no less a sum than fifty thousand pounds sterling. When the Colonies had grown into importance enough to attract the attention of the ministry at home, and restrictions were laid upon the trade of the Province, Mr. Wyborne withdrew from business ; and obtaining admission into the General Court, and afterwards into the Council, spent the remainder of his days agreeably enough in annoying the Governor, and doing his best to thwart all his favorite measures, and cut down his salary. In the intervals, however, of these useful and pleasant avocations, he found time hang rather heavily on his hands, and bethought himself of taking a wife to help him bear the burden. In those days, as now, it generally happened, by some chance or other, that a man with fifty thousand pounds in his pocket was not long to seek for a wife. Mr. Wyborne was no exception to the rule, and before many months he was the husband of Miss Armytage, a daughter of one of the oldest families in New England — or in Old England either, for that matter. I have heard my mother tell of the splendid style in which they lived in their fine house in King Street: there was no family in the Province who approached them in their manner of living. They had no children till the birth of Colonel Wyborne, in the year 1701.

"Mr. Wyborne died in the full prime of his life, in the year 1711, when his son was but ten years old; but his widow survived him for many years. Colonel Wyborne was reared in the usual style of that day; was flogged by Master Cheever at the Latin School into a competent knowledge of Latin; and, after the usual transmigrations from the fagging freshman to the dictatorial senior, he took his degree in the year 1720. He remained at Cambridge for three years, — till he proceeded Master of Arts, which was then a usual thing for those who could afford the expense. Having thus finished his academical course, he resolved to visit Europe, — an undertaking of no common occurrence in those days, when it was thought little less than a tempting of

Providence for a man to cross the ocean, unless it were to bespeak a cargo of English goods, or to look out for a grateful recipient of salt fish and lumber; which, of course, altered the moral bearings of the transaction altogether. Mrs. Wyborne most strenuously opposed her son's plan, and urged against it all the arguments which she could draw from the perils of the sea and the temptations of the shore, — a species of logic which I have remarked to make but little impression upon the understandings of young gentlemen who have been infected with a propensity to do as they liked, and had the power in their own hands of doing it. Dr. Cotton Mather, too, employed a whole afternoon and evening in attempting to defeat a project which would remove from his congregation one of its wealthiest members for an indefinite period, at the very time of life when his own influence might be most certainly fastened upon him, and who might not, improbably, return with a yearning after the more liberal atmosphere of the Manifesto Church. Maternal entreaties and ecclesiastical warnings were, however, in vain, and to London he went by the next ship that sailed for home. Not long after his departure, his mother consoled herself for his loss by marrying the Rev. Mr. Selleck, minister of the town of Sanfield, where Colonel Wyborne now lives. For a year or two after his departure, his young contemporaries and friends received frequent letters from him, giving full and glowing accounts of his success, beyond his hopes, in accomplishing the great objects of travel. A variety of circumstances, which I cannot now recapitulate, aided by his ample means, prepossessing appearance and address, and also by the novelty of his character as an accomplished transatlantic, introduced him into the brilliant circles of wit and fashion which distinguished the reigns of George I. and George II. He was well received by ' the wicked wasp of Twickenham,' was domesticated at Lydiard a few years later, and when in Dublin was admitted to a share in the somewhat unclerical frolics of the Dean of St. Patrick's. His success, however, was not confined to that disappointed though brilliant coterie; for he was admitted to the dressing-room of Lady Mary Wortley, had bowed at Sir Robert's levee, and was well received at court. His good fortune accompanied him to France, where he had an opportunity of witnessing, and, I fear, of partaking, the profligate revels of the Regent Duke of Orleans, and was well acquainted with Voltaire in his prime. The blandishments of Paris, however, did not detain him long from Italy, where he lingered for two years, seduced by its delicious climate and immortal ruins. At the end of two years he returned to England; but before this time his correspondence with his Boston friends had flagged, as correspondences are apt to do, and soon after breathed its last. His intercourse with his mother was kept up till her death; but, from the distance at which she lived, we in town gleaned but scanty accounts of his adventures. In fact, from

about the year 1726 or 1727, we almost entirely lost
sight of him ; and, as years rolled away, his image
grew less and less distinct in the mind's eye of his
best lovers ; and it was pretty well understood that
he had lived so long in the sunshine of courts and the
fellowship of wits, that he was unfitted to return to
the austere and somewhat pedantic society of New
England. The gentlemen who now and then went
home on business could only learn that he lived in
the north of England, for the most part, and but
seldom visited London. Fifteen years from the time
of his departure passed away, and all expectation of
ever seeing him again was abandoned, when one day
the ship 'Speedwell' was said to be below, from London. This was much more of an event in those days
than now, and the talk of the town for some time
before and after it occurred. My husband immediately took a boat, and visited the ship in the roads,
and soon returned with the strange news that John
Wyborne was on board; and that was not all, —
that he had brought his wife with him. Here was a
surprise. His wife ! Why, we had never heard
that he was married, or even thought of such a
thing ! Who was she ? How did she look ? Was
he much changed ? My husband, however, broke off
my exclamations and inquiries by the intelligence
that the returned prodigal and his English spouse
were to be our guests until they could take possession of their own house. This information threw
me into a little of a flutter, for I was but a young

2

housekeeper then; and though pleased with the idea of seeing my old playfellow again, and gratified at his choosing my house as his temporary home from amongst the many hospitable roofs of friends and relatives proffered to his acceptance, still, I could not but feel a little anxious, lest the difference should be too marked between the appliances of luxury to which he had been accustomed at home, and the more humble though substantial comforts which I could provide. And then his wife — an English-woman, too! However, there was luckily not much time for self-tormenting, for it was now one o'clock, and our guests were expected before dark. You may imagine how poor old Dinah, then a strapping wench, and Celia, who died before your memory, bustled about, not unassisted by me, to put the blue chamber overhead in due order, and to get all things in readiness for the due welcome of the coming guests. When all things were ready, or in train, and I had duly arranged my dress, I descended to the opposite parlor to await their arrival. Having now nothing more to do, I began making myself work by displacing and then re-arranging all the furniture in the room, and now and then giving an uncalled-for poke to the blazing fire, which Cæsar had just lighted on the hearth; for it was one of those delightful clear, cool days in autumn, when a good fire of an evening is relished as a luxury, and not regarded as a mere necessary of life, as in winter. At last, about six o'clock, they drove up, accompanied by your uncle, in the chariot, and, as soon as they appeared, I felt that all my previous twitter had been unnecessary: the first glance I had of them told me that.

"The fifteen years which had elapsed since I last saw John Wyborne had transformed the slight though graceful youth into an elegant man of mature age; but the hurried warmth with which he approached and saluted me, and the evident emotion which he felt at the sight of the familiar faces and scenes of his youth, assured me that he had passed through the ordeal of a European life without injury to the better feelings of his nature. He was now thirty-seven or thirty-eight years of age, but did not look a day more than thirty. He was more than six feet tall, and of a noble presence. His face beamed with manly intelligence; and his dark eye, which was at that moment quenched with emotion, at calm times sparkled with animation, or glowed with enthusiasm. His mouth was rather large than otherwise, but susceptible of the most varied expression, and his teeth were of the most glittering whiteness. But," continued my aunt after a short pause, shaking her head with a pensive air, "it is hardly worth while to describe so particularly what the ruins you are going to see once were; but all who ever knew John Wyborne in his best estate will tell you that they have never forgotten the fascination of his smile and eye."

"I assure you, my dear aunt," I answered, my curiosity being now fully awakened, "that you cannot be too minute for me; but, as time presses, pray give me some account of his wife. Was she as fine a creature as his wife should have been?"

"Indeed she was," replied my aunt: "at least, as far as one could judge from appearance and manner, she was well worthy of her husband. But there was some mystery about her which we never could fathom, and, where there is mystery, there must always be a degree of doubt as to the worthiness of the person, especially of the woman, to whom it attaches. But, poor thing, she did not live long to be the theme of the gossiping small-talk of the herd of society, or of the anxious and legitimate curiosity of her near relatives."

"Did she indeed die so early?" exclaimed I. "But pray go on with your story, for I am impatient to hear the end of it."

"That you will soon hear," my aunt resumed; "for there is but little more to tell. John Wyborne and his wife remained our guests for about six weeks, while the old family mansion in King Street was getting in readiness for them. This. time was filled up by a succession of gayeties in honor of their arrival. Governor Belcher entertained them at a grand dinner at the Province House, at which were assembled the most distinguished of the gentlemen and ladies of the town. All the principal inhabitants vied with each other in welcoming the new-comers with splendid hospitalities. The fine autumnal days which were free from engagements in town we employed in scouring the country round, sometimes in the chariot, and sometimes on horseback, to display the charming scenery of New England, glowing with the tints of a New England autumn. On these excursions we always stopped at some of the gentlemen's seats, which were sprinkled over the country in every direction, and the gates of which always stood wide open to invite the passing friend. Alas! too many of those hospitable portals have been closed by the cruel Revolution, or passed into niggard hands.

"Well, the six weeks soon passed away, and our guests left us, and took possession of their own house. And a fine establishment it was, being the result of taste combined with wealth; and yet there was no attempt to outshine their neighbors : everything was in the very best style of the town, and nothing more. When they were fairly fixed in their new abode, they gathered around them a circle of the choicest society; and that winter was a memorable one in the annals of anyone who was admitted within that charmed circle. Mr. Wyborne gave a weekly dinner on Wednesdays, which he managed to make a very different affair from the somewhat stiff festivities of set dinners at that time, or any other time either, for that matter.

"It was observable, however, after the first excitement of a new country and the first bustle of hospitalities were over, and they were quietly settled down by their own fireside, that Mrs. Wyborne was but ill at ease. Her form by degrees lost something of its symmetrical roundness, her brilliant complexion was exchanged for an alabaster chilliness, and her eyes gradually lost much of their peculiar beauty. Her husband seemed but to live for her, and there was no circumstance of watchful love and sedulous attention in which he was wanting. She, however, drooped from month to month so palpably as to excite the anxiety of her best friends and the lively curiosity of her common acquaintance.

" One thing was remarkable enough, and that was that neither she nor her husband ever made the faintest allusion to her parentage or history previous to their marriage. Mr. Wyborne so promptly and dexterously parried all attempts to extract any information on these points from him, and his wife met them with such a mournful embarrassment, that it was soon understood that they were forbidden topics in their presence; though you may well imagine that they were discussed in all their bearings, known and imagined, when they were absent. The circumstance, too, that she was plunged in double gloom upon the arrival of every fresh packet of letters from Europe, did not tend to damp the curiosity, or to extinguish the conjectures, of those kind inquirers who are more solicitous about the affairs of others than about their own."

" That certainly did look rather suspicious," interrupted I. "Did it not excite some doubts in the minds of the lovers of scandal as to whether they were married at all ?"

"That scandalous construction," Mrs. Champion replied, "would no doubt have been put upon their unaccountable behavior, if Mr. Wyborne had not, probably with a foreboding of such a rumor, taken good care to exhibit as an interesting autograph his marriage-certificate, signed by the famous Dr. Young, who performed the ceremony in London by special license. Matters went on thus for some months, their house being the centre of our limited sphere, and almost always thronged with company, which John Wyborne anxiously gathered round him in hopes of dissipating the growing melancholy of his wife.

"The winter wore on pleasantly enough to all except the fated mistress of the mansion. John Wyborne had received his library, the finest private one in the country, which he had collected abroad, and had arranged it entirely to his mind. Many valuable pictures, a few statues (rather shocking to the primitive taste of those days), and what was to us a rich collection of articles of *virtu* arrived, and added to the attractions of his house. A superficial observer would have pronounced John Wyborne a happy man. He had health, riches, taste, a well-cultivated mind, a splendid library, warm friends of congenial tastes, and a charming wife. What could man desire more? Surely he had clutched the rare boon of unmixed felicity. Alas, my dear boy! he was no exception to the general doom which condemns man to trouble. All the appliances of luxury, all the qualifications of taste, even all the leisure and ample means for gratifying a passion for elegant letters, bring no balm to the wounds of a gentle nature, inflicted by the sight of a beloved object consuming away before the sight of a mental malady beyond the leech's arts. Religion only, my son, religion only, has consolations adequate to support the soul under such a burden." She paused, for the memories of her own sorrows were painfully rising to her brain, and a phantom train of unburied griefs stretched in long perspective before her mind's eye. She, however, never long yielded to the painful influences of the past, and soon resumed the thread of her narration.

"Matters went on thus till the middle of February, when Mr. and Mrs. Wyborne, having their establishment now complete, issued cards of invitation to all their acquaintance to an entertainment given in return for the multitudinous attentions which had welcomed them on their arrival.

"It was bitterly cold, a glittering, clear winter's night, which well set off the genial and brilliant scene within. Your uncle and I dined there, and helped them to oversee the last preparations. By six o'clock all the company were assembled, comprising all the town which had any claim to admittance, from old Dr. Coleman down to the freshest and prettiest young girls just escaped from the nursery.

"The recollection of that scene is indelibly impressed upon my memory by the sudden change which soon was brought over it; though there is not half a dozen of the gay crowd which filled the rooms that night that now survive. What a strange thing is memory!—that I at eighty-three should at this moment be, as it were, in the midst of a brilliant and happy crowd of half a century ago, almost every one of which is now in the grave, except a few withered, weak old men and women just tottering on its brink. I could describe to you, if I had time, and you cared to hear it, every dress in the room, from the splendid brocade and diamonds of the mistress of the house, whose chief ornament, however, was her beautiful hair, falling in natural ringlets over her neck (for powder was not then in fashion), and from Governor Belcher's black velvet coat and breeches, richly embroidered waistcoat, point-lace ruffles, diamond buckles, and dress sword, down to the beautiful Mary Osborne, now old Mrs. Estridge, in her white watered silk, and glistening high-heeled shoes, which Cinderella might have envied, seated on the window-seat, half hid by the heavy damask curtain, listening to Ralph Estridge (whom she not long afterwards married), who had just returned from home, the image of a London petitmaitre, in a peach-bloom silk coat lined with white, pink satin waistcoat embroidered with gold, white satin breeches and white silk stockings, and a rapier with a steel handle, glittering like diamonds. Books, flowers, paintings, beautiful women, and elegant men, made it a picture to be recalled with pleasure, if it were not for the dark cloud which soon gathered over it.

"Well, everything went on well enough. All were

animated, and most were happy. The mistress of the house looked like herself again; the young people made love; their elders talked of the prospect of a war with Spain; some of the more austere of the elder school of New England manners privily shook their heads at the frightful havoc which luxury was making in the good old simplicity of the fathers. The most rigid of the reverend divines and honorable judges, however, smoothed their stern features on this occasion, and looked on with complacent smiles. At about half-past eight supper was announced, and we ascended to the supper-room, led by the Governor and the mistress of the house. It was a beautiful spectacle. The tables lavishly adorned with flowers, the luxurious banquet served almost entirely on plate, the lovely and graceful figures which were grouped around the board in the full flow of youthful spirits, and the venerable forms and beneficent countenances of the elder guests contrasting with them, made up a scene of enchantment which I have never seen approached since. The master of the feast seemed to be doubly inspired by the spirit of the scene, and never shone more brilliantly, both in his own proper powers of entertainment and his tact in drawing out the resources of others. My good old friend Dr. Byles, then a young and brisk divine, was in his element, and often set the table in a roar with his lively sallies; and many a sharp encounter of wits took place between him and his host. Suppers, however, like all other terrestrial things, must come to an end; and after about an hour and a half had been delightfully spent over the table, we returned to the parlor. Soon afterwards his Excellency, the clergy, and the more dignified portion of the company, took their leave, which was the signal for the appearance of the violins and the commencement of what was then a most unusual event — a ball. Mrs. Wyborne opened the ball with a minuet with Mr. Hutchinson (our late governor); and, that prologue being happily over, the country-dances began in good earnest, and were kept up with untiring devotion till nearly four o'clock, when the assembly gradually melted away. My husband and I, as we had been the first on the ground, were the last to leave it. As we walked through the deserted rooms with our charming hostess, and observed with pleasure how the excitement and success of the evening had recalled her vanished bloom, and rekindled her faded eyes, we little thought that the next occasion which would summon us to those apartments would be her funeral."

"Her funeral!" I exclaimed.

"Even so," she mournfully rejoined, "and so soon. She was taken violently ill the very next day, — probably from undue excitement, and unusual fatigue acting upon a frame already debilitated, — and in less than a week she was dead." She paused, and, as I looked at her, I saw that her aged eyes were wet at thought of the sad images which her story had recalled.

"And how did her husband bear the dreadful blow?" I inquired.

" His despair was frightful for the first few days," she replied. "He refused admission to his best friends, and would not be comforted. He shut himself up for hours with the beloved remains, and the anxious and affectionate servants listened with dismay to the tempest of grief which they could hear raging within. Such violence of sorrow, however, could not last long; but, when the first fierce paroxysms were over, the preternatural calmness which succeeded was scarcely less shocking than they. I can never forget, should I live a century longer, the dreadful change which that short week had wrought in his face: death had not thrown a more gloomy change over the features of the beloved dead,— his cheeks as hollow as a ghost's, his eyes of a stony vacancy, his pale lips quivering, and his whole energies apparently bent upon a mighty effort at calmness.

"That funeral was worth a thousand homilies. There she lay at length in her coffin, who, but a little week before, was the charm of all who saw or heard her; in the very room, too, in which she had led the dance, and surrounded by most of the very revellers who had basked in her radiant presence. It was a chastening though grievous vicissitude, from the house of feasting to the house of mourning, and from the garments of joy to the weeds of heaviness. The contrast of those darkened rooms, filled with mourn- ful countenances and suits of woe, to the glittering lights, splendid dresses, flashing eyes, and merry hearts of the time of their last meeting there, must have inscribed an ineffaceable lesson on the most thoughtless hearts. Nothing broke the sepulchral stillness but an occasional sob, which would find its way from some woman's heart, or a half-suppressed sigh from some manly bosom, till at length Dr. Sewall rose, and raised all our souls upon his eloquent prayers to heaven. When this impressive service was over, the last sad procession was marshalled to the tomb.

"It was one of those dark, gloomy winter's days, when the sky looks like a vault of stone almost resting upon the roofs of the houses. The ground was covered with snow, and a few flakes now and then fell heavily down through the still cold air. The pall was held by the lieutenant-governor and five other of the principal gentlemen of the time. Then followed the bereaved husband, supported by my husband and Dr. Sewall. Then came the governor and magistrates, succeeded by a long train of relatives and friends in the deepest mourning. Behind followed the family coach, the carriage, as well as the servants, in mourning, then the governor's coach, and next the carriages of almost all the gentry of the town and country round. As the black train swept through the streets, the common people, who thronged them to witness the spectacle, all uncovered as we passed, and showed none of the levity which I have sometimes seen to accompany great funerals.

"At last, after making a large circuit, in consequence of the numerous attendance, we arrived at the King's Chapel churchyard, and all passed round by the family tomb of the Wybornes, and took a last look at its latest and fairest tenant before its ponderous jaws closed upon her forever. Poor John Wyborne could bear up under his heavy grief no longer, but was supported by his anxious friends, almost insensible, to his coach. The rest of the melancholy attendants stood reverently by as the mourner was borne along, and then dispersed, and, entering the coaches which were in waiting, were slowly rolled to their various homes.

"The gloom of this event hung over the town for all the remainder of the season and for months afterwards. It seemed as if every family was mourning over some household death. The difference which it made to me, you may easily imagine. It was almost the first severe loss of the kind that I had ever encountered: Heaven knows it was not the last!" After a short pause, she resumed, "John Wyborne continued throughout the spring in a most pitiable state: the violence of his first grief was succeeded by an apathetic listlessness from which nothing could arouse him. He formed a plan for returning again to Europe, which was encouraged by his friends as the medicine most likely to be effectual; but he did not seem to retain enough of the energy with which he used to overflow to make the necessary preparations. At last, when May was well advanced, my husband proposed to him to visit Sanfield, the town in the Old Colony where his mother had spent the last years of her life after her marriage with the Rev. Mr. Selleck and where a considerable estate was going to decay for want of the eye of the master. As this excursion did not involve much expenditure of resolution or trouble, Mr. Wyborne consented to accompany Mr. Champion to the scene of his mother's later years. It was a most exquisite spring day when they went down, when the country was clad in its softest and freshest green, and the fields were white with apple-blossoms, and the delicious air seemed as if it might have been a balm even for a broken heart.

"Mr. Wyborne seemed to feel the benefit of the change of place almost immediately; and the appearance of his house and grounds, and of the village in its vicinity, seemed to strike his fancy. The house, which I will not describe, as you will soon see it, was somewhat the worse for want of inhabitants for a number of years, since the decease of his reverend step-father; but the avenue of fine elms and grove, which sheltered it from the sea, had grown up prosperously, though untrimmed and neglected. The garden was something like that of the sluggard, to be sure; and the sun-dial in its centre was almost hid by nettles and weeds, and the wall was in many places broken down, and the fish-pond was almost choked up with rubbish. I should have told you that the new part of the house was built, the trees planted, and the grounds laid out, by an English Church clergyman of fortune, who emigrated to this country about the beginning of the century, and who, finding small encouragement in his clerical capacity, had employed himself in the business and pleasures of a country life, and of whose heirs Mrs. Wyborne had purchased it on her second marriage.

"There was enough of native luxuriant beauty about the place to captivate the good taste of its owner; while there was an air of neglect and desolation about it which seemed to suit the present melancholy mood of his mind. My husband was well pleased to hear him avow his intention of putting the place to rights, and making it his residence for a part of the year. He encouraged him in his plan, and recommended that no time should be lost in putting it into execution. Accordingly they hunted up a farmhouse in the neighborhood, whose owners were willing to take him and his servant in until the old house could be made habitable. Rejoiced to have been the means of providing a healthful occupation for his friend's sick mind, my husband returned to town, expecting that he would follow in about a fortnight. A fortnight elapsed, and a month, and a year, and yet he tarried.

"He left his house in town for a couple of days, perhaps a week; and now almost half a century has passed away since then, and he has never once recrossed its threshold, or revisited his native town. He had found the first comfort which his wounded spirit had known among the old trees and green meadows of his new home and by the side of the ocean which washed his estate less than half a mile from the house; and he felt for them the love of a mourner for the tried friends of his affliction. Nothing, however, was further from his intention than making that sequestered place his permanent abode. But the first summer and autumn were insensibly wasted away in the pleasant tasks of bringing order out of the chaos of his grounds, and of restoring to the old mansion the comfort and elegance of which time and neglect had stripped it. Then, just as winter set in, his house was ready for his occupation, and he could not bear to leave this new home, which was invested only with happy associations, for that roof which was overshadowed by the gloom of his mighty sorrow, and under which he would be haunted at every turn by the ghosts of his buried joys. So the winter passed away and when spring returned he had made up his mind to make this his chief residence, and sent for his library. When winter again arrived, his attachment to the place had strengthened, and he determined to spend it as he did the last. In this way his habits of life became gradually fixed; his love for his new home, and his disinclination to return to his old one, increased with every year; and so his prime of manhood and his green old age have worn away in that retirement."

"Had he any society in his solitude?" I inquired.

"But little in his immediate neighborhood," my aunt replied, "except the clergyman and one or two country gentlemen. But for many years, during the summers and autumns, he had no lack of company from Boston: his house was scarcely ever empty, at those times, of his old friends and companions. Your uncle and I always paid him at least one visit a year, as I told you before, until I gave up the coach upon his death. By degrees, however, as his old friends died off, his younger ones grew less frequent in their visits. And then the Revolution came in to confound all old friendships ; so that for a good many years he has been thrown almost entirely on his own resources. I am told, however, by some old friends who are still constant to him, that he has acquired no cynicism from neglect, and gathered no rust from solitude, but is still, in his manners, dress, and way of living, a fine relic of the thoroughbred gentleman of the middle of this century."

The good old lady here ceased. I warmly thanked her for her story, and assured her that it had increased my curiosity to make the personal acquaintance of its hero a hundred-fold.

"I am glad you are going to see him," she resumed; "for you may never chance to meet with exactly such another specimen of the old school again : at least I do not know where his fellow is to be found."

At this point we were interrupted by the entrance of Dinah with the tea-things, which brought us down from our high converse about other days to a sense of present realities. After my good aunt had dispensed the fragrant infusion in china's earth, the sun began to remind me, by the peculiar mellowness of his light among the leaves of the trees, that it was time for me to set forth on my return to my rooms. My horse being accordingly brought round by Cæsar, I affectionately saluted my dear old friend, and, receiving from her a needless injunction not to fail to make my visit to Sanfield, I mounted my nag, and rode briskly back to my home among classic shades.

CHAPTER II.

MY aunt's history had made so strong an impression upon my fancy, that I became as impatient for the time of my visit to arrive as I had formerly been ingenious to invent excuses for putting it off. My strong curiosity to see the subject of her narration, actually sometimes inspired a kind of nervous apprehension that something would happen to prevent my visit, that I might be summoned in some other direction, or that the good old gentleman might in the interval exchange his quiet home for the vault of his ancestors. No such impediment, however, occurred. The autumn months melted gradually away, and at last brought round the annual festival of the Pilgrim Fathers. I obtained permission to leave Cambridge a day sooner than the regular holidays began in order that I might have a good three-days' visit, which I thought little enough for my purpose; the reverend president giving a ready assent to my application when he understood its object, for Colonel Wyborne was his old and valued friend. He intrusted to me a packet containing some sermons of his which had been recently printed, as well as a verbal message of friendly compliments; and having instructed me to call upon him on my return, with an account of his excellent friend, "he shook his ambrosial curls (of his wig), and gave the nod," which was the signal for my departure.

I louted low, and withdrew, inly pleased at the successful issue of an interview which was then considered as the most appalling of human ordeals.

On Tuesday morning of the last week in November, I bestrode the very indifferent beast which enjoyed the somewhat unenviable distinction of being the best livery horse in Cambridge, and set forth, like Yorick, with (not quite) a half-dozen shirts and a black pair of silk breeches in my portmanteau, on my long-looked-for excursion. Contrary to established usage in such cases, the day was fine and the roads excellent. It was one of those delicious, mild, soft days which sometimes occur at the very close of autumn, and seem to breathe a second spring in the very presence of winter himself; and to desire

> "Upon old Hyem's chin and icy beard
> To hang a chaplet of young summer buds."

As I rode over Brighton bridge upon a steed which had not yet got over the stimulus of his double allowance of oats, with my back turned upon my nursing mother, whose cares are but too often felt to be only vexatious till it is too late to profit by them, and a week before me unhaunted by the apparitions of dead authors and living tutors, I respired the bland air with a joyous feeling of young life, and felt as if there were no such thing as pain or trouble in the world. I trotted along the pleasant winding roads through Roxbury, Brookline, and Dorchester, with a heart ready and willing to receive pleasure from every object which struck the senses. The trees were almost bare, and the earth was sear and brown; yet the yellow light of the rejoicing sun seemed almost as beautiful as the leafy glories of their summer's estate. The farmhouses, with their roofs sloping to the ground; the sheds laden with the golden pumpkins, prophetic of pies to come; the corn-barns with the yellow ears peeping out from between the interstices of the sides; the wood-pile, suggestive of images of comfort and merry winter nights; the picturesque well-pole, not yet supplanted by the prosaic pump of these utilitarian days, — all were fruitful of happy thoughts and pleasant day-dreams. As I ascended Milton Hill, I saw for the, first time the magnificent prospect it displays, and checked my horse on its summit to admire the wide sweep of country, the tufted hills, the winding river, and the glorious burst of ocean, with here and there a white sail gliding along its blue surface, which it commands. On the other side of the road I saw the charming villa of Governor Hutchinson, with the fine plantations he had made, and the trees under which he had hoped his latter days would have declined in peace; and I felt that his exile from this beloved and lovely spot was punishment enough for his political offences as a public man. It is said, and I can well believe it to be true, that he died of Milton Hill. It must have been a bitter thing to have revisited its beloved shades, and gazed on its gorgeous view in the visions of the night, and then to have awoke a neglected, impoverished, despised exile, forever separated from the spot of earth which was dearer to him than all the world beside.

As I wound farther into the country, I often met, jogging cheerfully along, hale ruddy countrymen ; some young, some gray-haired, presiding over wagons groaning under the weight of the victims which had been sacrificed against the coming festival. Hecatombs of beeves, ghostlike forms of turkeys, partridges never again to rise on whirring wing, ducks fated to swim no more save in their own gravy, passed in long procession, like the shadowy train of Banquo's descendants. As I passed through the villages in my way, they had all a sort of pleasant holiday look. The labors of the year seemed to be over, and the inhabitants to be assisting one another to do nothing in the most neighborly manner possible. The boys, let loose from school, were playing football with all the energy which that manly game demands, but stopping in their sport to look at the passing stranger, and salute him, according to the good old custom, with uncouth demonstrations of respect.

At noon, I bated from my journey, though bent on speed, and drew the rein at the door of what was to me a most promising hostelry, being a farmhouse of the oldest description which New England affords, with its jutting second story as a "coigne of vantage" against the Indians, its diamond panes of glass set in lead, and its window-frames opening inwards like folding-doors ; and which was proclaimed to be a place of entertainment for man and beast by a most truculent portrait of General Washington, which hung in chains from a superb old elm before the door. I soon learnt that the hospitable proprietor was no less a person than Captain Crake, who had seen hard service both in the old French war and in the recent struggle for independence. The gallant captain did me the honor to invite himself to dine with me, and I found him an entertaining specimen of a large class of our revolutionary officers, who had superinduced the military frankness and ease of one conversant with camps upon the sturdy independent yeoman of the Old Colony. While I patiently exercised my molars and incisors in an almost hopeless attempt to subdue a beefsteak, which seemed as if it might have been ravished from the yet living flank of the sire of Abyssinian herds, I quite won the heart of my worthy landlord by the interest which I took in his descriptions of his campaigns and of the well-fought fields which he had seen. He exhibited with much satisfaction the honorable scar in his arm which he had received at the storming of Stony Point, and the sword which the Marquis de Lafayette had presented to him, and his insignia of the Cincinnati. He also displayed a richly chased gold watch, which had been given to him by a French

nobleman whom he had made the captive of his bow
and of his spear in Canada, I think at the taking of
Fort Niagara, as a token of his sense of the humanity
and courteous treatment which he had received at
the hands of his captor. During his long term of
service he had associated on terms of equality with
gentlemen of much higher rank in society than he
had been accustomed to know, except at a humble
distance; and he felt the loss of the company of his
old companions-in-arms most severely after the army
was disbanded. He had, as a resource against ennui,
rather than any expectation of gain, hoisted the head
of his beloved chief before his paternal door to invite
the passing guest; and the neighboring gentry always
made it a point to stop at the captain's door as they
passed, and gratify the veteran by treating him as
one who had bravely fought his way to an equality
with themselves at a time when the distinctions of
rank were still strongly marked. I subsequently
cultivated the acquaintance of the erect old man, and
extracted from him many a curious fragment of public and private history. But my horse is again at
the door, and I must return the military salute of
mine host with what grace I may, and hasten onward,
for I have no time to lose.

My horse, who, during the course of his long and
active life, had done little else than tread and retread
the weary round of what were in those days entitled
the great and the little squares, which were certain
roads encompassing Boston at a greater and less dis-

tance, began to show unequivocal symptoms of weari-
ness and disgust at my eccentric orbit. No logic,
either of whip or spur, could convince him of the
propriety of advancing at a more rapid rate than a
sort of shamble between a walk and a pace. To
crown all, he managed to cast a shoe at the most
inconvenient place possible, so that I had to lead
him for a matter of four miles before I could find
a blacksmith. All these untoward circumstances
combined to make my approach to the end of my
journey as gradual as might well be. Accordingly,
when the sun set, as sober suns will do, at a little
after five o'clock, he left me about five miles from
Sanfield. Now this distance I could have soon annihilated if I had been unincumbered with my impracticable companion ; but, as it was, I was obliged to
do as wiser men have been obliged in like cases to
do before me,

"And will again, pretend they ne'er so wise,"

even to succumb to the wayward humor of my ill-
conditioned helpmate, and to console myself with
cursing the evil hour in which I formed the ill-starred
union.

The day, which had been cloudless as a midsummer's noon, began, before the sun went down, to be
overcast with black clouds, portentous of showers.
A piercing north-east wind reigned in the stead of
the vernal breeze of the morning, and whirled the
brown leaves in rustling eddies like a miniature

tornado. As I stumbled onwards upon my journey, the twilight faded away, and was followed by a moonless night. I could scarcely distinguish my road, which seemed to grow longer and longer, under my feet. In something more than two hours, however, I was cheered by the ruddy blaze of a blacksmith's forge, which gave me assurance of being near a village. Upon reaching the smithy, I inquired of the son of St. Dominic as to my whereabouts, and was informed that I was on the confines of the village of Sanfield, and had ingeniously managed to take a wrong turning a few miles back, which had brought me more than a mile beyond my destination by a wrong route. Nothing remained for me now but to take the instructions of the worthy smith, and turn my horse's reluctant head in the opposite direction, and, having been put in the right way, to pursue it till I should come to the high trees, which were the mark of my journey's end.

My nag, contrary to my expectation, seemed to snuff afar off the comfortable provender which awaited him, and laid his feet to the ground with a speed he had not put forth since the morning. As I advanced, I earnestly bent my eyes into the thick darkness on my right hand, in hopes of distinguishing the friendly branches which were to point me to the termination of my weary way. I looked with the more earnestness as a few drops of a cold November rain began to fall, and to threaten no inconsiderable addition to the discomfort of my

benighted estate.   At last, however, as I descended a
considerable hill, I heard the sough of the blast stirring the boughs of many lofty trees on my right
hand, and could perceive lights glimmering through
the darkness at a considerable distance.   These I at
once knew must be the indications of the hospitable
habitation I sought.   The pitchy blackness of the
night compelled me to dismount, and grope my way
to the fence, and along it, in search of the approach to
the house.   This I felt to be prudent as I heard the
hoarse murmur of what seemed to be a considerable
stream near me.   I groped in vain, however, for the
carriage-road; and could find but a small gate, intended only for human ingress, about opposite where
the little candle threw its beams into the night, like
" a good deed in a naughty world."

In this distress I had nothing left for it but to tie
my horse to the fence, and follow the adventure on
foot.   Entering the gate, I proceeded onwards, with
the withered leaves crackling under my feet, and the
wind sighing among the bare branches over my head.
The rain now began to patter in more frequent drops
upon the dead leaves over which I walked, with the
peculiar clattering noise which is delightful to listen
to before a comfortable fire, but less musical to the
ear of an amateur of Nature's harmonies, when he is
·behind the scenes and in the midst of the performers.
As I neared my hoped-for haven of rest, I was
saluted by the fierce barking of a dog, who, if his
size were answerable to his voice, might be a match

for the shaggy "Dog of Darkness" himself. Now,
however sweet it may be

> " To hear the watch-dog's honest bark
> Bay deep-mouthed welcome as we draw near *home*,"

I put it to anyone who has tried the experiment,
whether it be an equally delightful sound as we
approach a strange house of a dark night. I venture
to say that the stoutest hearted despiser of dogs and
devils would feel some misgivings under such circumstances, lest his fate might be at least as hard as
that of the noble bard just quoted, who was welcomed
on his return to Newstead by having

> " His Argus bite him by the breeches."

It would not do, however, to be daunted by this new
lion in my path, which I afterward found was
chained, like the one in Pilgrim's Progress: so on
I fared, like any errant knight, resolved at all haz-
ards to achieve my adventure. The house seemed
to recede as I advanced, and I thought that I had
measured a good mile before I reached it : it was, in
fact, about a quarter of a mile. As, however, there
is an end to the disagreeables as well as to the agree-
ables of life, I at last stood in the porch, wet, hungry,
and tired, and made the brazen knocker give clamorous notice of my presence. The door was soon
opened by an elderly woman of respectable appearance, of whom I inquired if this was Colonel Wyborne's house, and whether he were at home ; to both
which interrogatories I received the expected affirma-

tive, together with an invitation to walk in. The good woman, eying me attentively, then said, in the negative-affirmative form in which inquiries are generally put in New England, —

"Sure' you are not the Mr. Dalzell whom the Colonel expects from college, are you ?"

I assured her of my confident belief in my identity with the individual in question; upon which she replied, —

"Well, the Colonel will be right glad to see you, sir, though he did not expect you till to-morrow, or he would have sent the chariot to meet you at Captain Crake's. But how did you get here, sir ? You surely haven't walked all the way ?"

I gave the information desired; upon which she promised to send the coachman for my horse, and requested me to walk into the parlor, where the Colonel was sitting. She accordingly threw open the door on the right as I entered the hall, and ushered me into an apartment, the lightsome cheerfulness of which was enhanced by the chilly, wet, famished condition in which I entered it. The master of the house, however, was not there ; though the chair drawn to the fire, the small mahogany table, covered with a green cloth, and sustaining a massive silver candlestick and wax candle, and the second volume of Sir William Temple's works in folio, showed that he had not been long absent. The housekeeper then left the room by the door by which we had entered, for the purpose of finding him, and announcing my arrival. The first object which attracted my attention was the noble fire which roared up the chimney, to which I incontinently rushed, and bathed my shivering frame in the genial warmth. When I had imbibed as much caloric as my forward man required, I turned what Lord Castlereagh used to call "a back-front" to the generous blaze, and took a survey of the apartment. The walls were panelled in oak, with a gilt moulding, now a little tarnished. Between the two windows opposite was a large mirror, framed in mahogany, with gilt sconces for lights. Under it was a table covered with a rich Turkey rug, which was well piled with books and papers, and beneath which appeared a couple of small globes. The closed window-shutters were well-nigh concealed, as well as the high window-seats of oak, by the depending folds of the crimson damask curtains. Between the two windows on my right hand was a card-table of mahogany, black with time, clasping heavy balls in its clawed feet. On the side of the room opposite to the card-table was a most luxurious easy-chair — a fit cradle for declining age — and a footstool, both covered with chintz protecting the crimson damask, which on occasions of importance was revealed, to match the curtains. In the nook on the side of the fireplace answering to the door by which I entered was a secretary, its looking-glass doors opening over what seemed to be a chest of drawers, but which, when drawn out, formed a writing-desk with pigeon-holes innumerable. Above the looking-glass doors were three smaller drawers; the inner one with fluted rays diverging from the middle of its lowest side to its edges; the whole crowned by a sort of pyramidal pediment, the polished wood reflecting the surrounding objects like marble, and the brass handles glistering like gold. A thick Turkey carpet covered the floor, and a sufficient number of inviting chairs, with carved frames and well-stuffed seats, expanded their arms to welcome the weary guest. It may be readily conceived that I took in this inventory in less than a tithe of the time it has taken to recount it, and had again turned to the blazing hearth. The chimney was one of those which men built when the forests grew up to their very doors, and it was their ambition to consume them as rapidly as possible. The fireplace was encircled with my favorite Dutch tiles, and surmounted by a capacious mantel-piece, which, as well as the panels over it, were covered with particular care.

While I was thus engaged in surveying these images of comfort, and basking in the blessed warmth, I heard a slight noise behind me, and, turning suddenly round, I saw before me my venerable host, who had just entered by a door which I have not mentioned, opening from the side on the left of the fireplace as I stood with my back to it. The apparition was one which might have startled one who might be taken by surprise. His face was furrowed with wrinkles, his teeth gone, his eyebrows bushy,

but of a snowy whiteness, under which his eyes
looked out with a keenness and brilliancy which
seemed almost preternatural. His head was covered
with a crimson velvet cap with a silk tassel in the
centre, under which he wore a linen cap, turned up
in front and at the sides over the velvet one, of the
purest white. He had on a branched-damask dress-
ing gown, pearl-colored silk breeches, a large flapped
waistcoat of the same, embroidered with silk, white
silk stockings, and black velvet slippers; his neck
encircled by a white stock clasped behind with a
large paste buckle. In his hand he bore the fellow
of the silver candlestick upon the stand before mentioned; and under his other arm he carried the mate
to the volume of Temple's works which I have said
lay open upon it.

It was plain that my arrival had not been announced to him, as, indeed, it hardly could have
been in the minute or two which had elapsed since
my entrance; and he stood for a moment gazing at
me from beneath his shaggy eyebrows with an earnestness which had the expression of sternness and
almost of austerity. I immediately advanced, and,
relieving him of his folio and candlestick, introduced
myself as his dilatory cousin, who had at last re-
deemed the promise which his parents had made for
him, of a visit to their much-honored relative. By
the time I had delivered myself to this effect, and
had deposited his honorable load upon the stand, he
had fully recovered himself, and, with a countenance

4

beaming with affectionate pleasure and hospitable joy, he took both my hands, and warmly pressing them, he bade me a most cordial welcome to his house, adding, —

".I am the more glad to see you, my dear boy, because your being better than your word in coming a day sooner than you promised shows that you were really in earnest to give an old man pleasure, and not merely induced by your dear parents' request. However, I am afraid that your ride hither has been a more fatiguing one than I had hoped to have made it, for I should have sent John and the carriage to meet you at Crake's. But however, here you are, and you cannot come too soon, or stay too long." Saying which, he again shook me by the hand, and wheeling his arm-chair, with my assistance, to ·the fireside, he motioned me to take a chair by his side, and we sat down and talked

> " Affectionate and true,
> A pair of friends, though I was young,"

and though my revered friend had the advantage of the Matthew of the poet by a dozen years. The punctilious politeness of the old school, informed with the soul of real kindliness of heart and the evident gratification which my visit to his solitude gave him, made me feel as much at my ease with him as if a draught from the Fountain of Youth had washed away threescore and ten of his years. We talked first and foremost of my parents, of whose well-being I gave

him what information I possessed, and in every
particular of whose way of life in their new home he
displayed the warmest interest. He then inquired
after the welfare of his old friend, my aunt Champion, and received with marks of hearty satisfaction
my accounts of her abounding in all that should
accompany old age, as well as the affectionate salutations of which I was the bearer. He then talked
about the college, in which he felt all that warm
interest which has in all times done honor to her
sons, with but few melancholy exceptions. I duly
presented the greetings of the president, and announced the advent of the sermons which graced my
portmanteau. Having suitably acknowledged these
favors, my venerable friend suddenly looked up in
my face, and said, —

"By the way, I am very selfish to be catechising
you in this way without remembering that you must
be almost starved. How long is it since you dined?"

I replied that I dined at Captain Crake's at about
one o'clock. "Bless me!" he replied: "that is seven
hours ago and better. Do me the favor to pull the
bell, and this matter shall be put to rights. Are you
not ravenously hungry?"

I should have done injustice to the sentiments of
my heart if I had replied in the negative, and accordingly assented to his proposition in its fullest extent,
and, having pulled the bell as he desired, heard with
unmitigated satisfaction his directions to Mrs. Wal-
dron, his housekeeper, to have supper anticipated, and

furnished forth with all despatch. Many minutes did
not elapse before that excellent person made her
appearance, and with the assistance of a gray-headed
negro brought in a small dining-table from the hall,
which was soon covered with a tablecloth of the
finest damask, and spread with a pair of nicely roasted
cold chickens, and a ham worthy of Westphalia itself,
a loaf of the purest of wheat bread, and some smoking
roasted potatoes, flanked with a decanter of old
Madeira, and a flagon of home-brewed beer. After
due justice had been done to these viands, they were
replaced by a pumpkin-pie of wonderful dimensions
and admirable composition, escorted by a cranberry-
tart, the white flaky paste of which was beautifully
contrasted with the celestial rosy red of the fruit, and
by a noble Stilton cheese. My hospitable entertainer surveyed my feats, as I rapidly made the good
things before me invisible with the appetite of a
hungry boy, with an air of complacent good-humor,
and as I approached the end of my labors, suggested
the medicinal virtues of a bowl of hot punch to my
consideration. I could not dissent from a proposition
emanating from such a source, and the motion was
carried by general consent. Peter, the gray-headed
negro just mentioned, was accordingly despatched for
the materials, and soon returned with the lemons,
sugar, shrub, and old Jamaica, and a small kettle of
hot water; which being deposited, he retired again,
and brought back with him the punch-bowl, of the most
precious porcelain of the Celestial Empire, and a fit

receptacle for the nectarous compound it was to receive. Peter, under the special eye of his master, concocted the mixture, and, having launched the last lemon-paring upon its bosom, consigned the precious burden to his master's hands. He, having touched it to his lips, passed the bowl to one who took a more liberal draught. Peter having removed the remains of the supper, and moved the table nearer the hearth, Colonel Wyborne and I drew our chairs closer to the fire and to each other, with the genial bowl between us (for the heresy of ladies had not crept in within the pale of good-fellowship), and we wore away the evening hours in most delightful talk.

The conversational powers of my host were unimpaired by years, and had just enough of a smack of what was then called the old school to give a racy flavor to his abundant small-talk. His remarks were rich and varied to a degree which I have never heard surpassed, though I have listened in my time to most of the famous conversationists of the age. His experience of life, which, though it had been completed a half a century before, was of the most extensive description, seemed to be as fresh in his recollection as if he had left the bustling scene but yesterday. The images of his early years and his European sojourn were as distinct and sharp in their outlines as if they were but just impressed; for the events of his retirement were not numerous or striking enough to have effaced or impaired them. His society, both on this occasion and all following ones, had a charm from this very circumstance, which that of no other man — even one who had enjoyed the same early opportunities, but had continued to mingle with the base crowd — could possess. He seemed to transport you by the magic of his words to an age that was past, and to a circle which had become historical, and many members of which had taken their niches in the temple

"Where the dead are honored by the nations."

The insignificant particulars which he now and then incidentally dropped of the habits and way of life of the illustrious acquaintances of his youth, gave a vitality to the cold ideas I had formed of them from books and their works, and almost seemed to evoke them from the shades to our presence. He delighted, too, as most old men do, to go back to his schoolboy and college days, and describe the boyish troubles and frolics of those hours when that flame burnt high and strong, which was now flickering in its socket.

Thus, in various converse, the hours flew imperceptibly away. Blazing logs had been reduced to a glowing mass of coals; the candles had nearly measured out their little span of life; and the great clock in the hall had tolled the knell of another day. The good housekeeper, who had several times made for herself errands into the room to see what was going on, at last entered, unbidden, with the chamber candlesticks, and, wishing us a good-night, withdrew. The Colonel then made a move to retire, declaring that he had not so egregiously violated the regularity of his life for many a year. He first desired me to ascertain whether the bowl was empty, and having been assured by me, in return, that " the tankard was no more," invited me to light the candles, and be shown to my sleeping-apartment. He accordingly, assuming one of the tapers, marshalled me the way that I should go, through the hall, up a pair of stairs properly so called, ascending in two flights with a spacious landing between, and as unlike as well as may be the corkscrew abominations which put in jeopardy the lives and limbs of the present generation. My chamber was in the front of the house, over the winter parlor in which I had spent the evening. My host, giving a general survey to the apartment, to see that all was in due order, shook me affectionately by the hand, and, enjoining it upon me to lie as long as I chose in the morning, bade me a good-night, and left me.

The appearance of my dormitory was quite in keeping with the specimen of the house I had seen, as far as I could judge by the light of my candle, assisted by the expiring rays of a few brands, which were all that were left of a cordial fire which had been lighted on my arrival. The bed was of ample capacity, swelling up with a downy buoyancy, and covered with a gorgeous quilt, evidently the handiwork of fair hands of other days ; the pillows were ruffled, and the sheets of a most inviting whiteness. Over the bedstead the tester was suspended from the ceiling, from which flowed on all sides thick curtains of green damask. An India cabinet occupied the space between the windows opposite the bed, yet redolent of the perfumes which it imbibed in Far Cathay, and displayed on its pictured surface the rich costumes and quaint customs of her inhabitants. Between the windows opposite the fireplace was a massive chest of drawers, upon which stood an old-fashioned oval dressing-glass, turning upon pivots on what had once been a white and gilded frame. The chairs were of richly-carved mahogany, without arms, the backs having a lotus-like expansion outwards at the tops, and the seats apparently the fruit of the same gentle labors which had produced the quilt. By the bedside was an elbow-chair, the brother of the one below, only this was covered with white dimity. Upon a table in the middle of the room I found my portmanteau, while the open door of a closet on the right of the fireplace displayed drawers already expanded for the hospitable reception of my integuments. On the other side of the fireplace was another closet, with a window opening into it, with water and the appliances of the toilet, and a shelf of books. The floor was covered with a comfortable English carpet, and green damask curtains hung heavily before the windows.

The gardens of Alcina would not have smiled more invitingly upon me at that moment than did that snug apartment. The extinguisher was soon on, and I was luxuriously buried in a soft valley between two mountains of down. I lay awake for a moment to enjoy the sound of the winter's wind howling around the house, and every now and then dashing the rain against the windows with a fitful violence, and sometimes roaring down the chimney, as if the fiend that rode the blast were in vain clamoring for his prey. These sounds, however, fell fainter and fainter upon my weary ear, and I was soon fast asleep.

CHAPTER III.

I SLEPT soundly through a dreamless night, and awoke about eight o'clock the next morning. I was at a loss, for a minute or two, to define where on earth I might be : soon, however, the scattered images of the day and night before began to group themselves palpably and distinctly in my recollection; and I began to realize that I was actually beneath the roof I had so strongly desired to visit. I sprang out of bed, and, having learned the hour from my watch, I despatched my toilet in all convenient haste. The cheerful light of the sun, peeping through the oval perforations in the tops of the window-shutters, informed me before I left my couch, that the complexion of the weather had changed since I had left the pelting, pitiless storm roaring about the eaves, and gone to the Land of Dreams. Upon opening the window-shutters in the front of the house, I saw the scene through which I had passed the night before in the blackness of darkness, all bathed in the living light of the blessed sun. The black, bare branches of the superb elm-trees, which rose high above the roof, and extended in two rows, one from each side of the house, to the roadside, were dripping with raindrops glittering in the morning ray. The brook, which I could now perceive brawling along just beyond the house on the right as I stood, was hurrying away to the sea, its dancing waters crowning its brink, but not over-flowing it, black as ink in the shade, but of a translucent amber-color where they were kissed

"With touch ethereal of Heaven's fiery rod."

On the left of the house I plainly discerned the carriage-road, which I had vainly sought the night before, the trees extending a canopy of boughs over it. It was separated from the lawn in front of the house by an ancient hedge of boxwood cut into the fantastic forms which were the delight of the English gardeners of the old school, and which Pope has immortalized by his satire, but which, nevertheless, my revered friend scrupulously preserved as a memorial of former times. The lawn was skirted on the other side by a double row of the verdant fence which guarded it on this. The lawn itself fell in a gentle slope, scarcely perceptible, to the roadside, and was now buried beneath the dishevelled tresses of the overarching trees, ravished from them by the winds of autumn. A low wooden fence, shielded on the outer side by a thick hedge of English hawthorn, divided the lawn from the high road.

These. observations were soon made while my toilet was making; and, as soon as it was finished, I hastened down to the parlor below, which had witnessed my hospitable reception. On entering the

room I saw that my venerable host was beforehand
with me, and that the breakfast-table was awaiting
my appearance. Colonel Wyborne was sitting by
the fireside in his elbow-chair, dressed as the evening
before, with the exception that a well-powdered bag-
wig had succeeded to the crown of his head in the
stead of the velvet cap of yesterday. He was busily
engaged in reading a large quarto, which I subsequently discovered to be the Greek Testament, and
did not immediately perceive my entrance. I cheerfully bade him good-morning, and desired him to
observe how punctiliously I had observed his parting
injunction to lie abed as long as I liked. He immediately rose from his chair, and, having laid aside his
book, shook my hand cordially, and, bidding me good-
morning, thanked me for having made myself at
home ; and all in a manner as if I were an honored
contemporary rather than a college lad, and with
that sterling courtesy of address which is the expo-
nent of true benevolence and kindliness of heart; a
very different thing from the base metal which too
often passes current in the world as the sterling coin,
but wanting the stamp of the heart. Compliments
being over, I drew a chair alongside of his, and answered the careful inquiries which he made as to my
comfortable lodging the preceding night. His hospitable anxiety on this subject being relieved, a touch
upon the bell-pull evoked our ministering spirits,
Peter and the housekeeper, from the culinary realms,
bearing in their hands the substantial and the more

ethereal components of that repast, which, when well administered, deserves the precedence which is conceded to it in the due order of the important events of every day. The breakfast which these worthy functionaries imposed upon the board bore no resemblance to the tea-and-toast abominations which usurp in these days that honored name, and to the prevalence of which I attribute much of the degeneracy which is allowed to have dwarfed the present generation. Peter marshalled the way, bearing upon a tray the massive silver coffee-pot, fuming like a courser, and diffusing a fragrance worthy of Araby the Blest. This monarch of the breakfast-table was surrounded by a cortège of dishes temptingly concealed from view by silver covers; which when duly set in order, and revealed to sight, displayed the luscious rounds of toast saturated with the most delicious of butter, the broiled chickens, the piquant sausages, the beefsteak, worthy of the famous Club devoted to its service. Then there was the egg-boiler full of the freshest of eggs, the honey, the smoked salmon, the wheaten loaf and the rye-Indian bread, the cream of the richest, and sugar of the whitest. All these, and other cates which I do not recollect, were all, too, for my especial eating; for at the heels of Peter followed the housekeeper, with a large silver salver, adorned with rich antique chasing, upon which she bore an ample bowl of the finest China, filled with a frothing sea of chocolate and a certain number of slices of delicately toasted wheaten bread, which was the long-established morning meal of the master of the house.

When all preliminaries had been adjusted, we commenced a well-directed and vigorously sustained attack upon the several divisions to which we were opposed, and soon effected a notable breach in the opposite ranks. My host hospitably encouraged me in my endeavors to do the amplest justice to his good cheer, and enlivened the meal with a description of the Scotch breakfasts which had cheered his journey through the Land o' Cakes, which had not then been transformed into a fairy-land of romance and poetry by the magic wands of Burns and Scott, but was regarded with the kind of belittling prejudice which afterwards stamped the pages of Smollett, and colored the mental vision of Johnson. He contrasted those justly famed repasts, which have disarmed even calumny and prejudice by their sterling virtues, and have surprised even the bitterest enemies into applause, with the *déjeuners à la fourchette* of France and the Continent, and gave the palm to the substantial elements of the northern breakfasts over the patés, grapes, figs, and sparkling wines of the south. He had evidently given the subject the attention which its importance deserved; and I have seldom had occasion in my experience of life to doubt the soundness of his opinions on this subject or any other.

After breakfast was over, and we had chatted on various subjects for half an hour or so, Colonel Wyborne proposed a walk over his farm, to which I readily assented. Peter, being again summoned to his master's assistance, helped him to substitute a pearl-colored broadcloth coat, embroidered about the cuffs and skirts with silk, for his morning-gown ; and having invested his feet with a stout pair of square-toed, high-quartered shoes with heavy heels, he brought from the hall his gold-laced cocked hat and gold-headed cane. Thus equipped, my venerable friend took my arm, and we sallied forth from the side door opening upon the carriage-way, and first took a survey of the exterior of the house. It was composed, in fact, of two houses of two different periods : the newer, as it were, growing out of and overshadowing the more ancient. The English clergyman, of whose heirs I have before said the estate was purchased by Colonel Wyborne's mother, had found a farmhouse of almost the earliest description of New England rural architecture ; its roof declining from two stories in front till it almost touched the ground behind, and a close porch projecting before, with windows on either side, and compacted of massy timbers of oak, on which the mark of the axe was in many places to be seen, knit together with a firmness and strength which showed that our forefathers built for their posterity as well as for themselves. The wooden walls of our ancestors would, if unmolested, survive, I doubt not, in many cases, the boasted strength of the granite structures of the present day. The original purchaser liking the situation of the house, but not thinking it worthy of his pretensions, built a new edifice, two stories high, with attics; its rear joining upon the side of the older structure, so that the original house was degraded into the servile condition of the habitation and offices of the servants. He in this way secured to himself an abode of capacious dimensions and convenient distribution, but somewhat of a heterogeneous appearance. The carriage-road, in which we were walking, turned abruptly away from the house before it had reached the end of it, and swept round a circle of trees and towering plants to the stables, which were, in the leafy time, effectually planted out of sight by the verdant screen. Immediately behind the house was a broad terrace of green sod, from which you descended, by a flight of stone steps with iron balustrades, to the garden. The transitory glories of this spot were of course vanished for this year; but the plan of the whole was plainly enough discernible. In the centre of the garden was a small fish-pond, with a neat stone curbing, which was filled with gold and silver fish. Immediately in front of the fish-pond was an ancient sun-dial standing upon a pedestal of stone, and preaching a lesson, by its silent shadow, of the irrevocable flight of the gliding hours, a thousand times more impressive than any told by

"The iron tongue of Time."

From the fish-pond as the common centre, radiated eight well-gravelled walks, extending from the centre to the boundaries, and intersecting a circular gravel walk which was described with mathematical exactness, halfway from the central point to the extremities of the garden. The sixteen portions thus marked out were of exactly the same size ; and in summer, when they were filled with flowers or vegetables corresponding to each other, must have answered Pope's description of an old-fashioned garden, where

> " Each alley has a brother,
> And half the platform just reflects the other."

The garden was surrounded by a thick English hawthorn hedge, which by age and constant trimming had become almost impervious to sight, even when stripped of its leaves. At the bottom of the garden a small gate admitted us into the orchard, which was of several acres in extent, and filled with apple and pear trees of every variety of sweetness and spicy flavor which distinguishes those gentle races. Of his fruit Colonel Wyborne was proud, with good reason ; for he had done much to introduce new varieties, and a better mode of cultivation than used to prevail. The orchard, and the whole domain indeed, was sheltered from the ocean blasts by a gently swelling hill, " feathering to the top " with a thick grove of various trees, which had now reached their full growth, having been planted by the first purchaser, with the exception of one magnificent aboriginal oak, which stood in the midst of the younger trees an acknowledged monarch, and which

5

had not yet disrobed itself of the gorgeous scarlet mantle with which autumn had invested it. Under this regal canopy there was a rustic seat, which allured us to its embraces. My aged companion seated himself upon it, while I took my place beside him, and we surveyed together in silence the brown meadows, and the trees with every bough and every twig standing sharply out, with all their fantastic ramifications, in the yellow sunshine of one of the last days of the Indian summer.

"There is something exceedingly captivating to my imagination," my venerable friend began, after a silence of some duration, " in the analogies between nature and the experience of human life. These you will apprehend and appreciate more and more as you grow older. They are among the many benevolent contrivances of the great Author of nature and life to make the never-dying soul contented and cheerful during its brief imprisonment in these frail bodies and this visible diurnal sphere. When I was of your age, I loved the spring with its budding promise and tender green ; for it was in unison with the consciousness of new life and springing existence which bounded in every vein. During my residence in England, and for the first years of my life here, I left my first love for the mature beauties of summer and of opening autumn ; and I delighted to watch the untiring, never-resting activity and life which informed all the grand and all the minute processes of the great system of nature, which goes on forever

in sublime silence, working out the beneficent purposes for which its Creator framed it. But now the
close of autumn and the snows of winter awake
the solemn echo in my heart more readily than all
the glories of spring or summer. Nature, though she
never rests, now seems to suspend her toils. The
business of the year is over. And the audible stillness of the fields and the sight of the trees, — which,
after their task is done, have thrown down the beautiful livery of their toil, — while they swell the heart
of man with gratitude, also seem to invite it to rest.

"On such a day as this, with this scene before my
eyes, I can almost hear a blessed voice whispering
me that my long, long year is almost over, and that I
shall soon be with them that rest. Like this old tree
under which we sit, I have outlived almost all my
contemporaries, and am surrounded by a new generation, which knows me not; and, though I will gratefully sustain the burden of old age which the great
Taskmaker has imposed upon me, still I shall bow
with joyful acquiescence whenever he shall direct
the axe to be laid at my root."

"You think, then, sir," I observed when he paused
in his observations, or rather his soliloquy, for he
seemed to address himself rather than me, — " you
think, then, sir, that the retirement of a country life
is a more fitting scene for the last act of a long life
than the exciting bustle of a great city and the pleasures of a various society?"

"To a well-constituted mind," he replied, "I think

it is; that is," he continued with a smile, "to a mind constituted like mine. There are natures which would show anything but wisdom in exchanging the busy throng and a tumultuous life for a solitude for the pleasures of which they have no tastes, and against the perils of which they have made no preparation. For my own part, I have never long regretted at any one time my withdrawing from the world. I have spent my many days pleasantly to myself, and not been wholly useless to others. At the beginning of the Revolution, indeed, I felt some visitings of remorse that I had reduced myself to the condition of a spectator, at a distance only, of that mighty drama; while so many of my contemporaries, and friends of a later generation, were shaking the scene, which was extended over a continent, before the admiring eye of the whole civilized world. These regrets, however, soon gave way to more wholesome suggestions. The brilliant part of the action was in the hands of the great men whose names are forever identified with it; but there was a subordinate but equally important portion of the business of the drama which I was in a favorable position to discharge. My relations with this part of the country enabled me to do something towards kindling and keeping alive the flame of patriotism; and I have the satisfaction to think that I was enabled to send many of the best soldiers and officers, too, to the battle, besides keeping the country-side in a state of self-defence. I could contribute, too, to one of the sinews of war. So I soon consoled myself by being useful for not being illustrious; for ambition was but an idle dream at the time of life to which I had then attained, if it be ever anything more than a will-o'-the-wisp. On the whole, then, I think that I chose wisely for myself in retiring from the world; but I would never advise any person whose heart has not been weaned from it to imitate my example."

"But can it be possible, sir," I said, "that you have never felt the want of the society to which you were admitted on such friendly terms in Europe? I should have thought, sir, that the choicest spirits you could have collected around you in the capital of your native province would have seemed tame and insipid after the circles you had left, let alone this seclusion in a remote country-seat."

"In the first place," he replied, "you must remember that I had had my fill of the society you mention: I had lived on intimate and friendly terms with the men about whom posterity will be the most curious of any of our age; so that the feverish thirst which at one time I felt to know face to face those illustrious men was entirely slaked. And in the second place, which perhaps you will scarcely believe, the familiar society of eminent men is in most cases not so very different from that of other well-bred and well-educated men of the same rank in life, and their intimacy is perhaps a pleasanter thing in recollection than in possession. For many years, too, I was in no lack of companions, and now in my old age I ought

not to expect to be exempted from the doom of out-
living my best friends, which is inseparably annexed
to an unusual extension of life. Still I am by no
means left alone in the world. My excellent friend
Mr. Armsby is an invaluable friend: although he is
speculatively one of the most rigid disciples of labor,
yet in his life and conversation he is one of the
mildest as well as one of the merriest of men. But
come," he continued, rising from his seat, "let us continue our walk to the seashore."

We accordingly skirted along the hill, and soon,
doubling its side, the wide ocean lay stretched before
us, broken by only one or two little islands in the far
distance. The waters were of the deepest and darkest
blue, with here and there a white sail stealing along
their surface. The beach was hard as marble; and
the surf, which yet felt the sway of the storm of the
night before, rolled slowly and heavily in upon it in
long and broken ridges. To our left, at about a quarter of a mile's distance, the brook which watered the
grounds about the house found its way to the ocean
after many meanderings: to the right, at a considerable distance, a wooded bluff came abruptly down to
the shore, and terminated the prospect in that direction. As we slowly paced along the sands, listening
to the voice of many waters, and watching the sea-
gulls as they hovered on dipping wings over the
waves, or rode lightly over their crests, Colonel
Wyborne said with a smile, —

"I hope that I have made a more rational as well

as a more happy use of these rolling waters since I
have lived by their side than did the pining and
discontented spirit of Tully during his exile, who,
you remember, spent his repining hours in counting
the waves as they danced to the shore, and sighing
for the Senate, the forum, and the shouts of the people —

'Bidding the father of his country hail.'

The voice of the ocean has never sounded in my ears
like an invitation to return to the world I have left,
but more as a friendly counselling that there are pursuits and pleasures higher and better than any that
world can give."

"Do you think, sir," I inquired, "that you could
be contented to live in an inland town, unless you
could occasionally visit the seashore ?"

"I should be sorry," he replied, "to be compelled
by duty or by poverty to try the experiment. There
is something about the grand features of Nature,
such as the ocean or mountains, which seems to
make an unfading impression on the hearts of those
who have lived from childhood in their neighborhood,
and which always excites the sensation of home-sick-
ness in their breasts when separated from them. I
have a good deal of the passion for the ocean which
the Swiss have for the Alps ; and, if I should be compelled to retire inland, I fear that the roar of the wind
among the forest-trees would be a *Ranz des Vâches* to.
my heart. I would not have you construe, however,
my young friend, my complacent review of my own

retirement into a recommendation to you to try the same plan of life. Fit yourself for the action of life, but do not set your heart upon success in it; for such are the chances and changes of this sublunary state, that the best accomplished for achieving a brilliant lot often fail in compassing the fulfilment of their ambitious hopes, unless they can woo fortune to be the handmaid of enterprise."

"Are not, however," I observed, "the chances of a man who is absorbed in great purposes and plans, embracing, perhaps, a continent in their scope, and reaching forward to distant posterity, better for true and exalted happiness than those of one who leads a useful and innocent life within a narrow circle?"

"I think his chances for permanent happiness less," replied Colonel Wyborne. "His moments of success may be more exquisite than any of the tranquil hours of the private man; but then the vexations and obstacles which he encounters, the calumny and detraction which assail him, and the too frequent failure of his best laid and most benevolently formed plans, which perhaps embrace the whole race, make up a mighty balance against the intense delight of those rare minutes. I grant you that there may be instances, as there have been a few in history, of minds so constructed, blest with such clear views of the true ends of human existence, and moved by such pure and sublime yet simple springs, that they make a happiness for themselves, even of disappointment and defeat, and regard nothing as worthy of regret but the being unfaithful to the powers and the purposes which Providence has committed to them."

" You do not believe, then, sir," said I, " that every man may be the ' architect of his own fortunes,' as has been stoutly maintained ? "

" Indeed I do not," he replied. " That is a fallacy which lures on many an aspiring youth, who mistakes ambition for ability, to miserable disappointment, and sometimes to ruin. We see men standing triumphantly at the goal with the wreath of victory on their brows, and remember, that, even at the starting-post, their prophetic souls had grasped the prize ; forgetting how many competitors, full at the outset of as confident hopes, have been outstripped in the course, and have turned broken hearted away. Every man may be and must be the architect of his own happiness, and every man may learn the alchemy which will teach him to extract happiness out of the bitterest fruits which overhang his path ; but let him not attempt to wrest the sceptre from the hand of the Disposer of events, and presume to dictate to him the precedence which he is to have in the ranks of his human servants."

" Surely, sir," I interrupted, "you are not a fatalist ! You would not take away the accountability of man by making him a mere blind, helpless tool in the hand of a higher Power ? "

" Nothing can be farther from my views or my wishes," he replied. " Man is accountable to the uttermost farthing for the use he makes of the talents bestowed upon him; but the number of the talents and the sphere in which they are to be employed are fortunately appointed for him by Infinite Wisdom. We find ourselves in this world, in this country, in this age, without any agency or volition of our own; we find within us certain powers and passions, differing in every man from his neighbor, and differing, too, in the opportunities for their improvement and the occasions for their right or wrong employment; and all this seems to be the work of accident. But no rightly judging mind can believe it to be so. The feeling of this truth gave rise to belief in the dark and inevitable fate, which, according to the Greeks, governed the destinies of gods and men. They attempted by this melancholy abstraction to solve the enigma of existence. They found themselves, they knew not how, in a various and inexplicable scene. Some found crowns on their brows; some, the philosophic gown upon their shoulders; some wielded the truncheon of victorious armies; and some swayed the fickle populace with their breath — and all these various fortunes growing from a combination of circumstances and events over which they had exercised little or no control. Surrounded by these impenetrable shadows, men in a later age attempted to derive some light from the stars to illuminate the darkness which was about them; and so astrology arose. They made the -blessed constellations an alphabet by which they endeavored to spell out the decrees of fate. And this was natural enough before the invention of the telescope had revealed the immensity of the universe;

for men could not believe that the glorious apparitions which looked down upon them from the heavens every night were made only to delight the eye; and there was something soothing to the bewildered mind of man in thus connecting his unaccountable destiny with those beautiful and fadeless orbs of light. It was a sort of antepast of immortality."

"You would then, sir," I observed, "had you lived two thousand years ago, have stood under the shadow of the Portico, and maintained the·non-existence of evil and the sufficiency of man for himself?"

"I believe I might have asserted the sufficiency of man for the creation of his own happiness," he smilingly replied; "but I think I should have maintained my doctrines beneath the living shades of the Garden rather than under the cold shadow of the Porch. There is nothing," he continued more seriously, "that fills my whole mind with such a certainty of the divine origin of our religion as the contemplation of its perfect system in comparison with those of the wisest of the ancients. The son of a carpenter in a remote and despised province founding a school of the divinest philosophy, which explains all the mysteries of our being, fathoms the depths of the human soul, directs the aspirations of the loftiest minds, and provides for the wants of the humblest, is to my mind a standing miracle. All the concentrated wisdom of all the wisest of the heathens collected around the intellect of Socrates as a nucleus, faded into nothing, like the morning star before the sun, when the divine mind of Jesus of Nazareth dawned upon the benighted world. Not all the sublime procession of prophets by which he was heralded, not all the stupendous apparatus of miracles which encompassed him, not all the noble army of martyrs which have borne witness with their blood to the truths he brought to light, bring such irresistible conviction to my mind as the simple contemplation of the teachings of the Master, limned out in his own life while on earth. The peasant of Galilee resolves the doubts which had perplexed the wisest of antiquity, explains the questions which the subtlest minds had raised, and establishes a system suitable to the wants of all the nations of the earth and to all the individuals which compose them, — a system to which the wisest of his disciples in the course of eighteen hundred years have been able to add nothing, and in which his craftiest enemies have been able to discover no fault. You, my dear young friend," he continued, turning his face towards me, and laying an affectionate hand upon my arm, " you are just launching away on the voyage of life which I have nearly finished. Do not refuse to listen to the counsel of one who has sounded all its depths and shallows: take with you the teachings of Jesus as your compass, and his life as your chart, and, fixing your eyes steadfastly on these unchanging guides, seize the helm with a firm hand, and steer right onward, fearing nothing that can befall you ; and then, whether your course be over a summer's sea or amidst threatening waves, whether you ride conspicuous in the eyes of your fellow-voyagers, or glide unobserved along, you will be sure at last of entering in triumph the haven of everlasting rest.

"And now come," he added after a short pause, "let us turn homeward, and I will show you my farmhouse and farm; for so far you have only seen my pleasure-grounds."

With these words he turned towards the farm-road into which we had entered after leaving the grove; and, following it along, it led us through wide fields, some of which showed as stubble-fields are apt to do at harvest-home: others bore evident marks of the recent disinterment of potatoes and other esculent roots. At some distance was a burly white man, guiding a plough drawn by a noble yoke of oxen under the influences of a tall black man in a white frock, preparing a place for the early wheat, which would spring up at the due time, unchilled by the snows of winter which had rested upon it for months. Five or six other men, some black and some white, were employed in various ways; some repairing fences, some spreading the compost of the barnyard, and one conducting a load of seaweed to that most necessary repository.

As we walked along, I inquired of Colonel Wyborne as to the economics of his mode of life, and how far he was dependent on the metropolis for his necessaries and luxuries. In reply, he told me that he procured nothing from town but his wines, liquors, tea and coffee, and such products as our own country does not afford. His own farm supplied him with bread, vegetables, the riches of the dairy, and in a great measure with butchers' meat and poultry. Wild fowl and fish were to be had for the trouble of shooting or catching them. His cider was the boast of the country round. His farm-people and servants were almost wholly clothed from the flax and wool which grew on his estate. His wood was procured from a range of well-timbered hills, which he pointed out to me in the distance. The finest of venison was brought to his door at the proper season, in any quantities, from the Sandwich woods. His life, as he described it to me, seemed to be one of the most relishing and enviable of lots, and put me in mind of Gil Blas' account of his life at Lirias; and I thought that I should be perfectly contented if I might look forward at the close of life to such a retreat, where I might inscribe upon my doors, with him of Santillane, —

> "Inveni portum, Spes et Fortuna, valete !
> Sat me lusistis, ludite nunc alios !".

But, alas ! no such white days were in reserve for me.

The farm-road brought us, after some windings among the fields, to his farmhouse, which was situated about a third of a mile from his mansion. The house was old, but in perfect repair, and stood in almost too immediate neighborhood of two modern-barns and an old-fashioned corn-barn. The barnyard was alive with fowls of all kinds — chickens, turkeys, ducks, guinea-fowl, and a gorgeous peacock. Beneath the barn farthest from the farmhouse was the piggery,

which might have served for the courtiers of Circe
herself. The barns themselves were filled to the
utmost of their ample capacities with the gifts of
summer and autumn. About a dozen cows were rumi-
nating in a large enclosure opening from the nearer
barn, in which were their stalls and those of the
farm-horses. A flock of about thirty sheep were sheltered in a fold about a stone's throw from the barn,
towards the shore. Under a shed open towards the
house was a cider-press, full of rural and festive associations; the dense mass of pomace yet remaining
beneath the relaxed pressure of the spiral screw speaking of a recent vintage. As we approached the farmhouse door, it opened, and the farmer's wife advanced,
with a child in her arms and a couple more clinging
to her homespun gown, peeping at the Colonel with a
mixture of bashfulness and of joy at the sight of their
old friend glowing in their ruddy faces. The good
woman invited us to come in and rest ourselves,
which proposition we declined, as it grew late. We
just entered the kitchen, and stood for a minute
within the enormous jambs of the chimney, on each
side of which was a comfortable seat of brick, built
for the accommodation of the more ardent worshippers
of the Penates. A settle of truly uneasy straightness
of back and narrowness of seat made an obtuse angle
with the fireplace, covered with towels of various degrees of whiteness and dryness. A sufficient supply
of rush-bottomed, red-painted chairs, in different
degrees of preservation, stood about the apartment.

A brilliant display of pewter graced a number of shelves on one side of the room. As I gave a glance up the yawning chimney, I discerned a black array of hams and flitches of bacon receiving the incense of the smoking fires below. The good woman made many apologies for her kitchen being in a litter, resting her main defence, however, upon its being the day before Thanksgiving, and the weight of duties which devolved upon her. Colonel Wyborne was occupied, while I was making my survey, and listening to the very unnecessary excuses of the good wife, in taking the youngest child in his arms, and patting the heads of the others, and distributing some of the little bribes which cheaply buy the affection of children, and which the kind-hearted old man was seldom without. I was struck with the sort of affectionate veneration with which the good woman regarded Colonel Wyborne, and with her self-respect, too, which she thought in no manner impaired by the most reverential observance of her kind landlord.

Freeing himself at last from his little friends, Colonel Wyborne bade Mrs. Davis a good-morning, and we set forth on our return to his house. The farm-road led us on to the stables, where we stopped a moment to inspect its arrangements. The black coachman was busy cleaning the chariot; the hind wheel, slightly raised from the ground, whirling merrily round under a shower from a watering-pot in the hands of the African Jehu. This worthy functionary had all the happy contentment beaming from his polished face, and grinning from his ivory teeth, which usually marks a well-fed and well-used negro. His master told me that he had been born on the place, and, together with all the other blacks which he had owned before the abolition of slavery in the State, had voluntarily remained in his service. He left his work to exhibit to my admiring gaze the horses over which he reigned; and as he displayed the glossy hides of the stout coach-horses, and the little nag for "massa's" own riding, and the old white pony which had retired on half-pay for the remainder of his life, he seemed to be filled with as honest a pride as ever swelled the bosom of a master of the horse. Having bestowed all due commendations upon this branch of the service, I accompanied my host along the sweep of the road to the house.

Upon gaining the door, we were met upon the threshold by the excellent housekeeper, who announced, with an air of no small importance, that Mr. Armsby, the clergyman of the parish, was in the parlor. Colonel Wyborne immediately hastened to open the door of the apartment indicated, and we perceived, standing with his back to the fire, waiting for us, the reverend gentleman in question. He was a tall man of about fifty-five, "or, by'r Lady, inclining to threescore," broad-shouldered, with the least in the world of a stoop, of a dark complexion, with thick black eyebrows beetling over a pair of sharp, austere gray eyes. He was suitably attired in a black cloth coat, waistcoat, and breeches, with a

6

pair of thick boots coming nearly up to the knee upon his legs, and a white bushy wig upon the excrescence formed by nature for that use. Colonel Wyborne received him with all the respectful courtesy which was due from a gentleman to an honored equal, and which the pastor returned with much formal politeness; through which, however, might be discerned by an accurate observer a priestly consequentiality, now, alas! but seldom seen, which told how much superior, in his own opinion and that of society generally, was the director of the spiritual affairs over the most honorable and honored of the laity. When the two gentlemen had concluded their salutations, Colonel Wyborne, turning to me, presented me in due form to his reverend friend as a young gentleman just from the arms of their common mother. Mr. Armsby, turning upon me an austere regard, without even the ghost of a smile upon his lips, and with the slightest imaginable inclination of his head, coldly extended his large hard hand to me in acknowledgment of my reverend observance and profound obeisance. Having surveyed me from head to foot with an annihilating scrutiny which nearly sunk me to the centre, he took a chair, in compliance with Colonel Wyborne's invitation, and, entering into conversation with him, apparently lost all memory of so insignificant an object as myself. They talked of the weather, the crops, the Thursday lecture the week before in Boston (which Mr. Armsby had attended), and of the fearful prospects of the times and of the country; both uniting in predictions of utter misrule, subversion of ranks, and destruction of property, which were shortly to ensue.

"Before this young man's career is over," said Colonel Wyborne, "these States will be split into rival monarchies, or else into anarchies inviting the foot of the foreign conqueror."

"Yes," asserted his reverend adviser, turning his severe eyes upon me, — "yes, young man, you will have a worse fight to maintain than we have had with England. You will have to contend with intestine factions, to strive for the protection of property, for the preservation of religion, for the maintenance of all that is worth having in this world. The old scenes of which you read at college in Grecian and Roman history will be acted over again in these new commonwealths before your head is gray."

"For my part," added Colonel Wyborne, "I rather incline to the opinion that our unhappy country is destined to be one of the dependencies of France. In the present humiliated condition of England, — bleeding from the disruption of her Colonies, and tottering under the weight of an overwhelming debt, — it is hardly to be supposed that Louis XVI. will not be encouraged to revive the old scheme of universal dominion which his ancestor, Louis le Grand, at one time seemed likely to bring about. England once subdued, the subjugation of the rest of the continent would soon follow, and then poor we would be but a mouthful to the ambition of the *Grand Monarque.*"

"True enough," replied Mr. Armsby. "No human wisdom can foretell what such a nation as the French, consolidated under a single absolute king, may accomplish. I confess I tremble for the cause of Protestantism in the world. Who knows but we may see a cardinal legate holding his court in Boston!" And the worthy divine shuddered at the bare imagination. Colonel Wyborne continued,—

"I think that the American Provinces, States, I mean, have yet strength and courage enough to resist a crusade under banners blessed by the Pope; unless, indeed, it should not be preached until our little jealousies and quarrels have ripened into serious hatred, and the lines of division have become too deeply marked to be filled up even by such a danger. The sooner such an attack should be made, the better I think it would be withstood; for every day seems to weaken the green withes which bind together the strong but jarring giants of the Confederacy. In a few years England herself might conquer us in detail, for all prospect of any permanent connection seems ˙desperate."

"It is too true," replied the clergyman; "and, bad as that would be, it would scarcely be worse than the utter dissolution of all the elements of society, which seems to hang over our heads, The industry of the country palsied, the land filled with sturdy vagabonds, law and justice mocked and defied, subordination a laughing-stock, religion and her ministers neglected, property uncertain, magistrates unrevered and disobeyed, — with all these things staring us in the face, what can we expect but sudden destruction or gradual ruin ? "

In this manner were these two excellent gentlemen pleased to make themselves unhappy, and to scare unhappy me with these hobgoblins which they conjured up. I was not then as used as I have become since to the croakings of such boding fowl, — which I have happily lived to see many times disappointed of the ruin they predicted, — and I felt serious alarm as to the instant safety of my purse, and ultimate integrity of my throat. The conversation, however, at length changed to books ; and, some allusion requiring a reference to some work which was not at hand, Mr. Armsby proposed going to the library in search of it. Colonel Wyborne, assenting, turned to me and said, —

" I believe that you have not yet penetrated to my adytum : so perhaps we will all go together."

We all accordingly left the parlor, and, following Colonel Wyborne across the hall, entered after him a door on the opposite side. Upon passing the threshold, I was surprised and delighted by a display of books which I had never seen equalled except in the college library. The library consisted of a room extending the whole breadth of the house ; the two rooms having been thrown into one for the accommodation of Colonel Wyborne's numerous collections. The walls were covered with well-filled shelves, tapering up from the massive folios beneath to the pygmy twelves at the top. Busts in marble of Homer, Socrates, Cicero, and Horace, stood on pedestals in the four corners of the room; and one of Lord Bacon and of Newton kept guard in the middle, where a portion of the old partition-wall yet projected from the sides of the rooms, carried into an arch in the centre of the ceiling. A study-table, covered with green baize, occupied the middle of one of these divisions. An abundance of well-stuffed chairs were distributed about in excusable confusion, and a set of library-steps stood against one of the bookcases. A fire-place filled up either end of the apartment; the panel over the one nearest to the door by which we had entered being occupied by a full-length portrait of a gentleman of about five and thirty, in whose form and features I could with difficulty trace any resemblance to the venerable wreck which I beheld before me. Fifty years had swept away almost every trace of the manly figure and handsome face which looked as if it might defy age and misfortune, and left a " withered, weak, and gray " old man standing and waiting on the shores of eternity; and yet here the cunning hand of the artist had bade the sun as it were stand still, and had bestowed a sort of immortality upon one hour — long since vanished — of the summer of his days. He was dressed in a hunting-suit, apparently the uniform of a hunter; and a fine hound was crouched at his feet. Behind him on the left of the picture were two pillars, with a crimson curtain depending from their capitals; while to the

right you saw a landscape representing a level country, well planted, with a river winding through it,
and terminated by misty hills in the distance. The
corresponding panel over the opposite fireplace was
filled by a picture answering in size and frame to
this, but concealed from view by a green velvet curtain which was drawn across it. My imagination
readily filled it up with the portrait of his beloved
and long-lost wife of whom my aunt Champion had
told me. Why it should be thus mysteriously veiled,
I could not conjecture; but the circumstance certainly had the effect of increasing my curiosity to see
it to the most intense degree.

While I was thus engaged, the two elders had
found what they wanted, and were returning to the
parlor. I was strongly tempted to frame some excuse
for remaining behind; but a secret awe of the clerical dignitary, and a fear lest my curiosity might be
obvious to Colonel Wyborne and give him pain,
deterred me; but I fully resolved to uncover the features concealed by that veil at the first opportunity I
could find or make. We accordingly returned to the
parlor; and, after a short sitting, Mr. Armsby rose and
took his leave, being accompanied to the hall-door
by Colonel Wyborne and myself, and reminded by
the former of his standing engagement to dine with
him on the following day. This was the first intimation I had had of the existence of such a prescription; and, lover as I even then was of old customs,
I confess that in this instance I should have been

better pleased with its breach than its observance. I did not at all relish the idea of having this uncomfortable third, with his stony step and hard eye, coming to the table, and displacing our mirth with his unseasonable severity. Colonel Wyborne, however, assured me that I should find him another man when we were a little better acquainted, saying that his excellent friend was one of that old school, which held that religion and virtue were most effectually recommended to the young by a harsh and forbidding exterior and deportment in their votaries.

" To-day," he added, " you have had a touch of his theory : to-morrow, I doubt not, you will see a specimen of his practice."

CHAPTER IV.

DINNER soon followed the departure of the pastor, and was sauced with discourse which I would that my limits would permit me to record. The afternoon and evening passed swiftly away, sped by "old wine, old books, old wood," and an "old friend." At an earlier hour than the preceding night, the chamber candles lighted us to bed, and my hospitable host shook me by the hand with a cordial good-night. After he had retired, I felt but little inclination for repose, and, as a good fire was blazing on the hearth, I procured a volume of Swift from the closet of my room, and sat down by the fireside to read. My thoughts, however, soon wandered from the page on which my eyes were fixed, and began to brood over the strangeness of the place in which I found myself and the singular history of my kind old host. I figured to myself the stripling parting from his mother's roof, and seeking the land of his ancestors. Then I saw him in the midst of the stir and bustle of London, and imagined his first palpitating interviews with Pope and Young and Gay. Then I would see him mixing in the hollow crowd of courtiers in the great man's antechamber, or joining in the fluttering throng which passed in review before the old monarch on a birthday, — that throng whose follies and vices are portrayed in fadeless colors upon the pages of Lady Mary Wortley.

The scene changed, and he was sitting between a couple of haycocks with Bolingbroke at Lydiard, or was listening to a chapter of pointed complainings at Pope's breakfast-table, or was chased up and down stairs by the Dean of St. Patrick. Another wave of the wand transported him to Paris, and plunged him in the recesses of the Palais Royal; and yet another, and he stood among the ruins of Rome. Again he was in England, and then came a mist over the mirror, and objects were but faintly and uncertainly seen in it. Among them, however, was a beautiful woman moving about, and busy with his destiny. She was now sitting alone in an old manor-house, gazing listlessly at the trees of the park as they spread their green canopies over the herds of deer, and at a single swan floating majestically in the stream which flowed beneath them. A sound is heard: she raises her head from her pensive hand, and shakes back her clustering locks, and eagerly listens. It is the tread of a horse galloping up the approach. She hastily rises, and with faltering steps advances towards the door. It opens, and Wyborne enters. Her gestures seem to entreat him to hasten away, for there is danger in his stay. He re-assures her with looks of joyful love. And now he seats himself by her side; her head droops upon his shoulder, and her passive hand rests in one of his, while the other, half-encircling her waist, plays with the tangles of her hair. Can there be any doubt as to the theme of their glowing discourse? But hark! What noise is that in the courtyard? Is it possible that the chase can be over? They both start up. She entreats him to fly: he moodily shakes his head. It is too late. The door flies open. A gray-haired man, but hale and ruddy, and of Herculean proportions, enters. He starts — turns pale with rage : his lips move with dire imprecations. His sword is out, and he advances furiously upon Wyborne, who puts his blade aside with his sheathed rapier. The old man stamps with passion, and seems to call for help. A train of liveried menials enter, and at their master's beck approach the intruder. Wyborne gently disengages himself from the clinging girl, and tenderly places her fainting form upon a couch. His steel glitters in the air. He describes around him a magic circle, which the baffled crew dare not pass. The door closes behind him, and, before the dependents can ask the further pleasure of their lord, the clang of his horse's hoofs is heard lessening in the distance.

Then again I saw them riding over the waves of the Atlantic, and I beheld her gentle form pining away on a distant shore, perhaps under the fatal ban of a father's curse — and then her funeral.

"I must see her picture before I sleep!" I exclaimed, starting up, strongly excited by my waking dream. "I must gaze upon her lovely features as they are feebly shadowed forth on the canvas below, or the phantom I have conjured up will haunt me till dawn." I opened the door softly, and listened: all was silent as the grave. I took off my shoes, and, snuffing my candle, prepared to descend. I have to confess that I was not at that time of my life free from the fumes of the superstitious lore which in my boyish days formed the chosen aliment of childhood, and which was employed by the ignorant nurses of those days both as a reward and a punishment. I own my curiosity more than half gave way when the hall-clock struck TWELVE as I was groping my way down stairs. I reached the library-door; my hand was upon the lock: I hesitated for a moment, and looked hastily over my shoulder. The lock turned, and, as the door slowly opened, I felt as if I should encounter some spectral form in the deserted apartment. All was still, however, and nothing was to be seen as I advanced into the room, but the white, ghastly busts in the middle of it, casting long black sepulchral shadows into the void beyond. I advanced stealthily along, shading my flickering candle with my hand, when I was suddenly startled with a shock and a noise. I had stumbled over a chair. Apprehensive lest the noise should alarm the house, I returned hastily to the door, and listened. But no sound broke the dead silence of the night, and I returned with more cautious steps to pursue my way. At last I stood before the mysterious curtain which concealed the features of the long-buried fair. I felt strangely excited ; I felt as if some appearance, natural or supernatural, would yet baffle my curiosity. The mantel-piece was so high, that I was unable to reach the curtain from the ground, and, putting down my light, I went in search of the library-steps, which I carefully arranged before the fireplace. Taking up the candlestick, I mounted the steps, and laid my hand upon the fringe of the curtain, and was in the act of withdrawing it, when I heard a rustling sound behind me. Turning suddenly around, I saw before me an apparition, which in such a place and at such an hour might well have daunted a stouter heart than mine. A figure in white drapery falling to its feet, a white covering upon its head, and its pale and withered features lighted up by a taper held in its long bony fingers, was looking sadly yet sternly upon me. My candle dropped from my hand, and I was near falling to the ground.

"Young man, what do you here ?" inquired a well-known voice. It was Colonel Wyborne, who had been disturbed by the falling of the chair at my first entrance, and who had descended as he was, in search of the cause. My confusion may be imagined : I would almost have exchanged his presence for that of one of the beings of another world, which for a moment I had imagined him to be. He stood looking at me with a kind of bewildered curiosity, and again said, before I had recovered from my confusion, " Young man, how came you here at this time of night ? "

By this time I had descended from my elevation, and had in some degree collected my spirits, and, thinking that the truth was the best excuse I could make, I apologized for having disturbed his repose, and accounted for my strange conduct by the strong curiosity which my aunt Champion's description of Mrs. Wyborne had excited in my mind to see her portrait. I added, that, as the picture was veiled, I had concluded that the subject was one upon which I was not to touch in his presence; but that my curiosity was certainly not diminished by that air of mystery, and it had perhaps got the better of my sense of what was due to my host; which certainly should have prevented me from prying into what he saw fit to conceal. I concluded by heartily begging his pardon for my unauthorized intrusion upon such sacred ground, and promising to offend no more in future.

I had gathered up my candlestick and broken candle, and was passing by him, feeling sufficiently foolish, when the kind old man laid his hand upon my arm, and gently detained me.

"Stop," said he, "there is no great harm in what you have done: your chief fault has been in not having told me of your desire to see all that remains to me of my beloved wife. I did not know that you had even heard of her; and she is a subject to which I never lead, unless I am sure of an interested auditor. Ascend the steps again, if you please, and draw the curtain."

Much relieved, I obeyed with alacrity, and the portrait was soon unveiled. The light of the two faint candles gave but a tantalizing view of a form of the softest grace, and features of the most bewitching beauty. There she sat in the bloom of early womanhood —

"In freshest flower of youthly years."

The side of her figure was presented to you; but her face was turned as it were suddenly to yours, as if upon some happy surprise; life and joy breathing from her half-smiling lips, and flashing from her dark hazel eyes. The graceful proportions of her bust, too, were brought skilfully into view by the attitude the painter had chosen. Her light brown hair, forming a singular but beautiful contrast with her dark eyes, fell in natural ringlets upon her shoulders, and shaded her pure brow. Her right hand rested upon the smallest of lapdogs, which (evidently a portrait, too) was apparently roused by the same cause which had excited his mistress, and was half standing upon her lap, and regarding you with a serious earnestness of expression. She was seated under a tree, as was usual in portraits of women of that day; and a landscape, which I could scarcely discern, formed the rest of the scenery of the picture.

I stood for many minutes gazing upon this lovely vision, — this being long since vanished from the earth, and yet here before me in all the rosy light of youth and joy. Colonel Wyborne did not interrupt my abstracted gaze till I drew a long breath, as if after a long draught of beauty. He at length broke the silence.

"It is like her," said he, " too like her, I sometimes think; and at other times I look at it till the resemblance seems to vanish in the stronger light of memory. It is for this reason that I have hung the curtain before it; for I find that the reality of the portraiture impresses me more vividly if it be presented only occasionally to my view."

" She must have indeed been a creature," I exclaimed, "to be remembered to the end of the longest life! I am sure that her image will never fade from my remembrance, should my days be protracted to the utmost verge of existence."

" You are right, my son," returned my aged friend : " you are right. She was one of those beings who bore the stamp of immortality upon her brow while she was on earth; and she breathed an undying remembrance into the hearts of all who knew her. We have been long parted ; but she has never been absent from me. And now this fleshly veil must soon be withdrawn, and we shall again see one another face to face."

As he was speaking, I turned my eyes from the lively portraiture before me to the living countenance at my side. His eyes were raised; the tears rolled down his wrinkled but unmoved cheek; his mind had, as it were, for a moment escaped from its prison-house, and rejoined the companion-spirit, the long-lost, but the unforgotten.

"The tears of bearded men," it has been said, and often quoted, "stir up the soul of him who beholds them with a far deeper, because stranger sympathy, than is called forth by the ready tears of woman." But what are they to the tears of extreme old age?

I was deeply moved, and, descending from my elevation, I advanced to my venerable friend, and, taking his hand, reproached myself for having thus agitated his aged bosom by my ill-timed curiosity. He looked at me, and seeing in my wet eye and quivering lip the sympathy which annihilated the years that separated us, he looked benignantly upon me, and said, —

"Nay, my dear boy, it is I who should apologize for having thus given vent to emotions which are far better confined in the breast. But you have taken me at unawares, and the strangeness of the hour and the unexpectedness of this interview quite disarmed me. But come," he continued, taking me by the arm, " we will live over together those long-gone years at some more seasonable time. And now let us betake ourselves to our chambers again."

With these words we slowly retired from the library, and ascended the stairs in silence. When we reached the door of my apartment, Colonel Wyborne expressively pressed my hand without a word, and left me —

"To chew the food of sweet and bitter fancy."

7

It was now near one o'clock. My fire was almost out, and my candle was flickering in its socket: so I speedily disposed myself for rest. It was long, however, before sleep consented to be wooed to my pillow. The figures of my aged host and of the bride of his youth for a long time flitted around my couch, and drove sleep away. At last, however, the twin-brother of Death waved his poppies over my head, and my senses were lapped in forgetfulness.

When I awoke in the morning, the midnight events, which were the first which occurred to my remembrance, seemed, like the visions of the night, to be "such stuff as dreams are made of." But the rays of the sun soon chased away the shadows which had lingered after sleep had fled, and I realized that I had actually had the singular interview with Colonel Wyborne in the library, which dwelt on my memory. I felt at first as if our morning meeting might be a little awkward after our midnight parting, and I resolved to make no allusion to the matter, unless my host led to the subject; but upon second thoughts I determined not to treat it as a circumstance of which I was ashamed, but as one which had excited a strong interest in my mind, of which I could not forbear to speak.

Upon my reaching the parlor, I found Peter busily employed in laying the breakfast-table, with an air of even greater importance than usual; which I accounted for by the fact of its being Thanksgiving Day. His master had not yet appeared. But a few minutes, however, elapsed, before the door opened, and he came in. He bade me good-morning in his usual manner, and I could perceive no trace of the agitation of a few hours before. When Peter had marshalled the last division of the multitudinous array of comestibles which were provided for my refreshment, and the housekeeper had duly furnished forth the simpler components of Colonel Wyborne's repast, and they had both withdrawn, I begged to know if my kind entertainer had experienced any ill consequences from his unusual exposure, of which I was the unintentional cause. He set my fears at rest upon that point, and showing no disinclination to the subject, I reverted to it, assuring him that it was an hour the remembrance of which would abide with me to my dying-day. He seemed pleased with my enthusiasm, and gratified to think that the memory of his wife, which he had supposed would have been buried with himself, would take root in a younger breast, and flourish for another generation. He inquired how much of his history I had learned from Mrs. Champion, and then added many particulars which she had omitted, from her having figured favorably in them, of his short residence in Boston. He also added, beginning at the breakfast-table, and continuing his narrative in a short walk in the garden, a succinct history of his first acquaintance with Maria Somers, the difficulties he surmounted, his clandestine marriage, and the reasons which made it expedient to transfer his residence from England to

America. His history, strange and eventful as it was, I must reserve for some opportunity which affords an ampler verge than is left by this too protracted though "ower true" tale. We continued sauntering up and down the gravel walks, and bathing in the delicious soft air and hazy light of a day better worthy of a place among the bright ring that circle in joyous dance around the merry month of May than to be of the train of the gloomy month which ushers in the winter, till the sound of the first bell reminded us that it was time to make our preparations for divine service.

My toilet was soon completed, and I occupied myself until it was time to go to church in a daylight visit to the library. The lovely features of Maria Wyborne were still unveiled, and smiled upon me even more sweetly than they had done the night before, as the rays of the sun seemed to penetrate the darkest recesses of the picture, and to bring boldly out all that was dimly seen at midnight. When I heard Colonel Wyborne leave his chamber overhead, I drew the curtain, and, having removed the steps from the fireplace to their appropriate nook, I issued out to meet him.

The second bell was just beginning to ring, and the carriage was already at the door; the sable coachman sitting complacently enthroned upon the dicky, while Peter, hat in hand, stood by the expanded door and unfolded steps of the old-fashioned chariot. Colonel Wyborne stood before me as he reached the lowest stair, the very image of a gentleman of the generation which was then just leaving the stage. His wig was elaborately powdered, and terminated behind in a black silk bag, which swung pendulously from shoulder to shoulder as he walked. His coat was of a deep claret-color, with gold buttons, and embroidered about the button-holes, skirts, and cuffs. His waistcoat, of the same material, richly laced about the ample pocket-flaps, opening in front, displayed a world of the finest lace waving in the breeze. Ruffles of the same gossamer fabric shaded his hands. His breeches and stockings were of black silk, and his shoes were graced with ample buckles of the purest gold. His gold-headed cane — full half as tall as himself, now only seen on the stage—and his cocked hat were brought by the vigilant Peter, who left his post by the carriage-door upon his master's approach. Having invested him with these ensigns of dignity, Peter took the cloak from the hands of the attendant housekeeper, and with fitting reverence enveloped his master's form in its ample folds. Alas for the scarlet cloaks of our fathers! They have vanished, with many of the other habits of our ancestors, and have carried with them to their last home much of the graceful reverence for age and rank of which they were the emblems. Peace to their shreds!

Colonel Wyborne, being at length invested with all his habiliments, leaned upon my arm, and somewhat painfully ascended the uncertain footing of the carriage-steps. I followed him, and the door was closed upon us by Peter, who duly took his stand behind the carriage. The heavy vehicle moved slowly forward, and, as we turned into the high-road, it might have been thought that one of the frontispieces to the old editions of Sir Charles Grandison was suddenly inspired with life, and had turned out the family coach of Uncle Selby, or the more elegant equipage of Sir Hargrave Pollexfen, or the mercurial Lady G., upon the king's highway. Turning to the left as we came into the public road, we ascended a considerable hill, from the top of which we saw before us the village meeting-house, forming, as it were, the centre of the little rural system. As we drove along the road we saw the inhabitants of the village issuing from their comfortable houses, and wending their way to church. They were mostly dressed in the productions of their own farms and looms, and had an air of substantial plenty about them, without any attempts on the part of man or woman to ape the manners and costume of the town. The road was also covered with the farmers who lived beyond walking-distance, mounted on stout farm-horses, with their wives or daughters seated on pillions behind them ; and now and then a heavy square-topped gig, or chaise as it was then called, looking like a sedan-chair cut in two and placed on wheels, came lumbering along, filled with an amount of humanity which proved to a demonstration the infinite compressibility, if not perfectibility, of human nature. The meeting-house was of the earliest style of construction ; the belfry in the centre of the roof, which sloped up on four sides to it : the principal door, which was opposite to the pulpit, was on one of the longer sides of the parallelogram, while the shorter sides were adorned and accommodated with porticos. As we passed by the cheerful groups of walkers or riders, — for, it not being the sabbath, they did not think it incumbent upon them, though going to meeting, to put on their Sunday faces, — they all made due reverence to Colonel Wyborne, who was universally beloved for his bountiful and courteous spirit. When we drew up at the church-door, many a brawny arm was proffered to assist him in his descent, which he acknowledged with the most perfect grace of good-breeding, and said something to each of his humble friends, which made them better contented with themselves, and of course with him.

I followed Colonel Wyborne up the broad aisle to his pew, which was the fourth from the door on your right hand and the nearest of the pews to the pulpit, the space between the pews and the pulpit being filled up with benches, upon which were arranged the aged parishioners who were not owners of pews, in order of seniority; the post of honor being the one nearest the minister. The pulpit was of oak, unpainted, and surmounted by an enormous sounding-board, looking like a gigantic extinguisher just on the point of putting out the luminary beneath. Beneath the pulpit, the deacons' seat embraced within its ample enclosure the dignified officials for whom it was designed, — one bald-headed, with an unquestionable squint, and the other with his thin gray locks falling almost to

his shoulders, and with a sharp face and meagre person ; both seated with their backs to the pulpit, and
their faces to the congregation.   Two galleries ran
round the walls ; one filled with women, and the other
with men.   Near the ceiling, on the left hand as we
sat, a phenomenon was presented to the inquiring eye
in the shape of an oblong hole in the wall, surrounded
by a sort of wooden frame in which was set a human
face, which glared upon the meeting-house door with
an earnestness almost supernatural.   About every
ten seconds the face of the apparition underwent a
sort of downward twitch, which was succeeded with a
sharp toll of the bell ; but the eyes were ever riveted
upon the door.   At length a twitch of more convul-
sive energy than usual was followed by an emphatic
clang of the bell, which said as plainly as the tongue
of bell could speak, "There, my work's done for to-
day!"   And, while its undulating sound was vibrating
on the ear, the Rev. Mr. Armsby walked majestically
along the aisle, and ascended the stairs; his well-
powdered wig diffusing a miniature snow-storm upon
the small precise cape of his black cloak.   After a
short pause, the services proceeded.   The prayers of
the revered pastor were admirable, eloquent, devout,
fervid, mostly clothed in the language of Scripture, or
at least in language which gushed from a mind deeply
imbued with the spirit of the Hebrew prophets.   As
the rich, deep tones of his voice uttered forth the recital of the blessings and bounties which this people
had received at the hand of Heaven, — of freedom, of

peace, of plenty, and, above all, of the knowledge of the true God and of Jesus Christ whom he has sent, — and then described their unworthiness and ingratitude and sinfulness, and deprecated the impending wrath of Heaven and the awful judgments which were reserved for an ungrateful, godless nation, all wrapt in the dark and terrible imagery of the prophecies, I could almost imagine that I heard one of the seers of old telling in thunder-tones his message of warning and denunciation to the chosen but erring race.

The innovation of a choir had displaced the good old custom of singing the hymns " line by line " by the whole congregation. Of this part of the service I will say nothing, except that it bore no resemblance which could shock the most rigid Puritan, to the choral symphonies of the Sistine Chapel, or even to the heathenish melody of that legitimate daughter of the old Scarlet Lady, the Church of England. A bass-viol grated its share of harsh discords in addition to those of the human instruments, all of which together, if the science of music does not lie, must have amounted to harmony. Colonel Wyborne, in the goodness of his heart and the abundance of his good-will to any persons who earnestly did what they could to assist at the service of the sanctuary, though himself an excellent judge of music, stood up alone during the performance, and encouraged the choristers by strict attention, and beating time, and, when they finished, by an emphatic, " Very well, very well indeed!" audible over the whole house. My gravity, I confess, received a severe shock, and I fully expected to hear a general titter run round the assembly ; but a hurried glance around satisfied me that it was a usual act of my admirable old friend, and was regarded with pride and pleasure by the singers and the rest of the congregation, and by no means looked upon as anything out of the common way. This circumstance brought Sir Roger de Coverley at once to my mind ; and, the idea being suggested, I recalled a good many points of resemblance between the warm-hearted old baronet and Colonel Wyborne ; though the latter was entirely free from any hallucination like that which sometimes sent Sir Roger's wits a wool-gathering.

The introductory services being over, the minister rose and took a prefatory look around at his flock. Before giving out his text, however, he desired the audience, in a tone of authority and decision which would have well become Dr. Johnson himself when he scolded Boswell for having a headache, not to interrupt the discourse by coughing or sneezing ; which ebullitions he assured them were entirely unnecessary. It may be well to add that his commands were strictly obeyed ; thus affording a new fact in support of Kant's theory of the power of the will over bodily ailments. This preliminary being adjusted, he announced his text, and proceeded with his sermon. It was a truly masterly production, and displayed those remarkable powers which not long afterwards procured his translation to the more congenial atmosphere of the metropolis. It was a work like one of the Pyramids; its foundations, broad and deep, resting on eternal and universal truth, and the superstructure tapering in sublime simplicity up to the blessed duty of gratitude,— massive blocks of sense and reasoning piled regularly in lessening rows upon one another, and clamped together by cogent quotations from the Greek and Hebrew Scriptures; all ascending upwards to a single truth, and making upon the mind, undistracted by meretricious ornament, an impression of oneness, the feeling of a grand whole. The music of his intonations and the harmony of his gesture are still present to my mind, as if it were but yesterday that he spoke. He was listened to with the most profound attention; and, when he ended, his auditory all seemed to take a long breath, and each man looked upon his neighbor with a flushed cheek and a dilated eye.

But one circumstance interrupted the solemnity of the discourse, and that was too characteristic a one to be passed over in silence. In the midst of the sermon an unlucky child in the women's gallery began to cry. The pastor stopped short, turned his severe eye upon the dismayed mother, and sternly said, "Take that child away!" In unutterable confusion the poor woman gathered up her descendant; and the urchin, kicking and screaming with an energy worthy of a better cause, quickly vanished from our sight. This little episode, however, attracted but little attention on the part of the rest of the audience, and, the moment it was over, they were as deeply absorbed as ever in the march of the discourse.

After the blessing had been pronounced, the whole congregation remained standing in their places, as was their invariable custom, until Mr. Armsby and Colonel Wyborne had left the house. While the clergyman was making his preparations for his departure, Colonel Wyborne left his pew, and kindly advanced to the venerable band of old men, and made friendly inquiries as to their well-being; and I could catch the sounds of their grateful voices thanking him for the bountiful gifts which he had bestowed upon them at this joyful season. When Mr. Armsby descended from the pulpit, Colonel Wyborne took his arm, and, giving me a signal to follow, slowly left the house, courteously inclining his head to the right and left in acknowledgment of the respectful salutations which he received from the sturdy farmers on either side. We all three entered the coach, which we found ready at the door, and were soon conveyed to the scene of the solemnities which yet remained to be performed appropriate to the great New England festival. On the way, the conversation was engrossed by the two gentlemen, and I confess that I regarded my reverend companion as a sort of a Mordecai at my gate, and looked forward with a kind of dismay to the cloud which he would bring over the joyous festivity which I had anticipated at the Thanksgiving table of my genial host.

Upon our arrival we were shown into the library,

at either end of which a blazing fire worthy of an English Christmas diffused a generous warmth through
the apartment. The cheerful heat had an evident
effect on the ice of the reverend gentleman's manners ; for, there being no provision made in those
days for warming churches, we were all glad enough
to greet the cordial welcome of the blaze. As we
walked from one fireplace to the other, and stopped
before each to imbibe a portion of its warmth, Mr.
Armsby, for almost the first time, turned to me and
said, " Well, young gentleman, how do you like being
between two fires?" — a jocular abortion which I
received with a laugh worthy of a better jest, with
an explosion which would not have discredited a
Schœpen in the eyes of a jovial burgomaster. The
worthy gentleman evidently took my laugh in good
part, and by being put on better terms with himself,
was disposed to regard me with more consideration
than he had yet done. He made some more rather
cumbrous attempts at jocularity, which being met
more than halfway by myself, we soon rapidly neared
one another, and before long, not unassisted by the
good-nature of our host, we were fairly engaged yard-
arm to yard-arm. My awe of him gradually melted
away, and, before Peter made his appearance with the
tankard of punch, I began to wonder that I could ever
have felt any.

As I have hinted in the preceding sentence, in due
time the door opened, and the excellent functionary
there alluded to was ushered in, bearing with fitting

solemnity upon a salver the silver tankard, which in those days ever heralded the serious business of the day. A grateful perfume arose from its brimming mouth, and filled the apartment. Colonel Wyborne received the fragrant offering at the hands of the sable Ganymede, and, having raised it to his lips, passed it to his most honored guest, who paid it the homage of a deeper libation, and then consigned it to my ingenuous hands. This harbinger of better things to come (now, I admit, better far removed) performed its orbit round our little circle with a rapidity and regularity which would have given a temperance society a fit of delirium-tremens, until the last drop was drained. Admirer as I am of old customs, I must allow that this was one which I am glad to have survived. The punch-drinking of a morning, which our ancestors looked upon in the light of an innocent amusement, not to say of a positive duty, is extinct, and with it have vanished in a great measure the gout, and a train of "immedicable ills" of which it was the fruitful parent. Since its disappearance, too, drunkenness is a vice almost unknown to the educated classes ; which was far from being the case in my time. On the present occasion, however, the bewitching draught seemed to unlock the secret source of a thousand sympathies till then unsuspected, and to bring to light a multitude of affinities, unfelt before, between the morning, the meridian, and the evening of life. Under its deceitful though delicious enchantment, the barriers which time and custom had raised between us, and which but a short time before seemed to be impassable, were levelled with the ground, and we stood side by side as friend by friend.

Precisely as the hall-clock struck two, Peter, re-entering, announced dinner, and, marshalled by that dark seneschal, we proceeded in due order to the dining-room. Mr. Armsby blessed the meal with a grace which seemed at least sufficiently long to a hungry boy, in which he did not omit, in the enumeration of blessings, the Governor, Council, the churches, the college, and the old Congress. When he had concluded, and we had taken our seats, the covers were removed, and displayed an array of dishes which would have seemed preposterous for the supply of three persons, did we not know that a multitude of retainers were assembled in the kitchen, eagerly awaiting whatever might fall from our table. A noble tautaug,[1] with his tail in his mouth, lay grimly before me, like the Egyptian emblem of eternity. At the foot of the table, Colonel Wyborne was intrenched behind a formidable round of beef *à-la-mode*. A roast turkey was stretched, victim-like, upon his back before the sacerdotal knife of the pastor ; while on the other side of the table a pair of boiled chickens lay patiently awaiting their immersion in the oyster-sauce which stood ready for the deed. Vegetables of every description filled up all the interstices of the well-spread board ; and decanters of white wine (for

---

[1] Vulgarly called black-fish by the many.

as yet red wine was not) kept watch and ward, like
tall sentinels, over the whole scene of action. Soon
the remains of the fish before me were decently removed, and replaced by an admirable haunch of venison, attended by all that should accompany that prince
of meats, — the sacrificial fires; the jelly, " sweet as
the smile when fond lovers meet, and soft as their
parting tear; " the thin parallelograms of toast, brown
as the Arabian berry. All our energies were soon
wholly engrossed in this new career of duty, which
we pursued with an untiring zeal and indomitable
perseverance, which should have entitled us to a high
place among the benefactors of mankind.

But, alas ! even venison may cease to please. At
least a foreboding of future good yet to be revealed
from the dark recesses of the kitchen prompted for-
bearance ere it was too late. At length the viands
which I have feebly attempted to describe were transported from our eyes, and a new generation occupied
their vacant places. The beef *à-la-mode* suddenly
gave place to the much-injured bird which saved the
capitol; the venison, with a sigh, yielded its throne
to a triple alliance of wild ducks; a pair of partridges
dislodged the reluctant turkey; while the boiled
chickens with the attendant oyster-sauce fled amain
before the incursion of a horde of lesser " fowl of
game." The transitory nature of all human things
is well illustrated by the sentiment of one of the heroines of "The Rovers, or the Double Arrangement,"
in the Anti-Jacobin, where she says (I quote from

memory), "The beef of to-morrow will succeed to the veal of to-day, as the veal of to-day has succeeded to the mutton of yesterday." But the flying courses of a single repast bring home even more forcibly to the reflecting mind the instability of our most substantial joys, and afford a lively picture of the fleeting generations of mankind, hurrying, like them, over the bountifully spread and richly adorned banquetiug-table on which Boon Nature feasts her children. The change which had just come over the scene before us was not destined to endure any more than the one which had preceded it. The shining face of Peter is again seen, full of busy importance, bustling about the board. And now the table is cleared ; and anxious expectation sits impatient on every brow. A pause ensues. The door opens, and, lo ! he comes, the Pudding of the Plum, Thanksgiving Day's acknowledged chief. He comes, attended, conqueror-like, by the dethroned monarch of Christmas Day, Mince-pie, who follows, crestfallen, in his triumphal train. Apple-pie, too, rears his " honest soncy face " in sturdy yeoman pride. Custard, no longer " blasphemed through the nose," receives the respectful deference due to fallen greatness. And thou, Pumpkin-pie, my country's boast, when I forget thee, may my right hand forget its cunning ! And Squash-pie, too, when I refuse to celebrate thy praise, may my tongue cleave to the roof of my mouth !

Then came the dessert, chiefly composed, from the necessity of the season, of dried fruits ; but then such

8

apples and such pears!—apples for which Atalanta
might well have lost her race, or which might well
have been thrown by Discord among the gods. The
pears, too!—St. Michael's spicy fruit, St. Catherine's
immutable glow,—"the side that's next the sun,"
—worthy the cheek of a cherub; St. Germain's celestial gust; and other gentle races which confer by
their virtues higher honors on their patron saints
than any they derive from their canonization.

Then, too, came from the subterraneous crypts,
where they had been confined for many years, the im-
prisoned spirits whom Wit obeys; not those fierce
demons which are called into being amidst the
fierce combustion of the still, and which soon tear
in pieces the victims whom they have singled out
for their prey, but "delicate spirits," like the gentle
Ariel, bursting into life in the year-long summer's
day of the Fortunate Islands, and summoned across
the Atlantic waves to impart their native summer
to Northern hearts. Alas that any magicians should
now be found who would fain exorcise them, and
condemn them to the fate of vulgar devils! But
then it must be admitted that the degeneracy of
modern times has reached even these ethereal powers.
The grapes of the present day do not express the same
juice which gushed from the veins of their progeni-
tors. Their thin potations have debauched this
washy generation. Did the French philosophy take
root amongst us before our clay had been soaked in
claret and champagne? Were we overrun with the

weeds of German metaphysics before the Rhine had poured an acid deluge over the land ?   Talk of the schoolmaster being abroad !   The heresies which infest this age were unknown until the wine-merchant went abroad.

I wish that I could find it in my heart to detain the gentle reader from the perusal of things better worth his reading, and recount the talk of that genial day.   But the milkiness of my nature forbids.   Besides, a separate essay will not be too much to devote to the oddities, genius, and virtues of Richard Armsby.   He was a choice specimen of that racy class of originals, the elder New England clergy ; men who were in a great measure raised above the control of public opinion, and the sharpnesses of whose characters were not smoothed down by the friction of society, and the excursions of whose eccentricities were checked neither by the inquisition of squeamish coteries nor by the censure of a fastidious age.   I have never looked upon his like since he entered into his rest.   He united the playfulness of Yorick and the simplicity of Parson Adams with the logical acuteness of Butler, the strong sense of Barrow, and the redundant imagination of Taylor; and all these shining and solid materials which went to make up the web of his remarkable mind were strongly relieved by the dark groundwork of the sternest Calvinism upon which they were woven.   And yet this man is forgotten.   His sermons, which should have constituted an integral portion of our literature, have been fated to "clothe spice, line trunks," or to fall into the sacrilegious hands of the "oblivious cook." Surely this was a man of whom the world in which he lived was not worthy.

That day is an epoch in my life, for it was the first time that I had ever listened to the table-talk of the highest description. I might have searched the world through, and yet not have met with two such men, so different and yet so admirable, as the two whom the chances of life had thrown together in the remote village of Sanfield. I have since listened to most of the celebrated men of conversation of our times, and the chimes of midnight have often fallen unheeded upon my ear as I yielded myself to the enchantment of their eloquence and wit; but the remembrance of that brilliant day still holds the first place among my convivial memories.

We remained at table till about six o'clock, when we returned to the library, where tea and coffee were served. After this ceremony was over, Mr. Armsby's pipe was brought, — "his custom always of an afternoon," — and taking, as it were, a new departure from this event, he swept gallantly on through a sea of talk, growing more and more brilliant as he went. At last, however, ten o'clock came. He knocked out the last ashes of his pipe, and, taking a glass more of wine as a stirrup-cup, he prepared for his departure. The carriage was soon at the door; and our charming friend, for such I could not but regard him in spite of his ministerial dignity, bade us a cordial good-night.   As I attended him to the carriage, he warmly pressed me, nothing loath, to visit him at his bachelor's house.

When I returned to the library, Colonel Wyborne begged to know whether I did not think that his prophecy the day before, of the change which a day would bring forth in Mr. Armsby, had not been fulfilled.   I replied with expressions of the warmest admiration of the qualities of his reverend friend. "And pray, sir," I added, "why did not you tell me how extraordinary a man he is?"

"Simply," he replied with a benignant smile, "simply because I wished to give you the pleasure of finding it out for yourself."

We soon separated for the night; but it was long after I had sought my couch that the clear tones of the pastor's voice died upon my ear.   The strange groups of thought, in which ideas that never before dreamt of meeting each other found themselves side by side; the freshness and beauty of his classic allusions, and the grotesque narrations of scenes and characters such as are only known in a simple and primitive state of society, delivered with a spirit and life which Matthews never surpassed, — all together produced a degree of pleasurable excitement which drove sleep far from my eyes.   The walls of my solitary chamber rung with the echoes of a foregone merriment; and, if my pillow were that night wet with tears, they were the tears

"Of one worn out with mirth and laughter."

CHAPTER V.

THE next morning, after breakfast, Colonel Wyborne proposed to me a drive to the parsonage to pay a visit to Mr. Armsby. I gladly closed with this proposition, as my experiences of the day before had excited a strong curiosity on my part to know more of that true original — in the best sense of the word. The coach having been ordered, my excellent host, at my request, commenced a short account of his reverend friend, which he concluded as we drove towards his local habitation. His history was not very different from that of hosts of other ornaments of the New England Church and State. His father was a painstaking farmer, who extracted by the alchemy of intelligent labor, from the rocky and ungenial soil of one of the least propitious portions of Massachusetts Bay, a plentiful and comfortable subsistence for a family of some twelve children. The early education of his son Richard had been in the school of agricultural labor. The plough and the spade were the earliest teachers his rugged intellect had known. During the leisure hours of "workless winter," indeed, he had picked up the rudiments of knowledge, and secured those branches of learning, which, according to high authority, "come by nature."

Having acquired the key to knowledge, he soon employed it to unlock all the stores which were within his reach.   His father's literary collections were not of a very extensive or a very various description.   A few books of Puritan divinity, and many printed sermons of New England divines, in loose pamphlets, formed the staple of his library.   These works, however, for want of matter more attractive, were eagerly devoured.   Among his father's books, however, was Cotton Mather's " Magnalia," which soon became his favorite author.   His admiration was excited by the display of learning which so liberally garnishes those curious pages; and his wonder was none the less because he could not detect the pedantry and bad taste of the load of quotations with which the author's original matter is overlaid, and of the conceits in which he delights to indulge.   To a boy in an inland town, brought up in Puritan habits, this book was truly fascinating.   The histories of the worthies who had founded or embellished the infant empire; the descriptions of the persecutions which they endured in England, and of the hardships which they encountered when they snatched their civil and religious rights to these bleak and inhospitable shores; the stirring descriptions of the Indian wars, which so often threatened destruction to the whole province, and of which there were many survivors in his neighborhood, full of traditionary lore; and especially the solemn recital of the mysterious phenomena of witchcraft, of the wiles of Satan for the extirpation of God's people, some of which, it must be confessed, did but little credit to the sagacity of the arch-enemy — all these topics formed fertile themes for winter evening study and for summer noontide dreams.

I do not wonder that the belief in witchcraft took such strong hold of our ancestors' imaginations, living as they did in a country but half explored, overshadowed with primeval forests — filled with heathen foes and with savage beasts — from the depths of which strange sounds came at midnight upon their ear, and whose varying shadows and lights assumed to the superstitious eye of the wayfarer the grotesque or ghastly forms of demons or spectres. There was an infinite deal more romance in the primitive days of our ancestors, planted as they were on a narrow belt between the ocean and the wilderness, than we can dream of in these prosaic days of steam and railroads.

Richard Armsby's love of books early aroused in his father's breast the ambition, which in those days lingered in every parent's heart, of seeing his son one of the clergy, one of the religious aristocracy of the land. His narrow circumstances, however, made the prospect almost a hopeless one, until one day the pastor of the parish, in one of his parochial rounds, discovered the young enthusiast busily employed with his favorite volume. It so happened that " the fantastic old great man " was a favorite with the good man; and his heart warmed towards the lad when he found how thoroughly he was acquainted with all that he could learn from that not too authentic source of the history of his country. His father's wishes and his own tastes were soon made known to their several advisers, and he undertook the task of preparing the young man for college. This was speedily accomplished by the vigorous intellect, and earnestness of purpose, of young Armsby. The work of preparation being finished, he was despatched to Cambridge, with but a small stock of money, but with an ample supply of faith and hope. His struggles in the cause of good learning were severe, and his heart at times almost died within him, and he was more than once on the point of abandoning his studies. In a happy hour, however, he went, one winter's vacation, to keep the village school of Sanfield, where he soon attracted the kind notice of Colonel Wyborne. The sagacity and knowledge of character which were almost instinctive with that excellent gentleman, soon discerned that the rough diamond he had lighted upon was a gem of the first water. From that moment, all his difficulties were at an end. His kind patron's liberality removed all obstacles from his way, and made the remainder of his literary path one of pleasantness. Soon after his college career was finished, the minister of Sanfield died; and Mr. Armsby was very soon inducted into his place, chiefly through Colonel Wyborne's influence. For the many years that had elapsed since that day, they had lived on terms of the most cordial intimacy; their esteem for each other increasing with their years. Mr. Armsby having never been married, their friendly intercourse had never encountered the interruption which the intervention of Hymen but too often works in the best-grounded friendships; and I doubt not that the minister's congenial society greatly contributed to cheer and prolong his aged friend's existence.

The substance of this narrative was just imparted as the carriage drove up to the parsonage-door. It was a very old building, unpainted, situated just on the edge of the village. It stood on a high bank, at some distance from the road, with two or three trees of aboriginal growth waving their twisted arms above its roof. The master of the house received us at the door with much formal politeness. On entering the front-door, we descended one step, which had nearly been a step too much for me, having never before been greeted with such a reception at any threshold I had ever passed. In front of us was a wooden seat, which opened on hinges, and displayed a sort of chest. The stairs ascended abruptly, almost from the very door. Turning to our left, we were ushered into the study, which was almost the only apartment which the solitary minister used of his whole house. It was a room of good size, but with a low ceiling, and a bare beam, rough-shaped with the axe, passing through its length. The walls were well covered with dingy-looking books, most of them formidable folios of controversial divinity, but relieved by excellent editions of the Greek and Latin classics (for Mr. Armsby was a ripe scholar and a good one), and by some of the sterling English authors.   There was the folio edition of Shakspeare, and the little shabby quarto first edition of " Paradise Lost," in ten books, and there was the first edition of Burton's " Anatomy," which I had ever seen.   A wooden arm-chair with a leaf to it was the throne of the sovereign of the domain.   A few wooden chairs — of various shapes, and apparently of different epochs in the colonial history, but none of which would have excited the envy of a Sybarite — were scattered about the room in a somewhat dusty confusion.   A deal table or so, and a woodbox, completed the furniture of the apartment.   The floor was unconscious of a carpet, and to all appearance had been long innocent of the knowledge of the virtues of soap and fair water.   The hearth was of red brick, on which was built a wood fire of exemplary brightness.   The bricks of the chimney-back, to be sure, had yielded to the hand of time (" What will not Time subdue ! ") but then one of them afforded a timely aid to one of the andirons, which, in the course of many years' service, had lost a leg.   The neatness of the whole establishment did not certainly afford much room for commendation ; but then, as no commendations were expected or desired, it was of the less consequence.

Our reverend host having resigned his chair of state to his honored guest, and provided himself and me with humbler stools, we all drew up cheerfully to the fire, and talked merrily over the day before.

Though the manner of Mr. Armsby towards me was not distinguished by the convivial freedom of the day before, still it was entirely free from the austerity and coldness which marked it at our first acquaintance. It was now just what the demeanor of a gentleman of his time of life, and standing in society, should be towards a lad of eighteen, — kind, affable, without being familiar or free; which made me feel perfectly at my ease in his company, and yet which made it perfectly impossible for me to forget the distance which separated us.

After we had discussed a variety of topics, which he treated in a manner to show that wine and wassail had nothing to do with his powers of entertainment, he inquired about my plans for returning to Cambridge. I informed him that I must set forth early the next morning in order to reach the arms of my Alma Mater before night. As, in the course of the conversation which ensued on the subject, I expressed no great satisfaction in the prospect before me, of a twenty-miles' ride upon a sorry hack, Colonel Wyborne seemed to be suddenly struck with a new idea, which he uttered to this effect: "It never occurred to me before; but I think that I can save you that tedious ride, if you have no objection to an expedition in a row-boat."

I assured him that boating was one of my choicest amusements, and awaited with some curiosity to know the nature of his proposition.

"If that be the case," said he, "I think, that, as

the weather is so fine, we can manage it in this way. I will take my boat, and accompany you to my farm on Vincents Island this afternoon, where we will spend the night ; and to-morrow you shall continue your row up to Boston, while I await the return of my boat."

" But my horse ? "

" Oh, John can take him home on Monday, on his way to town : it will be but a few miles out of his way."

The only difficulty in the way being thus obviated, I most heartily concurred in the plan, which promised to substitute a cheerful ride over the waves for a dreary one over the high-road, and, besides, to give me nearly a whole day to myself in Boston. These preliminaries being adjusted, Mr. Armsby was invited to make one of our water-party, with which proposition he readily closed, to our general satisfaction.

The conversation turning upon the early colonial times, Mr. Armsby displayed in that most curious portion of history a minuteness of erudition which I had never before seen exhibited. It was evidently his hobby, and he caracoled and curvetted upon it in a manner which excited my wonder and delight. He displayed many curious manuscripts of the fathers, illustrative of their history, and several of the old Indian deeds and treaties. In his library, too, were many books which the Pilgrims had made the chosen companions of their wanderings and exile, rendered more precious by copious marginal notes, which it would have puzzled the younger Champollion himself to decipher. In a walk which we took together round his house, he pointed out the scene of a bloody fight with the Indians, and showed many perforations in the walls of his house, made by the bullets of the savage foe. Then there was the pear-tree which Elder Brewster planted with his own hands, and the very oak under which Captain Miles Standish and his little company bivouacked on the night of their return from the discomfiture of Morton and his rabble rout at Merry Mount. The interest which I took in these relics of the last age, and the attention which I gave to his commentaries upon them, evidently raised me many degrees in his estimation, and laid the foundation of a friendship which only ended with his life.

After a visit of nearly two hours, we took our leave, having first arranged that Mr. Armsby should join me at dinner, so as to be ready for our excursion. We then returned home, and were duly joined at an early hour by our reverend friend. The airy prologue of the punch, the grave drama of the dinner, and the cheerful epilogue of the madeira, being over, it was announced that the tide served, and the boat was in readiness. We accordingly proceeded on foot to the shore, John and Peter following us with our cloaks and luggage. We took a little different route from the one which Colonel Wyborne and I had followed on the first day of our visit, and bent our steps towards the mouth of the little stream which washed his estate, on the banks of which the boat-house was built. On arriving at the place of embarkation, we found the boat launched, and the four boatmen — two black and two white — resting on their oars, awaiting our arrival. Our places were soon taken : Peter, with our luggage and a stupendous hamper of provisions and wine for the voyage, was seated in a grinning delight; and the "trim-built wherry" was speedily dancing over the crests of the wave.

The afternoon was more like one in May than one on the very brink of winter. The sun shone brightly; the sea was placid as a land-locked bay or inland lake; the sea-fowl hovered above or about us, or dived beneath the billows; while in the distance the white sails glided like happy spirits among the islands of the blessed. The scene was one full of quiet and of tranquillizing beauty, which rather provoked revery than conversation. A favorable breeze soon springing up, the mast was fixed in its place ; and the sail, given to the gale, soon made us leap forward on our course with a new alacrity. Our voyage was pursued in silence, only broken by occasional exclamations at the beautiful effects of light and shade caused by the floating clouds, and at the varying hues of the distant ocean. The sun set before we had reached our port, and, wrapping ourselves in our cloaks, we sat watching the stars emerging from their ocean-bed, and beginning the solemn procession which nightly moves in sublime order around " this dim spot called earth."

Colonel Wyborne seemed to be buried in deepest revery, sad yet not melancholy, as if the magic of the scene had conjured up to his half-dreaming eye —

> " The spectres which no exorcism can bind,
>   The cold, the changed, perchance the dead, to view
>   The mourned, the loved, the lost — too many, yet how few !

We respected the meditative mood of our venerable friend, and sat in silence till the boat reached her destined haven; when the oarsmen unshipped the mast, and pulled stoutly for the little mole which was projected into the sea.

We were soon disembarked, and on our way to the farmhouse of Colonel Wyborne, which was occupied by an excellent man and his wife, now just beginning to feel the hand of time, who had lived in the sea-girdled home for the chief of their days. They received us with many demonstrations of kindness and respect, and seemed in nowise disconcerted by our unexpected arrival. Indeed, the ample supplies of provisions which our commissary Peter brought along with him removed all hospitable apprehensions as to our due alimentation. We were received in the ample kitchen of the farmhouse, which was illuminated by a blazing pile of logs, roaring up a volcano of a chimney, and diffusing a ruddy light and cheerful warmth throughout the apartment. We were soon comfortably established by the genial fireside, while the goodwife was busily employed in preparing our evening meal. When our repast was ready, and we had taken our places at the table, Colonel Wyborne still seemed absorbed in his dreaming mood, and was evidently in spirit far away from the wave-washed islet where he was present in the body. His silence imposed an unavoidable restraint upon Mr. Armsby and myself. At last, however, he seemed to rouse from his revery, and, looking up at us, said, —

"I know that you will think dotage has come rapidly upon me, when I tell you of the resolution which I have been forming. But my mind is made up: I go to Boston to-night."

"To Boston to-night!" exclaimed in one breath both his companions; both, no doubt, a little suspicious that something was out of joint in the good old gentleman's intellectuals.

"Even so," replied he in his blandest but most determined manner. "It is now fifty years since I saw my native city, and I once thought that nothing could induce me to visit it again; but a strange impulse, which I have often felt before, urges me with an almost irresistible force to see once more, before I die, the scene of my early days and of the short-lived happiness of my prime of manhood."

"But why to-night?" inquired Mr. Armsby.

"Because," he replied, "it may be my last night. This strange possession often comes over me, sometimes in my solitary walks, or lonely musings in my library, but most frequently in those wakeful hours of nights which form a heavy share of the burden of old age. I feel that to-night the craving may be

9

satisfied, and that, if I neglect to use this night, another opportunity may never come to me."

"But I do not exactly comprehend your plan, my dear sir," observed his reverend companion.

"It is this," he replied. "The moon will rise in an hour: in three hours we may reach the town. I propose to land after all the inhabitants have deserted the streets, and to revisit my old familiar haunts by moonlight, and then return before the earliest stirrer is abroad."

Mr. Armsby in vain represented to him the fatigue, the sleepless night, the night-air, the mental excitement, which the execution of his scheme would bring upon himself. His heart seemed to be set upon the plan; and he expressed his determination to accomplish the adventure by himself, if we declined accompanying him. This, of course, was not to be thought of; and, his resolution being taken, we prepared to accompany him on his singular expedition. Mr. Armsby very evidently did not much relish the idea of exchanging his snug corner of the chimney in possession, and his comfortable bed in prospect, for a damp, chilly row of three or four hours by moonlight. I, on the other hand, was just of an age to enjoy anything which had the appearance of novelty and the air of romance.

Our trusty boatmen were speedily roused from their lair, and ordered upon this new and unexpected service. They were soon in readiness; and we all re-embarked, as well protected against the night-air as broadcloth could make us. As soon as we had pushed off, and cleared the shadow of the island, we saw the moon, " rising in clouded majesty " just above the waves, and shedding a long and tremulous line of light upon the dancing waters. The scene was truly enchanting. The slight murmur of the waves, the measured dip of the flashing oars, and the distant bark of the watchdog of the island we were leaving behind us, were all the sounds which broke the stillness of the midnight sea. The light, fleecy clouds which accompanied the appearance of heaven's " apparent Queen " were soon dispersed, and she shone forth in matchless lustre. The magic air which her silver light gave to the whole world of waters was the more charming to us who had just seen the orb of day sink in a sea of molten gold. The stars stood out from the firmament with all the sharpness. and distinctness of a winter's night; while the glimmering lights twinkled at unequal intervals from the line of coast along which we skirted, and the numerous islands amidst which we threaded our devious way.

Thus we sped along, for the chief of the way in silence, till at length we shot under the guns of the Castle, and the town lay before us, seen dimly in the uncertain moonlight. As we glided along to the measured music of the oars, Colonel Wyborne's eyes were fixed, with an earnestness almost painful, upon the shadowy mass of buildings in the distance. His thoughts were, doubtless, transported to the day, half

a century before, when he last approached his native
town by sea.   How different the circumstances under
which he approached it then and now !   Then, in the
pride of manhood, he walked over the waters in a
gallant ship, in the clear light of an autumnal day.
The wife of his love was by his side ; troops of welcoming friends stretched out their arms from the
shore to hail the wanderer's return.   Though he had
spent many years amidst the superb cities and magnificent ruins of Europe, and had dwelt as a familiar
friend in the bosom of the most gorgeous scenery and
time-hallowed relics of a classic world, still it seemed
to his true heart as if he had never gazed upon a
scene so lovely or so beloved as was present to his
filial eyes as he drew near his native land.   Now, in
the spectral light of the moon, he glided like a ghost
to haunt the scenes of his former happiness.   The
wife of his bosom, whose gentle hand was clasped in
his when he last moved over those waves, had been
for fifty years the latest tenant of his ancestral vault.
The numerous friends whose cordial grasp welcomed
him home were, with scarcely an exception, long
since gone from earth ; and the few survivors were,
like him, transformed from men of the prime to faint
old men just tottering on the brink of the grave.   A
thousand recollections of buried love, of vanished
youth, of half-forgotten friends, of well-remembered
griefs, of blighted hopes, of transitory joys, crowded
upon his musing soul.

At last the prow of our boat struck the stairs of

the Long Wharf, and our voyage was ended. Just at that moment, the clock of the Old South Church struck twelve, and was answered from the towers of all the other churches in long-drawn-out, but sweet and solemn tones. Mr. Armsby and I assisted Colonel Wyborne to disembark, who then, leaning upon our arms on either side, commenced his strange and melancholy pilgrimage. The fifty years which had elapsed since his departure from Boston had wrought none of those changes in the appearance of the town which the spells of modern speculation have in these latter days often worked in a single lustrum. The aspect of the place was almost unchanged. The population had scarcely increased during that period, and the small addition had been contented to fix their habitations upon the large extent of unoccupied ground within the peninsula, without laying their parricidal hands upon the roofs which had sheltered their fathers. As we slowly proceeded up King (now State) Street, there were to be seen on either side the same dwellings which our aged friend had left when he took his last leave of the metropolis. How different was that scene from the one which the same ground now presents! Now it is metamorphosed into one great granite temple to Mammon, whose pavements are worn by the frequent feet of his busy worshippers. The household gods have fled from its precincts; the fire is quenched on the domestic altar; the voice of woman and the laugh of childhood are there heard no more. But on that night, more than half a century since, the moon which looked down upon the sleeping city bathed in her silver beams a multitude of happy homes. The houses, substantial yet elegant, stood betwixt ample courtyards in front, and trim gardens behind. Old trees overshadowed them; shrubs and flowers in their season adorned them. Hospitality and religion sanctified them. Now how changed!

As we gained the end of the wharf, and entered the inhabited street, Colonel Wyborne seemed scarcely to notice the familiar habitations of his friends on either side, but with a hurried step pressed forward toward the house in which he was born, and which was his home during his brief abode in Boston. It was situated on the right-hand side of the street. It stood on the highest of three terraces of moderate height, and was approached by as many flights of stone steps, guarded on either side by iron balustrades, of the fashion of the beginning of the century. The grounds on either side were planted with evergreens, and numerous trees of ornament and shade. A heavy iron gate admitted you within the courtyard. The house itself was of brick, painted of a cream-color, Corinthian pilasters reaching from the ground to the eaves, and with grotesque faces looking from the tops of the windows.

When we had reached the house, our venerable companion paused in manifest emotion. For a moment he laid hold of the iron bars of the gate for support; but his spirits soon rallied, and he regarded the happy home of his childhood and of his married life with sad composure. Strangers now inhabited those apartments which were associated with his earliest memories. Other children played in the grounds which were his childish empire. Other hearts which he knew not, and which knew not him, were happy in the charities of domestic life within those walls that had witnessed his happiest days. Long he stood gazing upon that beloved home. He seemed to forget our presence, and to be in the midst of another age and a former generation. I have witnessed many strange scenes in the course of my pilgrimage; but none that I have seen returns upon my memory so often, or seems so extraordinary, as that moonlight walk. The attenuated form and pallid features of our friend might well have befitted an inhabitant of another world, returned to revisit by the glimpses of the moon the spot on earth he loved the best. The superstition which believes that the spirits of the departed hover over those places loved while on earth is one which even enlightened natures have loved to indulge; but it is a chimera born of ignorance and fear. The blessed spirit which has put off " the vesture of decay," and broken the fleshy chain that linked it to earth, yearns not for the little point of space around which its mortal affections clustered. If it ever returns to this visible sphere, it is the chambers of the human heart that it haunts; it is the beloved souls yet in prison that it visits, and strengthens for the struggles of earth, which are to fit them for the crowns of heaven.

As we stood gazing at the old mansion, a female form with a light in her hand passed across one of the windows, thus giving us assurance that the house was yet tenanted by more material forms than those of memory and fancy. The circumstance seemed to strike palpably upon Colonel Wyborne's heart, and to give vitality, as it were, to his dream of the past. It seemed for a moment as if he had only to open the door, and to walk into the midst of his long-buried household joys. But the mood soon passed away, and he slowly turned his fixed regard from his former home, and, resuming his hold upon his companions, proceeded up the street. He now observed on either hand the former residences of his early friends, every one of which had passed into other hands, through the lapse of time, or the chances and changes of the Revolution. He paused to contemplate the old Town House (then the State House), which was and is full of the memory of old colonial quarrels between the royal Governors and their Legislatures, and of the machinery which set the ball of the Revolution in motion. This historic edifice still stands, as little changed as could be expected when we know that it is at the mercy of a civic board.

We then stopped for a moment before the Old Brick Church, almost opposite the Town House, and surveyed with reverence the oldest building erected by our fathers for the worship of God. We then passed along Cornhill to the Province House, then degraded from being the residence of the representatives of royalty to some plebeian use, but still standing, unshorn of any of its externals of rank. The trees still waved in the courtyard; and the iron fence which had surrounded it for more than a century still seemed to tell the vulgar to keep their distance. Many a festive image was called up before the mind's eye of our companion by the sight of this scene of provincial grandeur.

We then continued our walk until we came to the house of my good aunt Champion, which had received him and his bride under its hospitable roof on his first arrival from Europe. This was almost the only one of all the habitations of his many kindred and friends which had not passed into strange hands. The sight of its well-remembered walls seemed for a moment to shake his resolution of returning to his retirement without revealing his presence to any of his friends. But the settled habit of seclusion was stronger than his wish to see his dear old friend. The thought, too, of the twenty years which had elapsed since they had met, perhaps brought to his mind the changes which years had worked in both of them, which would make their last interview on the shore of time one of melancholy emotions as well as of sad recollections. We then proceeded across the Common to the foot of Beacon Hill, a natural monument, which in an evil hour was torn from its firm base, and buried in the sea, to glut the insane cravings of the monster speculation, which threatens to swallow up our land.

At this distance of time I cannot recall all the particulars of our midnight ramble. I remember pausing to see the princely mansions of the Bowdoins, Faneuils, the Vassals, sleeping in the moonlight. Opposite the Faneuil House was the King's Chapel churchyard, in a distant corner of which slumbered whatever remained of Maria Wyborne. The gate was locked, so that we could not enter the gloomy precinct; but Colonel Wyborne pointed out to us the spot with an almost cheerful air, as he added, —

"But a few days, and the gates of the resting-place of my fathers will close forever on the last of their race."

We visited, too, the North End, then as now the most populous portion of the town ; and as we threaded its narrow streets, many well-known thresholds greeted the eyes of the time-worn pilgrim, which he had often passed in gay or in serious mood. Passing hastily by them, however, and stopping but a moment before the former residence of Cotton Mather, his early pastor, we hastened back to the wharf through some of the devious lanes which Colonel Wyborne seemed to remember as distinctly as if he had passed through them but yesterday. He seemed exhausted by the fatigue of the unusual walk and by the conflicting emotions which agitated his soul. We emerged into King Street from an alley about opposite his house. He stood earnestly looking his last at the place he loved so well, and then turned sadly away to return to the home of his declining years. His heart seemed too full for words; but, as he slowly walked down the wharf, he pressed my arm, and said almost inarticulately,—

"Tell my dear friend, Mrs. Champion, what I have done and seen to-night, and tell her that I shall spend the remainder of my few days in more content and satisfaction for this night's ramble. The earnest longing of my heart to see once more these beloved scenes is satisfied, and I shall die content."

When we had reached the spot where our boat was in waiting, my revered friend tenderly embraced me in his aged arms, and, giving me a tremulous "God bless you!" sunk into his place, and supported himself on the shoulder of his faithful servant. Mr. Armsby took his leave with a cordial grasp of the hand, and hastened to assume his seat. The oars fell with a sudden plash into the water, and the boat was soon gliding over the waves far from the shore. I stood and watched its departing course as long as the flashing of the oars in the moonbeams indicated its pathway. At length nothing was to be seen but the gleaming of the moonlight on the waves, and I turned away in an inexplicable frame of mind, in which it seemed to me as if I were but just awaking from a strange mysterious dream.

I returned up the street, with my portmanteau in my hand, and after some difficulty procured admission at the Bunch of Grapes, a hostelry of no mean fame in its day.   The next day I spent with my good aunt Champion, whose faith was hardly sufficient to make her credit my story of her old friend having actually, but a few hours before, been looking up at her windows.   Before night, I returned to my chambers at Cambridge, with a fund of cheerful and of sadder images over which to brood at leisure, and which, at the end of half a century, still return in clearest vision upon my memory whenever I call to mind my visit to AN OCTOGENARY FIFTY YEARS SINCE.

THE HAUNTED ADJUTANT.

THE HAUNTED ADJUTANT;

A TRADITION OF THE SIEGE OF BOSTON.

CHAPTER I.

" BY Jove, the ghost has a good taste in quarters!"
exclaimed the young Captain Hazlehurst, as
he stood with his back to a rousing fire (in " a gentle-
manly attitude," like Mrs. Todgers), and complacently
surveyed the comfortable apartment of which he had
just taken possession. And indeed there were few
gentlemen of his rank in his Majesty's army that
were better lodged than he. It was a spacious room,
on what Americans call the second, and Englishmen
the first, floor of a large old-fashioned house, situated
in a narrow street leading out of Hanover Street, far
down in the depths of the " North End " of Boston.
The house had been the residence of a patriotic gentleman, who had found it convenient to take his
departure in such speed from the town, as the siege
was fast enclosing it in its iron embrace, that he had
left all his furniture and appliances of luxurious life
behind him as they stood. Several officers of higher
rank than its present occupant had successively in-

habited it, but, on one pretence or another, they had all of them in succession exchanged it for other quarters. They gave no credit, not they, to the foolish stories which were rife among the common people and the soldiery, to the discredit of the character of the house. They begged it might be understood that it was no superstitious folly that caused the shifting of their quarters; but then, it was too far from parade, or it was in too confined a situation, or the kitchen chimney smoked, or there was some other very sufficient reason for the removal.

And let no one think the worse of those gallant gentlemen, if their actual motives did not exactly correspond with these plausible pretences. Many a hero has been afraid to go to bed in the dark, and many a fire-eater, who would storm a battery of cannon without flinching, might be frightened out of his wits by a white sheet and a drag-chain. At least it was so in the good old times, before ghosts were snubbed, and sent to Coventry; when they were welcomed with a fearful joy to the drawing-room fireside, and before they were injuriously driven thence, first to the nursery, and thence again to the servants' hall, and at last reduced to scour out kettles, on their knees, with the fat, foolish scullion in the kitchen. Dear souls, you are a much abused generation! It is no wonder that you are cowed, and are ashamed to show your faces in good company. Confound this march of mind! It has hardly left us a good comfortable superstition to our backs!

Be this as it may, there stood the gallant Captain
Hazlehurst, looking round upon his new domain.
And a comfortable-looking domain it was, as I said
before. The walls were panelled in longitudinal com-
partments, each bordered with the " egg-and-anchor "
carvings in which the souls of our forefathers delighted. Two portraits adorned the side of the room
opposite the fireplace : one, of a beautiful girl of eighteen, of that peculiar style which combines dark
flashing eyes with blond hair, the exquisite glow
of whose skin, and the inimitable finish of whose
point-lace ruffles could have owned no other hand
than Copley's ; and the other, an elderly gentleman,
in a full-bottomed wig, and formal cataract of cravat
pouring down over his laced waistcoat, plainly the
work of an earlier and an inferior artist. Between
the windows on your left, as you turned what Lord
Castlereagh used to call " a back front " to the fire,
was a tall mirror, in a frame of tarnished gold, surmounted by a bird of nondescript characteristics,
which a naturalist might class with eagles, with peli-
cans, or with herons, at his pleasure. Beneath the
glass, stood a low, curiously carved chest of drawers,
the handles and key-holes flashing back the fire from
their glittering brasses. Upon this stood a Japan, or
rather a Chinese dressing-case, with curious drawers
in the centre, and comical little doors at the sides,
and gold mandarins, " with women's faces," and man-
darinesses, " with yet more womanish expressions,"
taking tea all over it with much contentment, upon

10

a glossy background. Opposite the glass stood the bedstead, none of your modern French abominations stuck upon the side of the wall like a hornet's nest, but a substantial, solid, imposing four-poster, with chintz draperies above, and draperies below, which I am not upholsterer enough to describe. The bed itself puffed up in all the elasticity of feathers, as beds of any character were wont to do, before *paillasses* and mattresses came in from France, with Jacobinism and thin potations. The table in the centre of the room was round, of shining mahogany, its edges scalloped, its legs clasping large balls in their claws, as if about to engage in a game of bowls. The chairs were heavy and hair-seated, the backs presenting a sort of mahogany lace-work, of a strange pattern, and unfolding themselves outward at the top in a bell-like expansion.

And then, if you turn and examine the mantelpiece, it will reward your trouble. The curious carvings of grotesque heads on either side, and the delicate sculpture of fruits and flowers in the centre were the work of no mean artificer. And then the Dutch tiles guarding the orifice of the fireplace! Heavens! it is strange that so much piety should have been left to our ancestors, when their earliest ideas of saints and patriarchs were derived from those earthen tablets! What bandy-legged kings, and dumpy queens! What squat prophets, and squab apostles! I see now, in my mind's eye, King David ogling a Bathsheba, from the roof of his house, whose portraiture excited my youthful horror at the taste, rather than at the crime, of his Hebrew majesty. But there they were in blue and white, grim, grisly, and grotesque; the blazing logs below lighting up their square faces and repairing their halos with a light not their own. The andirons, too, and the shovel and tongs were well worthy a description; especially as they are likely soon to become an extinct generation, whose very name will be a puzzle to future antiquaries.

But my story is waiting for me, and will soon get impatient. Still, you must take a glance at the roaring wood fire, which goes crackling up the chimney, and acknowledge its superiority over the pitiful grates and subterranean furnaces, which are drying up the present generation to mummies. If flesh be indeed grass, anthracite will soon desiccate the American public into a very creditable *hortus siccus*. Was there anything else in the room demanding notice? Oh yes, there was the carpet, a heavy Turkey one, half worn, and evidently promoted, "like a crab, backward," from the parlor to the best chamber. On either side of the fireplace was a closet, each with a window and a window-seat, the one on the right-hand side large enough to contain a bed for the Captain's servant, who had stipulated for this arrangement before consenting to accompany his master to a house of so dubious a reputation.

"By Jove, the ghost has a good taste in quarters!" exclaimed Captain Hazlehurst, rubbing his hands, and then giving them one gentle pat together, expressive of infinite content. "It is certainly much to his credit to prefer such snug lodgings as these to a mouldy church-yard or a damp, dilapidated old ruin."

Then drawing up the easiest of the chairs to the front of the fire (it is a strange instinct which always tells a man which chair is the easiest!) he established one foot on either andiron, and resigned himself to the comforts of his situation in an attitude rather redolent of ease than grace. But a handsome young fellow of two-and-twenty may twist his limbs into any posture without much danger of criticism.

And it was a night fitted for the intensest comfort. The wind roared down the chimney; the snow was dashed against the windows in fitful gusts; the old elm which overshadowed the house groaned and creaked as it tossed its huge arms about in the storm. Tibullus himself could not have wished for one more congenial to his notions of enjoyment, as he has recorded them in his immortal couplet. Having thus taken a survey of his new dominion, and imbibed as much caloric as his sitting man was fitted to take in, he naturally began to think about his supper.

"I wonder where that rascal John can be," said he, a little testily; "he has had time enough to go to the Green Dragon and back again fifty times since he went out. But there he comes," he continued, in a milder tone, as he heard a man's step ascending the stairs; "but how happened it that I did not hear him open the hall door?"

The steps ascended the stairs slowly and heavily, and then came "tramp, tramp" along the entry, till they appeared to stop at the door of the room.

"Come in, can't you!" called out the impatient Adjutant (for he was adjutant, as well as captain, as you shall presently hear). "What the devil are you stopping for?"

Then recollecting that John might by possibility come with both hands full (though fortune never does), he jumped up, and incontinently flung the door open to its utmost capacity of swing. And was not John obliged to him for this timely assistance? Why, bless you, he was n't there! No! Who was there, then? If anybody, it was that personage well known in the best regulated families by the name of Mr. Nobody. In short, there was nobody there.

"Whew!" softly whistled the Captain, "if this is the ghost, he is a heavy-heeled lubber, and it 's hard if I can't catch him, and lay him,—if not in the Red Sea, at least in some of his own claret."

With these words he took a candle from the table, and a stout regimental cane, such as officers wore in those days at drills and off duty, from behind the door, and proceeded coolly to search the hall and the chambers opening out of it. But it was all to no purpose. The ghost, if it were one, had vanished, and not left so much as a "melodious twang" behind it.

"It 's very strange," he soliloquized. "Could it be that villain John, making game of me? If it be — but no, it 's impossible!"

And the impossibility was soon put beyond a doubt, by a multitudinous stamping and kicking in the porch, such as indicates a return from a walk through a deep snow-storm, and then by a sudden opening of the hall door, which admitted John, and a furious draught of wind and snow by way of accompaniments. The doors above banged to, the Captain's light blew out, and a fresh stamping, kicking, and shaking bore noisy evidence that the new comer was none other than John himself in the flesh. Captain Hazlehurst stole back into his room, not caring to acknowledge the extreme civility of his disembodied visitor, in making him a call so very early after his arrival; though, in his secret heart, he could not but think him "most infernally polite." He had scarcely resumed his chair and relighted his candle, when the veritable John made his appearance, his shaggy great-coat white with snow, and making altogether a spectral appearance in very good keeping with his whereabouts.

"Why, John," said his master, "I thought the ghost must have got you, and my supper into the bargain."

"Oh dear, your honor," cried John, setting down his basket, and taking off his great-coat, "please don't talk in that sort of way. The ghosts are made quite mad-like when they hear themselves made fun of. I was almost afraid to come up those creaking stairs. My grandmother once "—

"Never mind your grandmother just now, John,"

interrupted his master, "but let me see what you have got in your basket; for I am hungry enough to eat a ghost myself, if it should appear in the shape of a boiled scrag of mutton, like the one at Oxford, which was laid by eating him with mashed turnips and melted butter."

John groaned in spirit at this blasphemy against the powers of the air, as a Methodist may do when some unlucky scapegrace raps out an oath in a stage-coach. However, he proceeded to lay a snowy napkin over the table, and then to produce from his basket a cold chicken, some slices of ham, and bread and butter and cheese, which he duly disposed upon the board. From a yet lower deep he evoked a string of sausages and a dozen potatoes in the prime of their age. With a precision, which showed him to be an old campaigner, he next deposited the potatoes in the ashes upon the hearth, and taking down a small saucepan from the closet, began to fry the sausages, which soon sent up an aromatic perfume, that might well summon to the presence any spirit yet in the body, whatever its effect might be on one that had shuffled off his mortal coil. When these conjurations were over, he deposited the result with the other comestibles upon the table, and then intimated to his master that there was nothing to wait for.

While the young soldier was carrying the war with spirit into the enemy's country, his faithful squire was not idle in his yet unfinished vocation. He took down a silver tankard, with a heavy lid falling back on its hinges upon the solid handle, and slicing the lemons, and heating the water, and mixing the sugar, and pouring (I grieve to say) the rum, he compounded that insidious concoction with which our sires welcomed the noon, bade farewell to the departing sun, and chased the shades of night. When the ingredients were duly mixed, and the whole made "slab and good," he set it down upon the glowing coals, to acquire a new fire from without to reinforce that within.

His supper ended, and his libation poured, Hazlehurst prepared for bed. He could not help revolving the sounds he had heard over in his mind, and he was fully of the opinion that there was some trick designed him by his comrades or some waggish rebels. He thought it was entirely contrary to the etiquette of the spirit-land for its accredited envoys to go creaking about in clouted, hob-nailed shoes, like a live plough-man. "Gliding," "skimming," "floating," "sailing," he well knew to be the appropriate mode of ghostly locomotion, but as to stamping and *clumping*, he believed them to be unworthy of any goblin of good breeding and a liberal education. So he was resolved to be upon his guard. John lingered about his master's toilet as long as he could, and seemed loath to depart.

"And so your honor does n't believe there is any ghost at all?" he suggested.

"Ghost!" his master responded, as he untied his right garter, "I believe there 's no ghost but has a head to be broken, and a — hinder man to be kicked; and so I advise all such gentry to keep out of my reach!"

"Oh, Lord! I wish your honor would n't talk in that sort of way. My grandmother"—

"Plague take your grandmother," cried the Captain peevishly, slipping his left leg out of his scarlet unmentionables (they called them breeches in those days), "you are half a granny yourself. I tell you no ghost will dare to come within the reach of these magic circles" — pointing as he spoke to the muzzles of his pistols; "if they do, they 'll find that there is a spell in them that will soon send them packing to the Red Sea."

He spoke thus in a raised tone of voice, and then cocked and uncocked his pistols, that his words and their "strange quick jar" might fall upon the ears of the walls, if, peradventure, as often happens, they were provided with them.

"But, Lord bless you! what good will they do, sir?" persisted John. "I heard of a ghost once that caught a brace of bullets in his hand, and flung them back in the gentleman's face that fired them at him."

"Then, I shall save my lead, at any rate," rejoined the Captain, laughing; "but to bed with you, for I am tired and sleepy." With these words he turned into bed, and the unlucky John, after replenishing the fire, and clearing away the things, was fain to do likewise.

But though Captain Hazlehurst pretended to be asleep, he was never more broad awake in his life. He lay for a good while watching the flickering phantoms which danced in the light of the wood fire upon the panels of his chamber. And then he thought a multitude of thoughts, for there are no such promoters of thought as night and watchfulness. The steps which he had heard in the evening certainly suggested some of his meditations; but he was not superstitious, and believed they appertained to some being of flesh and blood, whom it was his business not to be afraid of. As he had seen the door carefully bolted, and had, beside, double-locked it and put the key under his pillow, he felt tolerably secure from any visitants, other than such as might make their entrance through the keyhole, without some sufficient warning of their approach. These thoughts, then, soon vanished from his mind, and his imagination was soon a thousand leagues away, disporting itself in the glades of the park of his ancestors, watching the deer in the fern, the swans on the stream, or the whirring coveys as they rose from the cover. There he saw himself, and perhaps a fairer form or two, wandering through its paths, or sitting at the foot of its old trees, in the light of that farewell sun which ever sheds a Claude-like glow around our last day at home, when we live it over again in other days and distant climes.

And, perhaps, the scene changed to his ancestral hall, and it was evening, and the lights shone bright upon his father's erect form and thoughtful face, upon his mother's placid brow and calm smile, upon the manly figures of his brothers, and the graceful shapes of his sisters, as he saw them all on the night before his departure for America. And there were those other forms, too, that had been with him in the park (who were not exactly sisters, but who would have been almost as much missed from the dream-circle as they); they were there, too, and he was leading down with them the contra-dance (for, alas! the waltz, and even the quadrille, then were not), with interludes in the intervals of the dance, which are very well to dream about, but which it would be a breach of the confidence reposed in me to reveal. And then he thought, too, of the charming, the perplexing Clara Forrester, his latest flame (for I grieve to say that my hero was *un peu volage*), who had made more of an impression upon him than he cared to admit, even to himself, was within the power of a provincial beauty. His visions, however, grew more and more indistinct, and, like many a sleepless lover before him, he was soon sound asleep.

He had not been long asleep when he was aroused by a hurried shake, and a gasping entreaty to awake. He instinctively seized his pistols, and was near putting them to their natural uses without further inquiry, when he was stopped by the voice of John.

"Don't fire, Captain — don't fire, your honor. It's the ghost — the ghost!"

"D—n the ghost!" exclaimed the Captain, provoked, as gentlemen are apt to be, at being waked out of their first sleep, "I 've a great mind to make a ghost of you, you blockhead."

"But don't you hear him, your honor?" cried John, in an agony of terror, "don't you hear him walking about over our heads, as if "——

"Hold your tongue, can't you, and let me listen," said his master, whose attention was thoroughly aroused by this intimation of the character of the ghostly visitation. He listened, and heard the same heavy tread, stepping backward and forward, with slow and measured step, in the chamber directly over his head.

"Give me my cloak, you villain," exclaimed Hazlehurst, as he leaped out of bed and ensconced his feet in his slippers, " and light the candle and come along with me."

"And where are you going, sir?" inquired John, with woe-begone face and chattering jaws.

"Going?" was the reply. "Why to see who it is that is making that infernal noise upstairs, and make him choose some other place for his promenade."

"Oh, Lord! your honor, pray don't—pray don't! perhaps he 'll fly away with the side of the house if we provoke him."

"Never mind," replied the Captain coolly, "the house don't belong to me. But make haste, and come along."

"Oh! but I am afraid to go, indeed I am! Pray,

don't go, sir, for God's sake! I shall die if I go, indeed I shall."

"Then stay, and be"— blessed, the Captain would probably have said, as he snatched the candle which John had just lighted out of his hand, had he not interrupted him to say that if he were resolved to go, he would go with him, as he was a good deal more afraid to be left alone.

"Come along, then," said the Captain, as he led the way, a pistol in one hand and his sword in the other, followed by John with the candle up the creaking staircase.

Reader, was it ever thy hap to be awakened in the dead of the night by a mysterious noise in the kitchen ? and, urged by the instances of thy wife or sister, hast thou descended, poker-armed, to the eerie spot ? I doubt not thou art a valiant man, a proper fellow of thy hand, but tell me true (for doth not an author stand to his reader in the relation of a father confessor ? Fear not that I shall betray the secrets of the confessional !), did not thy manly heart go pit-a-pat as thou approachedst the fatal door and puttedst thy hand upon the lock, the turning of which might reveal to thy sight a ferocious band of robbers, whiskered to the eyes and armed to the teeth ? And didst thou not wish in thy secret soul that thy desire to appear a man of prowess in the eyes of thy womankind had suffered thee to lie quietly, with thy head covered in the bed-clothes, saying unto thyself, "·Lo ! is it not the wind ?" And when, on opening the door with a desperate thrust, thou hast discovered a whiskered robber, indeed, and one well-armed, but of the feline, not felon, race, with her head stuck in the cream-jug, its milky whiteness on her sable fur testifying to her crime, and a heap of upturned trays bearing evidence to her desperation, didst thou not feel thy bosom's lord sit lightly on his throne, and didst thou not receive the gratulations of thy fair instigators, and sip thy creamless coffee the next morning, with more contentment than if thou hadst sacrificed to thy insulted household gods a hecatomb of burglarious varlets ? If such has ever been a part of thy experience, thou canst appreciate the sensations of master and man as they ascended with noiseless step the stairs which led to the next floor.

Pardon this digression, dear reader. Your confessions in the premises shall be sacredly kept secret. But it was necessary for the due preservation of the unities (for which I am an Aristotelian stickler), that my characters should have time to get upstairs. As they approached the door the steps ceased suddenly, as if the owner of them had paused to listen. Who could he be ? It clearly could not be the cat. For, first, they had no cat; and, secondly, no cat could have made such a fearful tramping, unless, indeed, it had been the prime minister of the Marquis of Carabas, the redoubtable Puss in Boots himself.

I have the greatest tenderness for my hero's reputation, but my duty as a faithful historian obliges me to say that there was the slightest possible nervous

contraction of his left arm as he seized the lock of the
door, to throw it open, having slipped his sword under
his arm to enable him to do it. He had led his company up Bunker's Hill without flinching, to be sure,
but this was an entirely different case. There is a
wide range allowable to tastes in the matter of throat-
cutting, as well as in the rest of the fine arts. A man
may be ready enough to submit to this elegant deple-
tion on a field of battle, with all the enlivening con-
comitants of such a scene, who might reasonably
object to the operation at the top of an old house, in
the middle of the night.

However this might be, he flung open the door to
its utmost extent, at the same moment recovering his
sword and presenting his pistol. He was prepared
for the worst, and resolved to encounter the enemy in
whatever shape he might appear. He presented a
figure at once civil and military ; his night-cap, and
night-gown fluttering under his cloak, fairly representing the *toga*, while the " sword and pistol, which
did come at his command," as at that of the celebrated
Billy Taylor, might well stand for the *arma*, — for
making which last yield to the first, Tully was so
well quizzed by the Edinburgh Reviewers of his day.
There he stood, ready to kill, slay, and destroy any
and every antagonist, however formidable. And for
whom was all this energy so well got up ? Who was
the object upon whom this well-cooked wrath was to
be bestowed ? Bless you, nothing at all ! The very
identical Mr. Nobody who had walked up stairs early

in the evening, and stopped at the door below on his way up! There was no sign of any mortal creature near!

"The devil!" exclaimed the Captain, as he lowered the point of his sword and the muzzle of his pistol, and drew a long breath.

"O Lord! sir, don't mention him, or perhaps he 'll come back again," ejaculated the trembling John, who was peeping, with a foolish face of fear, over his master's shoulder.

"It is very strange!" monologized that gentleman. "What can be the meaning of it?" And stepping gently into the room he examined it and its closets with all care, but without any clue to the mystery.

But just as he had completed his search, probing the darker recesses with his sword, "and wounding several shutters and some boards," without any satisfactory result, his attention was arrested by a tremendous crash in the room below. One leap brought him to the door of the room, two more to the head of the stairs, and a hop, skip, and jump in addition, to the door of his own chamber. And there he saw a scene of confusion which might well have roused the ire of Moses, the meekest, or of Job, the most patient, of men. The bed-clothes were stripped off the bed, and coiled up on the floor like a spectral boa constrictor. The andirons lay lovingly together on the top of the deserted bed. The tongs bestrode, like a Colossus, the dressing-case on the chest of drawers under the glass, while the shovel seemed to regard its old companion's exploit with a chuckling laugh of satisfaction, from the easy-chair in the corner of the room. And to complete the scene, the table in the centre of the room was overturned, and, with all its miscellaneous contents of books, glasses and *etcetras*, lay in one wide heap of ruin upon the floor.

All this was not at first visible, as the fire was almost out, and panting John toiled after his master, if not in vain, at least so slowly as to put him entirely out of patience. But when the candle came, and the chaos was revealed, who shall paint the rage of the master or the dismay of the man? "The *devil!*" exclaimed the choleric Captain, with added emphasis, and I am afraid I must allow that he made use of other expletives of more significance and weight, as he danced about the apartment in a most heroic passion. For it is a melancholy fact that the British armies did "swear terribly" in America in Captain Hazlehurst's day, even as they did "in Flanders" in that of Captain Shandy. If the recording angel undertook to write down all the oaths the gallant Captain uttered, he must have gone nigh to have written up his wings; and if, in consideration of the provocation, he should have attempted to drop a tear upon every one of them, to blot it out forever, he must have infallibly cried his eyes out. Whatever may have been the proceedings in Heaven's chancery, I am afraid that just where he was, Captain Hazlehurst would have maintained that he felt the better for the effort.

11

But, be that as it may, as soon as his first transports of anger and amazement were over, the Captain made a minute examination of the chamber and the house, but without finding any trace of the perpetrator of these deeds.   He was all the more convinced that he was made the victim of a practical joke, as he could not believe such pranks worthy the gravity of disembodied, or the dignity of evil spirits ; but he could not refuse to allow that the joke, if it were one, was well done.   Poor John, on the other hand, whose notions of the moral or the social proprieties of the inhabitants of a world he knew very little about, were much less exalted than his master's, laid the whole blame upon their airy shoulders.   It was as much as he could do to command himself sufficiently, after the Captain had finished his researches, to put the room to rights again, fearing lest some spectral hand should resent his interference with the admired disorder it had created.   But no such displeasure was manifested, and after the bed had been readjusted, the Captain retired to it again, marvelling much at the events of the night.   He lay long awake pondering upon them, and neither he nor his man fell asleep till the neighboring clock had told that the small hours were fast growing into the larger ones. It is no wonder, then, that they overslept themselves, and that, when he awoke, his curiosity as to his adventures of the night should be merged for the moment in his fears of being late at the morning parade.   His hurry would allow no time for remark from his attendant, whose mind was full of nothing else, while the business of the toilet was proceeding. Captain Hazlehurst, however, found time to enjoin it upon John, as he was giving the last sprinkle of powder to his plastered and pigtailed head, to say nothing about the night's adventures, as he valued his favor, till he had his permission. His determination was, he said, to sift the matter thoroughly, and, in the mean time, he wished no reports to be spread of what had happened, as it might interfere with his investigation. With these injunctions he left the mortified John in great vexation, as he had been reckoning on the pleasures of telling the ghost story as his only compensation for his fright, and hurried with all the speed he could command to the parade-ground on the Common.

CHAPTER II.

"YOU were late at parade this morning, Captain Hazlehurst," said Lord Percy to his young adjutant, as he called for the orders of the day, immediately after breakfast.

"I have no excuse to offer, my lord," was the deferential reply, "excepting my removal to new quarters at the other extremity of the town ; for I am afraid that my having overslept myself would be regarded by your lordship as rather an aggravation than a palliation of my dilatoriness."

"To be sure, to be sure," answered his lordship, who was somewhat of a martinet, "but be more careful in future ; that's all. But where are your new quarters, Hazlehurst ?" he continued, his disciplinarian gravity relaxing into a friendly smile, for Hazlehurst stood high in his good graces.

"At Mr. Vaughan's house, at the North End, my lord," responded the Captain.

"What, the haunted house !" exclaimed Lord Percy, laughing, "why, you are a bolder fellow than I took you for, my lad. I hope the ghost did the honors of his mansion like a gentleman, and treated you with becoming hospitality."

"I had no reason to complain, my lord," was the guarded response.

"I trust that your oversleeping yourself this morning had nothing to do with any nocturnal merry-making with any honest fellow of the last generation, or flirtation with any of the rebel grandmothers, who look so temptingly down upon us from some of these old picture-frames," pointing, as he spoke, to some lovely forms with which the pencil of Blackburn had decorated the walls of his parlor.

"Nothing of the sort, I assure you, my lord," replied Hazlehurst, "no boon companions and no ladye love, whether in the body or out of the body, had any thing to do with my tardiness this morning, which I shall take care shall not occur again."

"Right, right," said the son of "Duke Smithson of Northumberland." "I have every reason to be satisfied with you in every respect. But, by the way, how is Miss Forrester?" he proceeded, for his lordship had a discursiveness of discourse, and a talent for knowing all the details of the garrison gossip, which vindicated his hereditary claim to cousinship with royalty.

"She was well, my lord," answered Hazlehurst, "when I had the honor of seeing her last. But that was not yesterday, nor the day before."

"Lovers' quarrels — lovers' quarrels," said his lordship, laughingly; then added, more seriously, "but, my dear Hazlehurst, pardon me if I ask whether you have considered what may be Sir Ralph and Lady

Hazlehurst's opinion of a New England daughter-in-law, should you be disposed to present them with one ? "

"I have not given the subject any consideration at all, my lord," replied Hazlehurst quickly, "because I have no intention of subjecting them to any such trial at present. I beg that your lordship will give no credit to the talk of the mess-table or of the assembly-room on such subjects, at least where I am concerned. My sword is my bride till this war is over, and I shall suffer no rivals in my affections, of flesh and blood."

"Bravo ! bravo ! Hazlehurst," answered Lord Percy; "these be brave words. Only I hope that you will not have to serve for your bride of steel as long as Jacob did for Laban's daughter. Excuse my caution, which I am glad to know is not wanted. But I advise you to do as I used to do when I was addicted to falling in love."

"How was that, my lord ? "

"Always to take care to be in love with two or three at the same time. You will find it an excellent rule, I assure you."

Hazlehurst joined cordially in the laugh with which the stout earl uttered this apothegm, and assured his noble commander that he would not neglect his advice.

"Here is your orderly book," added his lordship, handing it to him; "I take it for granted we shall meet at the assembly to-night, where I trust I shall see you reduce my instructions to practice."

"Never fear, my lord, but you will find me an apt scholar in love as well as in war. I only wish I could hope to rival your lordship in either service."

To this his lordship replied only by a good-natured nod, which the adjutant understood to be his signal to take his leave, which he accordingly made haste to do.

"Confound that Clara Forrester," soliloquized Captain Hazlehurst, as he walked slowly along Hanover Street, after he had discharged his regimental duties, "what is there about her that plays the devil with me, in a way that no other woman ever did before ? It can't be her beauty or her accomplishments, for I have seen her superiors in both. I don't know though, on the whole, as to her beauty," he said to himself, in a tone of more deliberation. "It's a peculiar style, to be sure, but she's devilish handsome, there is no doubt about that. And as to her accomplishments, what have they to do with the matter, I should like to know ? It must be this cursed siege, which shuts us all up so close together. Well, I have not been to see her for these three days, and I sha'n't be in a hurry to call on her, after her flirtation with that puppy Bellassis, I can tell her. She shall see that I am not dependent upon her, that I'm resolved upon."

As the gallant Captain had just made this valiant resolution, he found himself opposite the house of the Hon. James Forrester, one of his Majesty's council, &c., &c. This house was situated in Hanover Street, just before you come to the turning into Duke Street, in which were Hazlehurst's quarters. For in those days you must know that the North End was (pardon the Hibernianism, my maternal grandfather was an Irishman) the West End of the town. There did the great body of the colonial court and aristocracy reside. Far be it from me to insinuate that this circumstance of juxtaposition was any element in the determination of the Captain to take up his new quarters. But so it was. And as he accidentally raised his eyes to the window of Mr. Forrester's house, just as he was internally ejaculating the doughty resolution just recited, he caught a glimpse of a pair of sunny eyes smiling upon him from between two flowering shrubs, which stood upon the window seat, and the next minute he was standing in the porch thundering away at the knocker.

People may say what they please about dreary dilapidated houses, haunted by old dead men, but if I had a young son, or nephew, or ward (which, God be praised, I have not), I should warn them to avoid the bright and cheerful homes haunted by young live women. These are the haunted houses to be afraid of. And, no doubt, they would take my advice. At least, I am sure I did whenever my grandfather, or uncle, or aunt gave me any such admonitions, "in my hot youth, when George the Fourth was King." "Never mind the *old* witches," a gentleman celebrated in civil and military life, of the last generation, used to say, when speaking of the witches of his native town of Salem, "never mind the *old* witches, it is the *young* witches that do all the mischief!" And I incline to think that he was more than half right.

I have a great mind to seize upon the opportunity, while my hero is waiting for the knocker to be answered, to give my friendly readers some account of him. I have been waiting for a chance to put in a word on the subject ever since I began. But the tide of events has swept me on with such resistless force that I have not had a moment to take breath. Indeed, my plan is epic. I have plunged *in medias res*, and it is about time for the hero, sitting over his wine with his mistress, or some Phœnician Amphitryon, to relate his birth and parentage, "his breed, seed, and generation," and all the surprising adventures that had preceded his appearance in their domains. But lest I should find no passage recorded in this true history to that effect, I think I will fill up this pause in the march of the story with the little I know of his previous history. And little enough it is. If any reader asks me for his story, I can only answer in the words of the knife-grinder —

"Story! God bless you, I have none to tell, sir!"

My hero then, in short, bore the baptismal and patronymic appellations of Charles Hazlehurst. He was the eldest son of a Somersetshire baronet. He was six feet high, with broad shoulders, a deep chest, and a clean leg. I can't tell you the color of his hair, for I never saw it without that powder which has passed away with so many of the virtues and graces of the last age.

"God bless their pigtails, though they're now cut off!"

When to this I add that he had a round, ruddy face, clear blue eyes, and the most perfect of teeth, I trust my readers will take my word for it that he was as dangerous a *Cupidon déchainé* as ever disguised himself in a red coat and breeches, wore epaulets instead of wings, and used a regimental sword for a bow and arrows. In addition to this you will please to remember that he was but two-and-twenty, which is an essential item in the inventory of his perfections. I am well aware that objection will be made to his claims as a lady-killer, on the score of his rosy cheeks and blue eyes. But you should recollect, my dear madam, that your thin, black-eyed, sinister-looking, "sublime, sallow, Werter-faced men" had not then come into fashion. And so you must excuse the taste of your grandmothers, who thought health and good humor main ingredients in manly beauty. As to the number of times he had been in love, I am unable to say with anything like accuracy, as I have not as yet received returns from all the towns where he went on the recruiting service, or was stationed in garrison, before his regiment was ordered to America. Should they arrive in time, I shall add them in an appendix, reduced to a tabular form for convenience of reference. If there is anything on which I do pride myself, it is the business-like manner in which I do up my work.

So much for love; and now for war. He had
" fleshed his maiden-sword," — figuratively, for he
did n't kill anybody, — at the modern Chevy Chase of
Lexington,

" Made by the Earl Percy."

He attracted attention by his good conduct on that
unlucky occasion, but he chiefly distinguished himself at the battle of Bunker's Hill. On that famous
day he led his company up the hill, under the mur-
derous fire of the rebels, twice, his captain having
been killed in the first attempt to dislodge the enemy
from their entrenchments. As a reward for his gal-
lantry on that occasion, he obtained his captaincy ;
and, the adjutant of his regiment being killed at the
same time, and the number of officers being sadly
reduced by the fatal aim of the American marksmen,
he was appointed to fill that station also, until other
arrangements could be made.

But it would be cruel to keep him waiting on the
steps any longer, in one of the coldest days of that
bitter winter. However, he felt warm enough, nor
did he feel in any violent hurry to have the door
opened. Have you no recollection, my reader, of
the queer sensation, — after you had rung the bell at
the door of your particular princess, and when you
had a feeling as if you might be left to do something
desperate, if you got in, — with which you awaited the
servant's approach, hardly knowing whether to be
glad or sorry to hear that she was not at home ?
There is nothing like it, unless it be the odd feeling

when you have rung the bell at the door of your particular friend, for the purpose of asking him to accompany you to the "tribunal of twelve paces," at daybreak the next morning.   But I postpone any further reflections until my chapter on bell-pulls.

After a rather longer interval than was usual in that well regulated household (I once knew a famous man who used to say that he judged of the domestic management of a house by the space which intervened between the ringing of the bell and the opening of the door), the portal was expanded by a particularly ugly negro, whom Hazlehurst did not recollect to have ever seen before about the premises.   Upon asking whether Miss Clara were at home, the new porter made an inarticulate sort of sound, which the visitor chose to consider as an affirmative, and walked in without further ceremony.   He was left to open the parlor door himself, for the attendant spirit took no further notice of him.   He accordingly ushered himself into the comfortable apartment where Miss Forrester sat, diffusing an air of cheerfulness throughout it, even beyond that (at least our adjutant thought so) dispensed by the good logs that blazed upon the hearth.   The scarlet curtains, the pleasant window-seats, with their velvet cushions, the plants that were placed upon them to catch a glimpse of the wintry sun, the thick Turkey carpet, and all the appointments of the parlor (for in those days drawing-rooms were not), spoke to the heart that comfort was a word understood in New England at least, if nowhere else beyond the precincts of the fast-anchored isle.

The front windows looked into the street, as my readers may have partly gathered, and those on either side of the fireplace opened upon a thin slice of garden which extended down to the street, and stretched and expanded itself far behind the house, the shrubs and fruit trees all glittering, to the finest ramifications of their smallest twigs, with the snow which had fallen the night before. On one side of the door, opposite the fireplace, was a large mahogany book-case, with glass doors and resplendent brasses, containing the library of Miss Forrester, the books bound uniformly and stamped with her name. There was the pabulum upon which our grandmothers nourished their intellectual natures. Good, hearty food, i' faith! None of your modern kickshaws which the pastry-cooks of the circulating libraries supply to tickle the palate withal, but solid substantial viands, such as good master cook furnishes forth to replenish the heart with its best blood.

There the Spectator sat with his club, in his short face, long wig, rolled stockings and high-cut shoes, over a squat bottle of wine, in the frontispiece of his closely printed twelves. The Tattler, too, was to be seen in his original fine-paper quarto. History, also, there was good store, and biography, such as those days afforded. And was not Shakspeare there, and Ben Jonson, and Spenser, and Milton? Sir Charles Grandison, too, looked ready to step down and bow over the hand of his fair mistress, so like was the scene to the dear cedar parlor of " the venerable circle." I don't know whether it will do to say it, but so it was, there stood Tom Jones and Joseph Andrews and Roderick Random and Peregrine Pickle, as bold as lions, alongside of Tristram Shandy, who did not look the least bit ashamed of himself. My fair readers must excuse my heroine for keeping such rollicking company, for they must remember that she had not the privilege they enjoy of the pious conversation of Sir Lytton Bulwer (or Sir Edward Lytton, or whatever title please his ear), or of Monsieur Victor Hugo, or of the epicene George Sand. She had no choice, poor thing; and, upon my word, I never could perceive that she was a jot the worse for their society. In the other corner of the room, answering to that filled up by the book-case, was what was in those days termed a *buffet*, a closet without doors, with its shelves loaded with the curious old plate, and rare glass and China, which had been accumulating for generations in the family.

Miss Forrester sat upon a curiously carved settee, with devices of flowers and birds in choice mahogany on the back, which looked like one uncommonly broad-bottomed arm-chair, or, by 'r lady, like two single chairs rolled into one, cushioned with green damask, and drawn up to the table in the centre of the room, and inclining in an angle of—I am not mathematician enough to tell the exact number of degrees, say forty-five — to the fire. Her work-basket was by her side, which she graciously removed to the table, and made room on the settee for Captain Hazlehurst, when he had made his advancing bow, — a very different thing, let me tell you, from the shrug and jerk, performed chiefly by the antipodes of the head, with which your modern exquisite " shakes his ambrosial curls and gives the nod," when he enters a room. And when they were sitting there side by side, I protest, I don't believe that there was a handsomer couple in all his Majesty's dominions. Clara Forrester was — but I won't describe her. I never could describe a pretty woman. And, for that matter, who ever could ? Suffice it to say, she was a blonde, with a profusion of fair hair, I doubt not, but its color was concealed by that plaguy powder ; and yet I can't say the effect was unbecoming to her pure brow, her blooming, downy cheeks, and sweet mouth. And that morning cap had a most coquettish and killing air.

"And then her teeth, and then, oh Heaven ! her eye !"

It was as wicked and roguish an eye as you would wish to see on a winter's day looking into yours by the side of a good fire. And then her hand, and her foot, and her shape ! But I won't go on. If you can't see her, just as she was sitting there, it's of no use for me to be trying to fit your mind's eye with a pair of spectacles. It's your fault, and not mine, reader, if you don't see her sitting in that old-fashioned room, in the glittering light of that clear winter morning of seventy years ago.

I don't know how it was, but Hazlehurst had not sat by her side a minute, when he felt all the wrath he had been nursing for three days, to keep it warm, oozing out of the palms of his hands, like Acres's courage, and no more recollected Major Bellassis (whom he had just before, in violation of the articles of war, and of the respect due to his superior officer, irreverently styled a puppy) than if there had been no such dashing sprig of nobility in existence.

I might give the details of their conversation; but I don't know that it would be quite fair, as it was communicated to me in confidence. But there was nothing particular, — that is, *very* particular, — upon my honor. They talked of the news of the siege, of the advances of the rebels, of the probabilities of repulsing them. And then they diverged to the small talk of the garrison, the rise and fall of the flirtation stocks, and the variations of the match market. Then they talked of the last review, and of the comical figure that Colonel Cobb, the *ci-devant jeune homme,* cut when he was thrown from his new horse, and could not get up again, — not because he was hurt, but because he was too tightly girt. And the assemblies, too, and the private theatricals, afforded endless topics of mirthful discourse. Though there was not much that was enlivening in the siege itself to those who were shut up in the narrow limits of the beleaguered town, still youth and good spirits would make their way, and find a thousand divertisements for speeding the weary hours. God bless them! what would this working-day world be without youth and good spirits ?

"And so I hear," said the fair Clara, at last, when they had pretty well exhausted all the topics which a three days' absence had accumulated, "and so I hear that you have come into our neighborhood. And, pray, how do you like your landlord ?"

"My landlord !" exclaimed Hazlehurst in some surprise. "I am as well satisfied with him as a man usually is with himself; for I am the only landlord that I have to my knowledge, unless indeed it be the quartermaster-general."

"Ah, you put it off very well!" persisted Miss Forrester; "but be honest now, has not Captain Honeywood paid his respects to you yet ? He is much too fine a gentleman, I am sure, to have neglected it."

"I have not the honor to understand you, Miss Forrester," replied the Captain. "It was never my chance to hear the gallant Captain's name before. Pray, in what service might he be ?"

"Oh, in the sea service, you may be sure," answered the lady; "but did you never hear of the noble Captain, who makes continual claim, as papa says" (papa was a lawyer), "to the Vaughan house ?"

"Never, upon my honor," protested Hazlehurst. "And I shall feel myself especially obliged if you will introduce me to his acquaintance."

"Heaven forbid!" exclaimed Clara, laughing, "but

I have no objection to talking a little about him behind his back."

"That is better yet," said Hazlehurst. "It is to be hoped then that his character is bad enough to be well talked over."

"Bad enough to gratify your warmest wishes, I assure you. I believe he was as wicked an old villain as you could possibly desire to see," replied Clara.

"Many thanks for the compliment to my taste," answered the Captain, bowing, "but did you ever happen to know this amiable individual?"

"Know him?" cried Clara. "Good Heavens! why, he's been dead these sixty-five years!"

"Bless me!" exclaimed Hazlehurst, "dead sixty-five years, and yet lay claim to a good piece of real estate! What an unconscionable old dog! I only hope his example will not be very extensively followed."

"It is to be hoped not," responded the lady, "but if you really do not know about the claimant to your premises, I will tell you all I know about him, which is little enough."

"You will lay me under everlasting obligations," bowed the Captain, as he inclined his ear to her in mock seriousness.

"Well, then, all I know about him is," resumed Miss Forrester, "that he was a master of a vessel out of this port, some hundred years since, who went to sea, and was gone five or six years without any tidings being heard of him. At last, however, he returned in a ship from Europe, telling that his vessel was lost in the East Indies, and no soul was saved but himself, who was taken up by a Dutch vessel, and, after various adventures, found his way home again. This story would have done very well, had he not soon made a great display of wealth, among other things building the house in which you (and people do say *he*) now reside. This went on for a few years, and by dint of giving good dinners, going regularly to meeting and Thursday lectures, and being eminently liberal to one or two of the most influential ministers, he was getting to be in very good odor with the Boston public. There were those, to be sure, who still marvelled whence he got his wealth. Some thought it must be witchcraft, but the majority, more charitable, believed it to be only piracy and murder. Their suspicions were confirmed by the occasional moody and depressed turns to which Captain Honeywood was subject. People thought that there was something weighing upon his mind. This, however, did not prevent a young lady of one of the chief families from being willing to marry him, and the ceremony was about to be celebrated with all the pomp which the times permitted, when they were prevented by an untoward occurrence. It so happened that the very night before the marriage was to take place, a sloop of war came into the harbor, with orders to arrest our amiable friend, and carry him to England for trial, on a charge of murder and piracy. It seems that a sailor had been arrested for a recent impropriety of this sort, who had purchased his own pardon by revelations touching our valuable townsman. The Captain of the sloop-of-war came up to the Province House, and communicated his orders to Governor Phipps, who, with the sheriff and other officials, proceeded to effect the arrest. But on arriving at the scene where it was to be completed, they found themselves too late. The bird was flown. They searched the house and the neighborhood, and offered large rewards, but all was in vain. The Captain was never heard of again. The disaffected in the colony hinted that notice was given to Honeywood, by persons in authority, of the design to take him, in time to favor his escape. Others, and this was the opinion of no small number, believed that the devil had for once helped a friend upon a pinch, and spirited him away. Some supposed that he had concealed himself in some secret place designed for this emergency in his house, and had there starved to death. At any rate, he was heard of no more. In due time sentence of outlawry was passed upon him, and his house, with his other property, declared forfeited to the crown. When it was sold, and the purchaser took possession of his estate, it was found to be more than the crown of England could do to give him a quiet possession. The pranks that were played, the noises that were heard, the sights that were seen, among them the apparition of the very Captain himself, are not to be told. The intruder was soon forced to quit the premises. All who subsequently ventured to occupy the house were ejected in a like summary manner. For years it stood untenanted. Property in the street fell in value, and people were afraid to pass through it after nightfall. After many years had elapsed, an elderly man arrived from England, with the avowed intention of spending the rest of his days here. He could not be suited to a house to his mind, and at length pitched upon this deserted one. He bought it at a low price, and, in spite of its ill name, fitted it up for his residence, and there spent the remainder of his days. He shook his head when questioned as to the claims of its former possessor, and gave people to understand that he could tell much if he chose. So the ill-repute of the mansion continued unimpaired. It was a singular fact that he found the lady of the love of the former inhabitant still unmarried, and by some strange coincidence they married each other, and lived together in as much comfort as the ghost of his predecessor would allow. That is his portrait that you may have seen in the chamber over the right-hand parlor"—

"And who," interrupted Hazlehurst, "is the young lady in the same room?"

"That," replied Clara, "is the portrait of his granddaughter, the only child of his only daughter, the child of his old age,—my dear friend Fanny Vaughan. For you must know that after his death his heiress married Colonel Vaughan, and this is the way in which the house came into the Vaughan family."

"And, pray," inquired the Captain, "did this inexorable claimant continue to keep up his claim to his property under the Vaughan dynasty?"

"It is so asserted and believed by the common people," said Clara, laughing; "it would be a pity to spoil so good a story, and any disclaimers on the part of the reigning family have been always received with a proper degree of incredulity. But here ends my story, and I must say that I think it a passably good one."

As she ceased speaking, she stretched out her hand to the bell-pull and gave it a gentle pressure. Hazlehurst thanked her gayly for her narrative, which he protested was one of the best authenticated ghost stories he had ever heard. As he was speaking, the same negro who had opened the door for him entered with a salver of wine and cake.

"Where is James?" inquired Miss Forrester, with an air of the slightest possible vexation. The servant replied by a succession of grotesque gestures, and some sounds which seemed to be unintelligible gibberish to Hazlehurst.

"Very well," said the young mistress, and dismissed the uncouth attendant.

"You seem to have a new page of honor," said Hazlehurst, smiling. "I do not think I have ever seen this groom of the chambers before."

"No," replied Clara, a little confused at the exposure of this unseemly appendage to her well-appointed household, "I dare say you have not. He never before made his appearance in the parlor when any one was here. I suppose James was sent out by my father. He was a servant of a family that we knew well, and that left the town at the latest allowable instant, in such haste as to leave this faithful follower behind, who happened to be out of the way at the moment. He was the most devoted creature, but is a little unsettled in his intellects, in consequence of a blow upon the head received in defending his master from an attack from some street ruffians late at night. My father found poor Peter in great distress, and took him home out of humanity to himself and friendship to his master. He has been even stranger than usual since he has been with us, in consequence of missing his old friends, but we make him as comfortable as we can."

"I am sure that it is highly to your honor and that of your father," said Hazlehurst, with feeling; "but I see that it is about time for me to repair to the mess-room, if I have any regard for my dinner. But before I go," he continued, rising as he spoke, "will you permit me to ask the honor of Miss Forrester's hand at the assembly this evening?"

The lady smiled an assent, and the young officer took his leave cheerily, and walked up the street towards the Green Dragon with a much better opinion of human nature in general, and of female nature in particular, than he had entertained when he walked down it.

On arriving at the mess-room, he found himself very closely examined as to his experiences of the night before, especially by those officers who had been his predecessors in his quarters. He parried their importunities, however, as adroitly as he could, and kept his own counsel most religiously. He slipped away as soon as he could after the cloth was removed, and hastened home to dream over his morning with the gentle Clara. He found everything in proper order, and John awaiting his commands. On interrogation, that worthy asseverated that he had stoutly denied that anything unusual had happened. "He hoped he had not been an officer's servant so long without knowing how to tell a lie upon occasion."

"Very well, John," said the Captain, "I don't believe the truth will suffer in your hands. So you may now go where you please, only be here at six o'clock to dress my hair."

John departed, and his master sat down to think over the doings and sayings of the morning. He could not but examine the portrait of the former inhabitant of the apartment, and think of the strange thoughts that must have haunted him while he sat in that place; and at the picture of his lovely grandchild, and compare her charms with those of her lovely friend,—I need scarcely say to whose advantage. The adventures of the preceding night troubled him not; he was haunted by another and more dangerous phantom in that solitary chamber.

At length he was aroused from his revery by a knock at the door, which, when opened, revealed his orderly-sergeant, whom he had directed to come to him at that hour, with the best padlock he could find in Boston, and all its appliances. The man had been a blacksmith, and he soon affixed it with its staple to the door of the room and departed.

"If the ghost come to-night, while I am gone," said Hazlehurst to himself, "he shall not come in at the door if I can help it!"

When John had returned, and the toilet was finished, Captain Hazlehurst proceeded to set forth for Concert Hall, the yet surviving scene of many a pre-revolutionary festivity. He dismissed John with instructions to meet him at the Hall at twelve o'clock. As he was leaving the room, his pocket struck against the side of the door.

"There's no occasion for carrying my orderly-book with me, that I know of," said he, carelessly, to himself, and, as he spoke, threw it on the table in the centre of the room. He then locked and double-locked the door, and to make assurance doubly sure, applied the padlock, and, with both keys in his pocket, walked cheerily up the street to the scene of action.

I wish I could indulge my dear readers with a description of that brilliant assembly, but the inexorable limits of my chapter (which I have already

overstepped) forbid. You would not have supposed
that the scene of that bright and gay festival was in
a besieged and straitened town. One of the finest
bands in the British service discoursed its sweetest
music to inspire the dance. The Hall was admirably
lighted, and decorated with flags and other loyal insignia. The Governor, the General commanding the
troops, with their brilliant staffs, the officers of the
various regiments, comprising many of the younger
branches of the best families of England, the principal civil functionaries, and the loyal gentlemen of
the town, all in the rich costume of the days when a
gentleman was known by his dress, were present.
And there, too, were the dashing wives of the married officers, and the flower of the provincial beauty
that still remained loyal to its king. The appointments of the supper, the plate-chests of the several
regimental messes being laid under contribution for
the purpose, were of the completest description, and
the table was covered with viands and wines which
showed that the sea was yet open to the beleaguered
army. All was joy and mirth. Every one seemed
determined to shake off whatever of despondency
the darkening prospects of the siege might urge upon
their hearts, and to be happy for at least one night.
Ah! What a glancing of scarlet coats and of gold
lace! What a rustling of damasks and brocades was
there! But of all the brilliant assemblage, I will
maintain it *à l'outrance*, there was none that surpassed in beauty or in grace my Clara Forrester and

her Charles Hazlehurst. It was a blessing to see them glide down the dance, and to look upon their beaming eyes. Lord Percy shook his head, when he saw how his young favorite had taken his advice, and smiled inwardly as he watched them without looking at them. But then it was no concern of his. He had discharged his duty in putting Hazlehurst on his guard. He must now take his own course, on his own responsibility.

But such evenings (alas! that it should be so!) cannot last forever. At a late hour the signal for breaking up was given, and the party dispersed, "shut up in measureless content." Hazlehurst handed Clara into her carriage, and, I am afraid, found it necessary, as it was a slippery night, to hold her hand rather closely as he performed this duty. I recollect *I* used sometimes to find it unavoidable. However, she drove off, and Hazlehurst, followed by John, walked down Hanover Street to his quarters. So absorbed was he in his meditations upon the hours just fled, that he thought of neither ghost nor goblin till he found himself at the door of his room. Reminded by the sight of his padlock of the reason of its employment, he said, laughingly, "I flatter myself that I have been rather more than a match for his ghostship to-night! But we shall see."

With these words he unlocked his various fastenings, and, followed by John, made his way into the apartment. A few embers yet glimmered upon the hearth, and John soon lighted the candles. Hazlehurst cast his eyes around the room. Everything was in its proper place and order. He chuckled inwardly at the success of his plan, and rubbed his hands with internal satisfaction. Everything was right, no intruder had been there. He glanced at the table in the centre of the room. He started forward, and gazed upon it yet more earnestly. He stood silent, and motionless with astonishment. BY HEAVEN, THE ORDERLY-BOOK WAS GONE!

CHAPTER III.

THE orderly-book was gone ! Death and furies ! What was to be done now ? The pranks of the night before, though, like most practical jokes, more amusing to their perpetrators than to their victims, seemed to have been but the prologue to a more serious jest, — one of those jests which are paradoxically but truly called " no joke." As long as the ghost was content to confine the overflowings of his animal spirits to new combinations of the tables and chairs, to a novel arrangement of the bed-clothes, or to a summary divorce of the shovel and tongs, his effervescences, if not absolutely agreeable, were at least not positively mischievous. But to meddle with what was none of his business, but, on the contrary, with what was emphatically the business of his Majesty's —th regiment, was an entirely different affair. The ghost could not be a loyal ghost, that was plainly to be seen. Old Honeywood, to be sure, had no particular reason to love a government that intended promoting him to the yard-arm, if it could have laid hold of him ; but it was not handsome in him to resort to such a pitiful revenge as this, particularly in his own house. It was hardly fair to visit the sins of Queen Anne's Lords of the Admiralty upon an unoffending captain and adjutant in the army of King George.

It is plain that he was a rebel at his heart, and, had he been in the flesh, would have waged war in the name of the Colonies against his liege sovereign, with as much *gusto* as he did against mankind in general on his own account, especially if there happened to be any rich London or Bristol ships within range of his guns. He had a natural taste for such pursuits: his only mistake lay in interfering as an amateur in what was strictly a professional monopoly. There is great virtue in a commission or letter-of-marque. A piece of sheepskin and a pair of epaulets make all the difference in the world in the moral qualities of actions. In many cases it makes all the difference between a hempen cord and a red ribbon round a man's neck. Many a hero has gone out of the world in the embrace of a halter, his achievements only recorded in the Newgate Calendar, who, had his noun substantive been only qualified by an adjective or two, would have received " the Senate's thanks," have glittered with medals and orders, and been commemorated by world-famous historians and poets. Such is luck! But it is none of my business to moralize in this way. All I have to do is to relate this true passage of history with the most absolute accuracy of detail. *Revenons à nos moutons.* Let us to our muttons again.

While we have been indulging in these profitable reflections, our hero has been through a variety of evolutions. First he stood aghast, as if, instead of gazing upon nothing at all, his sight had been blasted by some particularly ill-favored apparition. This was the only idea that his look and gesture communicated to his trusty squire, who turned his eyes with difficulty in the direction of his master's in the confident expectation of being rewarded by the vision of a raw-head and bloody-bones at the very least. Disappointed, however, of any such pleasing spectacle, he was by no means so ill informed in the very rudiments of demonology, as not to know that it did not necessarily follow, because *he* could discern nothing beyond the common, that his master was equally unfortunate.

"What is it, sir? Where is it, sir?" inquired John, in a voice of hollow emotion.

"The orderly-book, you scoundrel! the orderly-book!" responded the Captain, in a low, concentrated tone.

"The orderly-book, your Honor!" returned John. "Well, sir, I never heard of the ghost of a book walking before! What does it look like, sir?"

It is evident that John was not a reading man (the march of mind had not then been taken up, nor had the schoolmaster gone abroad), or he would have known that nothing is more common than for the ghost of a book to walk. Indeed, what is a book but the ghost of the man that writes it? Oh, blessed necromancy of reading, mightier than that of the Governor of Glubdubdrib, or the Island of Enchanters, once visited by that only truthful traveller, Lemuel Gulliver! For whereas his could only command the departed for the space of twenty-four hours, thine can summon them to the presence at all seasons and for any time. But John did not know this, and so he asked what the ghost of the orderly-book looked like.

"Look like, you villain!" somewhat testily answered Hazlehurst. "It looks like nothing at all. It's gone, you dog!"

"Gone already, sir!" exclaimed the astonished John. "And where was it, sir?"

"Exactly in the middle of the table there, with its right cover leaning against the candlestick, its hinder end cocked up upon the inkstand."

"Bless my soul!" shuddered John at this picturesque description. "And how long ago is it since your Honor saw it last?"

"Just as I was going to the assembly this evening," replied his master.

"O Lord! is that all?" exclaimed the man, much relieved. "I thought your Honor had just seen it, when I could see nothing at all."

"Confound your nonsense!" returned the Captain sharply. "I wish to God that I had seen it! What under Heaven I am to say about it to Lord Percy to-morrow, God knows! But light all the candles in the room, and let us have a thorough search for it, though it is not likely that it is here."

This foreboding was but too true. His prophetic

heart had told him an ower true tale. They looked above, around, and underneath. They crawled over the floor on their hands and knees, and, like the serpent of old, "upon their belly did they go" under the bed. They looked into every drawer, and inspected the most impossible places. But it was all in vain. The mystic volume was not to be found in the wood-box, nor did it drop from the inverted jack-boots. The window-seats were ignorant of its whereabout, and the window-curtains wotted not of its presence. The cooking utensils knew not of it, and their basket and their store was not blessed with its possession. Where the devil could it be? It seemed as if the devil only could tell.

There was no sign of any other disturbance in their premises. This made the matter look the more mysterious. It was a much more awful affair than if the disappearance of the book had been accompanied by any of the gambols and *funniments* of the night before. That looked like fun : this looked like earnest. The orderly-book contained information relating to the strength and state of the royal forces, which it was of the last importance should not fall into the hands of the rebels. And beside this there were loose papers, given to our hero by Lord Percy to be copied, as he acted in some sort as his private secretary as well as adjutant, which were of a still more secret nature ; such, for example, as his lordship's reply to the requisition of the commander-in-chief for the opinions of his principal officers as to the state

13

of affairs in the town, and the best course to be pursued. This, and other documents, involved an amount of intelligence as to facts and opinions, which might be of infinite mischief if they fell into the enemy's hands. Hazlehurst knew too well what a mass of disaffection existed in the town, not to feel that the worst was but too probable.

After every place, probable and improbable, had been ransacked, and to no purpose, the search was abandoned for the night. The room was secured as far as locks and bolts were concerned, though they seemed to be of but little moment in this chamber of bedevilment, and Captain Hazlehurst retired moodily to bed to seek for such rest as he could find. It was an uncomfortable night, to be sure; not from any renewal of the disturbances of the night before, for all was quiet, but from his harassing thoughts and internal vexation. His sleep was broken by visions of his interview with his commander, in which he should communicate this provoking occurrence. Words of censure and reprimand rung in his ears. He even saw himself, in the phantasmagoria of his waking dreams, standing without his sword before a court-martial detailed to try him for neglect of duty. In the confusion of his thoughts he could not very accurately determine what would be considered the exact measure of his military offence; but he could not help feeling that it would be no advantage to him in his professional career, even in the most favorable event. He cursed the evil hour in which he sought these unlucky quarters, and heartily wished them, and everything connected with them, at the devil. He perplexed his thoughts in vain with conjectures as to the motives and the method of the trick that had been played him ; and though he resolved not to rest until he had plucked out the heart of the mystery, still he feared that the injury to the service and to his own prospects would be completed before he could accomplish his purpose. It was a miserable business altogether. If he escaped with a reprimand from headquarters, and with the dread laugh of the mess-table, he would be a lucky fellow.

I have often wondered how much the beaming eyes and laughing mouth of Clara Forrester mingled in these visions of the night. I am afraid that all the little loves by whom he had been escorted down Hanover Street, after he had put Miss Forrester into the carriage, were sent to the right about by the first tempest of his astonishment and vexation. But they are volatile creatures, and, though easily brushed aside for a moment, soon return again to the charge. Like flies, it is easy enough to drive them away ; but, before you can congratulate yourself on being rid of them, back they are again. There is one villain, for example, that has been buzzing about me all the time I have been writing, and evidently takes an in-telligent pleasure in tormenting me. " Get out, you scoundrel !" There he stands on my paper, rubbing his hands, and shaking his head, in perfect diabolic glee at his success. Ben Jonson and the old dramatists knew what they said when they called a familiar spirit — a young devil, saving your presences — "a fly." Just so the little loves come fluttering back again after you think you have effectually scared them away. But there the analogy ends; for although they do mischief enough sometimes, still, like my Lord Byron, "I cannot call them devils." They played the devil with me, to be sure, a good many times in my hot young days, but I don't believe they meant any harm. At any rate, I should then have been devilish sorry and still should be (but that is between ourselves) to miss their gentle ministrations altogether.

Be this as it may, I have the best reasons for believing that they returned before daybreak, and buzzed merrily about the pillow of Hazlehurst. The mosquito-net is not yet invented that can keep them out. I cannot depone positively to the exact proportion of his waking or of his sleeping dreams that was of their weaving; for I am scrupulous never to state any fact in an historical document like the present, which I am not prepared at any moment to authenticate by affidavit before any·magistrate or justice of the peace. But I am quite certain that those soft eyes and that bewitching smile floated before his mind's eye, mixed up even with his least pleasant anticipations. In case of the worst, youth and nature would suggest that there might be some comfort yet left him. Though his cup might be a bitter one, still there was at least one cordial drop at the bottom of it. Though censure or derision might visit his misfortune, still there was one whose soft bosom would feel with him, and who would view it with the eyes of love, and not of discipline.

Perhaps the events of the day and evening had encouraged this state of feeling; for, to be candid, she had been tolerably encouraging. He felt more sure that she loved him than he had ever done before; and, although he could not exactly define his own views and intentions in the premises, still he yielded (and who can blame him?) to the delicious dream of love. If any of my readers can recall to recollection the time when he first truly believed that he was beloved by a beautiful young woman, and yet can find it in his heart to wonder that Hazlehurst should have gilded the gloomy hours of that unlucky night with dreams of Clara Forrester, I wish he would just do me the favor to lay this true history aside. He is not worthy to be my reader. But then it is impossible that there should be such a man.

The hours of the night wore on, and at last the morning came. It was a black morning to poor Hazlehurst; but he resolved to meet the unpleasant consequences of his mishap with the best face he could. As his candle-light toilet was proceeding, the orderly-sergeant called for the book.

"I shall call myself upon Lord Percy, Williams, immediately after parade : so you need not wait."

The veteran stared a little at this deviation from

routine; but it was his business to obey: so he bowed and retired.

It was a bitter cold morning, and the keen wind was improved in sharpness by the broad expanse of frozen water which then separated the Common from the country beyond; but Hazlehurst felt warm enough in the prospect of what was before him. There is no external or internal application of a more calorific tendency than the inevitable necessity of doing a particularly disagreeable piece of work at a certain specified hour near at hand. It makes the heart seethe like a caldron, and the boiling blood is sent bubbling through the veins.

The parade was over: the troops were dismissed. Hazlehurst was moving slowly towards the mess-breakfast, thinking of the duty that must follow it, when he was aroused from his revery by hearing a horse reined up suddenly by his side. It was Lord Percy himself.

"So Williams tells me, Hazlehurst, that you have something to say to me. Come and breakfast with me, my boy, and you will have the best of opportunities to say it. I shall be quite alone."

"It will give me infinite pleasure, my lord," replied Hazlehurst, "and I will be with you immediately."

"Right, right," said his lordship: "punctuality at drills and at mess is a great military virtue. I shall expect you in a quarter of an hour."

With these words he cantered along the frozen road

(for it could hardly be called a street then) that led to his excellent quarters.

I am afraid that my hero lied the least in the world, when he said that it would give him infinite pleasure to breakfast with his noble friend and commander. Not that he had any fears as to the quality of his breakfast or of his society; but the thoughts of the sauce which he brought to both plagued him in advance, and he wished that a longer time and a wider space could have elapsed before it was necessary to administer it. But delay was useless and impossible: so he strode toward the quarters of his host with a firm tread, and ascended the long flight of steps that led to the house, and gazed upon the trees and shrubs in the courtyard, all glittering with ice, with as easy and careless an air as he could assume.

The breakfast-room, into which he was shown, was a spacious wainscoted apartment, with a low ceiling, but an air of great comfort. A blazing fire of logs roared up the chimney; and the breakfast-table, with all its appliances of luxury, was drawn into a comfortable proximity to it. The winter's sun looked brilliantly through two windows of the room. Fresh plants stood in the windows, and old pictures looked down from the walls. It was not Alnwick Castle, nor Sion House, to be sure; but it was a very inhabitable place, for all that. An older campaigner than his lordship might have thought himself well off in worse quarters.

In a few minutes Lord Percy appeared,—having exchanged his uniform coat for a brocaded dressing-gown, and his military boots for Turkish slippers,— and, after a cordial welcome to his young friend, rang the bell for breakfast. The tray was brought; the coffee was poured; the eggs were cracked; the toast was crunched. The breakfast was despatched with the appetites of young men sharpened by a daybreak parade with the thermometer at zero. Their discussions were confined to the good things before them and the things to which they were naturally allied, until the table was cleared and the servants withdrawn. Then Lord Percy, drawing his chair up to the fire, and comfortably nursing his left leg placed over his right knee, turned to Hazlehurst with an air of comic gravity.

"Well, my lad," thus his lordship opened the palaver, "so you have somewhat to say to me? Faith I thought as much last night!"

"Last night, my lord!" exclaimed the adjutant. "I don't know that I rightly apprehend your meaning."

"Oh, of course not," replied the Earl. "But you can hardly suppose that I failed to observe how carefully you followed my advice last evening. You must not suppose that Cupid has bandaged all our eyes as effectually as he seems to have done yours."

"Ah, yes!" replied our hero, "your lordship alludes to my little flirtation with Miss Forrester. I was only following your own advice, to fall in love with two or three at the same time. But you know

my lord, that it is necessary to begin with one. Now
I begin with Miss Forrester."

"Bravo, bravo, Hazlehurst!" said Lord Percy, laughing. "A ready answer is a good thing, in love or in
war. Well, well, you understand your own affairs
best, and are old enough to manage them for yourself. Upon my honor, I can hardly blame you, young
man. I was half inclined to fall in love with her
myself last night. She is a fine creature."

"One does not often see a finer, indeed, my lord,"
answered the lover; "but you are quite at liberty to
enter the lists with me, if you choose," he doughtily
continued: "I have no pretensions to any monopoly
in that quarter."

I believe the fellow knew he lied when he said
that; but these, I believe, are the sort of lover's per-
juries at which Jove laughs. You will see this idea
illustrated and enforced in my folio on the subject,
now in the press. Whether Jove laughed at this or
not, Lord Percy did, as he replied, —

"Very likely, very likely. Thank you, thank you!
I do not know that I should like to run the risk,
were I not armed in proof on that side. Then I suppose your business of this morning does not relate
to this matter, as I thought at first it might."

"No, my lord," answered Hazlehurst, plucking up
his courage, and determined to have it over at once
— "no, my lord. I am sorry to say that my errand
is of a much less pleasant character; and it relates
rather to war than to love, and to me than to Miss

Forrester.   It is not the loss of my heart, but of your orderly-book, that is in the question."

"The orderly-book lost, Hazlehurst!" exclaimed Lord Percy. "What the devil do you mean?" in a tone of the utmost surprise a little mixed with incredulity.

"Exactly what I say, my lord," replied the adjutant, waxing cooler as he went on. "The orderly-book and all its contents is gone; and what is worse I see no sort of prospect of ever recovering it again."

"What do you mean? what do you mean?" repeated the Earl in great astonishment. "You know very well that this is a serious matter, and can hardly be jesting."

"I was never more serious in my life, I assure you, my lord," asseverated the young officer. "I wish it may turn out to be a jest in the end. Sorry as I should be to be guilty of any disrespect to your lordship, I would willingly encounter your displeasure for an untimely jest, so that the service were in no danger of mischief from this unlucky business."

"But how could it be lost, Captain Hazlehurst?" his lordship replied a little sternly. "How could it be lost, when it was in your custody, and you could not but know the vital importance of keeping it safe? How came it lost, sir?"

"I am well aware, my lord," replied poor Hazlehurst, "of the importance of this matter to his Majesty's service, as well as to my own honor and prospects — if I may mention them in the same breath.

I beg your lordship to listen patiently to the story I have to tell you; and I beg that you will pardon the apparent nonsense of the first part of my narration, as you will see that it leads to a serious termination. I presume I need bring no other evidence of the truth of my statements before your lordship's tribunal than my own assertion. The evidence of my servant will be ready to corroborate them before less friendly judges, should the matter end as seriously as I fear it may."

He then proceeded to relate to his commander the whole history of his two last nights, from the mysterious footsteps to the vanishing of the orderly-book. His lordship looked grave as the story proceeded, and, rising, walked thoughtfully about the room after it was finished. At length he thus addressed his young friend, who sat in anxious expectation, —

"This is a strange business, Hazlehurst, a very strange business. I am afraid there is mischief in it. At first I thought it might be a mystification of some of your messmates: but they would hardly have ventured upon such a *dénoucment*."

"That is my own opinion, my lord. The pranks of the night before were all fair, though a little rough play. But I do not think that the *ennui* of a garrison life, however much it may sharpen the wits of its victims, would lead them to commit an action which might injure the service, to say nothing of the character of a brother-officer."

"That is true enough, Hazlehurst," resumed his

lordship. "I think it must be a contrivance of some of the disguised rebels in this cursed town to assist their rascally friends on the other side of the river. My God! I would have sooner lost the best horse in my stables than have had those papers fall into the rebels' hands."

"I hope that your lordship does not look upon my part in this unfortunate business as amounting to culpable negligence, or neglect of duty," Hazlehurst humbly ventured to suggest, seeing that his commanding officer was in a milder mood than he had apprehended he would be.

"Why, as to that matter, my friend," replied his lordship, "you can hardly think, that sitting here with you as my fellow-officer and companion, when off duty, I can attribute any moral blame to you for this accident. Whether you may not be regarded as responsible in a military sense for the loss of this valuable book, is a question I can express no opinion about here and at this time, as I may have to form one officially on the subject before long. The book was properly in your custody: if it be not forthcoming when regularly demanded, the question will arise, *Why?* · And it is not for me to decide now whether the facts you have stated will be considered sufficient to discharge your responsibility."

"Will your lordship have the goodness to advise me what course to pursue under these circumstances — as a friend, as one gentleman advising another in a case of difficulty, and not as my superior officer ?"

"Why, my dear fellow," returned the stout Earl, sincerely feeling for his young favorite in his awkward predicament, "the best advice I can give you is to ferret out these rascals, and find the orderly-book again before it is missed. When that fails, we will see what can be done next."

"But how much grace have I to make search, even if I could get a clew to the villany, before it must be reported at headquarters ? "

"I can give you only till next Saturday, when I must make up my full weekly report to General Howe. There is no need of saying anything about it before then ; and it gives you four whole days to work in, as it is now only Tuesday morning. Leave no stone unturned, my good fellow, to get at the bottom of this affair. Much may be done in four days."

"I am heartily obliged to you, my lord," said Hazlehurst gratefully, for he felt much relieved and comforted by the kindness of Lord Percy's words and manner, "and you may be sure that I will lose no time in sifting this matter to the best of my abilities. And you may be sure, also, that your lordship's goodness and consideration for me will be gratefully remembered by me as long as I live, whatever may be the event of this affair."

"Keep up a good heart, my lad," returned the Earl kindly, "and hope bravely for the best. You may rely upon my doing all I can for you consistently with my duty. And now you had better set about your inquiries, as there is no time to be lost. And when Williams comes to you, send him to me, and I will have a new orderly-book ready for you before evening parade."

With these words the heir of "the Percy's high-born race" bowed his visitor out of the room. Hazlehurst descended the steps with a lighter heart than when he had ascended them, and he felt, what we have all felt in our time, how much more unpleasant the discharge of a disagreeable duty is in the anticipation than in the actual performance. His actual position was in no wise changed, and yet he felt as if it were bettered. Such is the relief of the communication of a secret sorrow, and such the magic of a kind thought fitly clothed with words of kindness.

There is a great deal of one very excellent thing in this world. There is at least one article which everybody is ready to give away, though there are comparatively few who are ready to accept it. I mean there is a great deal of very good ADVICE floating about. James Smith, I think it was, once suggested the formation of "A Society for the Suppression of *ad*-Vice." But I am sure I should not encourage such an institution. Why, bless you! I don't know what my neighbors would do if my issues of advice were stopped or curtailed. The interest I take in their affairs is worth much more to me than the ten per cent I get for my money. I really don't think the neighborhood could get along at all without my advice. "It's unknown" what good I do, as were the tears Mrs. Malaprop shed at the death of her poor dear Mr. Malaprop. I consider the benevolent Howard as a hard-hearted villain in comparison with me. No, no! it will never do to suppress advice. The difficulty in this branch of benevolence lies in finding out how to apply the advice to practice. But that is the concern of the party benefited. If he do not know how to avail himself of your good advice, that is no affair of yours. Dr. Johnson settled it long ago, that no man should be expected to furnish ideas and understanding at the same time.

Now, here was a case in point. Lord Percy had given Captain Hazlehurst some very excellent advice: the perplexity was to know what to do with it, now he had got it. It was very easy for his lordship to say, "Hazlehurst, ferret out these rascals, find the orderly-book again;" but it was quite another affair for the gallant Captain to reduce his instructions to practice. However, he resolved to do his best; and, as safety is said to be found in a multitude of counsellors, he thought he might as well take some more advice — on the homœopathic principle adopted by the philosopher of Islington for the recovery of his eyes after they had been scratched out in his celebrated leap into the quickset hedge. So he thought he would take into his counsels some of his trustiest comrades and especial cronies.

Calling at Captain Lyndsay's quarters, he was so fortunate as to find him at home, and his Pylades, Major Ferguson, with him. Dr. Holcombe was speedily summoned to the council; and Hazlehurst soon laid the matter, under strict injunctions of secrecy, before them. It was a grave matter, requiring all the aids that reflection or art could afford. Accordingly, they lighted the calumet of consideration, and sought for illumination in the circling clouds of smoke that curled around their heads. In those days, dear reader, cigars were not; but pipes daily reminded frail mortals that they, too, were made of clay, and that their lives were but as a vapor of smoke, that soon vanisheth away.

But as suffumigation, though a powerful agent, did not seem to be alone sufficient to summon the powers most needed, the worthy surgeon, as one well skilled in potent mixtures, brewed a smoking caldron, in which he mingled many opposite ingredients, of various kingdoms of nature [to make the mixture "slab and good"]. When his incantations were ended, the magic bowl was placed in the centre of the circle, and was solemnly passed round from mouth to mouth of those who sought from it wisdom and inspiration. In those primitive days, the heresy of ladles had not yet entered the pale of orthodox good-fellowship. The genial mother-bowl was not then split up into as many sects as there were disciples. I beg to be distinctly understood that I by no means sanction this concoction of the " medicine-man," nor do I wish to imply that the spirits thus summoned to their aid were the best assistants in council or in action. I merely relate the fact, and leave it for others to form their own opinions about it. It is not my fault if they drank punch, and smoked pipes, in the morning. But what would posterity say to me, if I suppressed so important a feature of this important consultation, from a wish to whitewash their characters in the eyes of this water-drinking generation?

"By Jove, Hazlehurst!" said Major Ferguson, knocking the ashes out of his pipe, "this is the most extraordinary ghost I ever heard of, and one that will take a bishop, at least, to lay him."

"In default of a bishop," suggested Lyndsay, "here is the Doctor, who as a university man, and one of a learned profession renowned for making ghosts, must serve us for want of a better man."

"This is the first time," said the Doctor, setting down the bowl, from which he had been, in a most unprofessional manner, engaged in swallowing his own prescription — "this is the first time in my life that I was ever taken for a conjurer. But, as Ferguson justly remarks, as this is a case calling for the piety of a bishop, I am certainly the only man in company fit for the adventure."

"I wish to Heaven you would undertake it, then," said Hazlehurst, who thought his friends rather inclined to make light of a serious matter. "It may be sport to you, but it is" —

"Not death to you, my dear fellow," interposed the Doctor: "you are not so easily killed, as the d—d Yankees knew, when they saw you running up Bunker's Hill faster than they ran down it. Besides, you

14

should never mention death in the presence of a doctor. You might as well talk of cabbage to a tailor.
It's professional, my dear fellow, it's professional."

"I wish, then," resumed Hazlehurst, "that you
would bring your professional artillery to bear upon
the villain who has stolen the orderly-book; and you
may call in the aid of your natural ally, too, if you
please."

"I should like to have the treatment of his case,"
said the Doctor thoughtfully. "I think that I could
manage it."

"And I should like to have the qualifying him for
your treatment, Doctor," said Lyndsay. "I am quite
sure that I could manage *that*."

"No doubt, no doubt," replied Holcombe. "Any
fool can break a head. It takes a wise man to mend
it again."

"And what," retorted Lyndsay, alluding to an
operation he would persist in considering as unnecessary, in consequence of a knock over the head
at Lexington, — "and what if, in mending the hole,
he makes two?"

"He puts at rest forever," replied the Doctor
gravely, "the disputed question, whether or not the
party had any brains. There were not much, to be
sure; but it can never be denied again that there
were some."

"Truce to banter," said the graver Major Ferguson,
"and let us see what can be done to help poor Hazlehurst out of this scrape."

"With all my heart," resumed the Doctor. "It seems to me that the thing to be done is to set a trap for the thief. But what the deuce shall we do for bait? — unless, indeed, the commander-in-chief would lend us his private papers for the purpose."

"He cannot be a vulgar thief," said Ferguson, "or he certainly would not have left your tankard and spoons behind him, Hazlehurst."

"Not only the plate," said Hazlehurst, "but my watch and purse, lay full in his sight. So plunder could not have been his object."

"He is an extraordinary fellow, certainly," said the Doctor, "and we must as certainly contrive to catch him, if it be only for the curiosity of the thing. — What is your plan, Ferguson?"

"I can suggest nothing better," said the Major, "than to keep a strict watch for a few nights, both within and without the building; for it seems to me our only chance is to find him at his old tricks, or prowling about the premises, as we have no idea of where else to look for him."

"I can see no other plan that we can follow," said Hazlehurst.

"Nor I," said Lyndsay. — "Can you, Doctor?"

"We can try it, at any rate," returned the leech. "We shall probably have plenty of time, in the intervals of his visitations, to devise other schemes. I am ready for my share of the watch; that is, if Hazlehurst's punch and tobacco are what they should be."

"You need have no fears on that point," answered Hazlehurst; "for John will brew you an Atlantic of punch, and pile you up a Chimborazo of tobacco, when he knows that you have entered into an alliance, offensive and defensive, against the ghost."

"I am your man, then," cried the Doctor, finishing the punch, "and I will bet you a supper at the Green Dragon that I am the first man to see the ghost."

"Done!"

"Done!!"

"Done!!!"

And the session was adjourned.

CHAPTER IV.

AFTER the conference at the quarters of Captain Lyndsay was broken up, our hero walked deliberately down Hanover Street toward his own abode. He was busily planning operations in accordance with the result of the council as he walked along. But he was not so much absorbed by his own affairs or his own meditations, as to be unconscious of his approach to the habitation of his ladye-love. In those days it was an essential part of good breeding for a gentleman to call upon his partner on the morning after a ball, "and humbly hope she caught no cold," though he had to canter over half a county in the service. It was not likely, therefore, that Hazlehurst would pretermit the performance of this duty when his path took him past her very door. So he knocked boldly, and was speedily admitted, and ushered into the presence of the fair Clara, who, of course, was expecting his visit. She wore her apple-green silk that morning,—a color I would not recommend to my lady-readers, unless they are very sure that their complexions can bear it,—and, by Heaven! she did look divinely. It is provoking to see how the most unbecoming colors will set off a complexion and eyes that need take no thought for themselves. But I am not going to rave. I only state the simple truth in saying that she looked divinely: at least, I never saw anything prettier than the sweet glow of consciousness that mantled over her cheeks and neck, and the smile that kindled in her eyes, as she met the ardent gaze of her advancing lover. At any rate, I am quite sure that he agreed with me in this opinion; for he hardly seemed to know whether he was in the body or out of the body, as he walked up the room. Lovers are foolish creatures — at least, so I have heard, for I was never one myself. But for the life of me I can't conceive why that silly Hazlehurst should have gone and seated himself in the arm-chair on the other side of the fireplace, when the gentle Clara had taken pains to leave plenty of room for him on the sofa by her side. I am sure I never should have done that. However, he did, and it is my business to relate, not to account for, the fact.

They were soon seated *vis à vis*, with nothing but the little work-table between them, and there seemed to be no reason why they should not make themselves agreeable to one another. And I am by no means sure that they did not, although they had very little to say for themselves apparently. What Hazlehurst might have whispered to Clara the night before, at Concert Hall, as they stood apart, sheltered by a battalion of card-playing dowagers, and covered by the full burst of a regimental band, I am unable to say, for I was at that time engaged in overhearing what

General Howe was saying to Governor Gage at the other end of the room. But I think it must have been something that altered their relations to each other in some way, for they were not half as chatty and conversable as they were the day before. And yet it could not have amounted to a full understanding, or that stupid Hazlehurst would not have been sitting two yards away, looking at her pretty foot (not but what it was well worth looking at) as it rested on the edge of the footstool; nor would she have kept her eyes fixed upon her embroidery all the time with the prettiest confusion you ever saw. And I don't believe that they would have talked over the night before in a sort of way that made it perfectly plain that they knew nothing at all of what they were talking about, if they had felt quite at ease in their own minds. It was clear that they were thinking of something else than their words. Poor Hazlehurst was evidently in the state of mind of an unlucky moth that has been well advised by its wisers and betters, that candles are dangerous things in general, and especially that specific candle in particular, and who yet cannot keep itself away from the shining mischief. The attraction of the brilliant object before him was quite too much for any dimly remembered warnings of his distant family against American beauties, or for the fresher hints of his friendly commander, to keep him from flying at last into the flame.

I can't tell you how it was, my dear reader, but somehow or other, in less time than I have been writing these lines, Hazlehurst was by the side of Clara, his left arm encircling her slender waist, their right hands clinging together, and her sweet head gently drooped upon his shoulder. It was a charming group, I do assure you. There are many more disagreeable situations in the world than that of young Hazlehurst at that moment. It was a grand pantomime of action. No words could have expressed their meaning more eloquently. It was not a time for words: they would have been impertinent and superfluous. Accordingly, their lips gave utterance to no sound. Whether their lips did anything else to the purpose, it is not my intention to disclose. I am "trusty Mr. Tattle" as to all matters which should be kept private. Nothing of that sort was ever wormed out of me. The ladies need have no hesitation in placing the most entire confidence in my discretion.

But this silence, though deep and delicious, could not last forever. Alas that it could not! Murmuring words soon displaced it, and the faith of two true young hearts was plighted to each other forever. Ah, holy troth plight! Thine is the true marriage, the era of the mystic union of souls, of which the blessing of the priest is but the statement and proclamation. Woe to those who profane its mysteries by levity, by covetousness, or by falsehood!

As soon as their young joy had subsided into a sort of tumultuous calmness, how they sat, with their hands locked together, talking over their love and their hopes! They traced with fond curiosity the course of their true love—"Great Nature's Nile"— up to its small beginnings and unsuspected springs. Bruce himself could hardly have surpassed them in zealous or minute investigation. And then the more dubious future—how were its uncertainties turned into realities, and its doubts transmuted into sanguine hopes, by the potent magic of youth and love!

> " Ah, love, young love ! bound in thy rosy band,
>   Let sage or cynic prattle as he will,
>   These hours, and only these, redeem life's years of ill."

Clara's doubts as to her reception into the family of her lover were eagerly driven away by his earnest assurances of a cordial welcome. Sir Ralph and his mother were the best of human beings, and had no earthly wish beyond his happiness; and was not his happiness wrapped up in her? Such is the logic of youth and love, and it easily prevailed over one willing enough to be convinced. The best of human beings sometimes take very different views of the component elements of earthly happiness from their children : at least, so it is said. They were too happy to fear. The future would take care of itself. The present was enough for them.

But such interviews, though they live forever, must come to an end in time and space. The time came when the plighted lovers were to part for the first time since they had exchanged their sacred vows. Dinner-time will come round on the day of rejoicing and on the day of mourning, and interpose

its material demands between our souls and soft
emotions of tenderness and grief. The necessities
of the body often afford a healthful distraction to
thoughts too highly strung to sensations of joy or
of sorrow. The body is a "homely nurse;" but it is
a faithful one, if it be not maltreated, and does its
best to guard and help the immortal child that is
intrusted to it to be carried in its arms during its
days of infancy. So the time of parting came, and
they parted; not for any interminable space of time,
to be sure, but it was their first parting. It was
not, as I just said, an eternal separation, for there
was to be a great sleighing-party that evening, and
Hazlehurst had already engaged Clara to be his
companion. With as many last words as if they
were to part for years, he at length departed, with
quite unnecessary entreaties to her not to forget the
evening's engagement.

It was all over. The irreparable step was taken.
The Rubicon of life was passed. The hour that was
just expired would tinge with its hues every future
moment of his life. He felt that it was no light thing
that he had just done, and, though he was conscious
of a deep happiness, it was no boisterous joy, and
it was not only with ease, but with satisfaction,
restrained within the limits of his own breast, until
the due time of disclosure. It was a pleasure to feel
that he had a secret hoard of happiness, known only
to himself, which he might count over with a miser's
joy, but with none of a miser's guilt or folly.

One thing, however, was remarkable. The idea of the orderly-book, or of the ghost, had never once crossed his mind after he had found himself hurried on to the catastrophe of the interview. He was sorry that he had not made Clara the confidante of his troubles, and resolved to repair the omission at the first opportunity. Confidence should not be kept back first on his side. He rather rejoiced that he had a misfortune which she might share with him. Perhaps his philosophy would not have stood him in such good stead, had his misfortune been a little greater than it was. But everything helps to feed a healthy love. It is your feeble, rickety brats, that expire of the first unsavory mess of earthly pottage.

The mess-dinner was over. There had been some quizzing on the subject of Miss Forrester and of the ghost; but it was all evidently at random, and they had no idea how very near the wind they were going on either tack. Hazlehurst and his friends kept their own counsel, and after dinner met by appointment at Dr. Holcombe's quarters to finish the plan of their campaign against the midnight forager of orderly-books. They had, as they had agreed upon, selected a number of picked men, on whose secrecy and fidelity they could rely, who were to keep watch and ward, duly relieved, by night and day, without making any noise about it; so that if the ghost should return, clothed in his "vesture of decay," to the scene of his former operations, he would be pretty sure to be laid by the heels. The officers themselves also agreed to mount guard, by turns, in the Captain's chamber, so that it should never be without a sleepless eye on the lookout. Arrangements were made that the sentinels and their officers should rendezvous quietly in the neighborhood, at a small inn, as if by accident, and the men be shown their posts of observation without any bustle to attract notice; John and Orderly Williams being left in garrison of the haunted building until it was properly invested. Everything happened at the time and in the order that it should, and the arrangements were carried into effect with military precision. One man walked up and down the street, with injunctions never to lose sight of the front of the house. The three other sides were in charge of three other trusty men, so placed that no approach could be made to the house on either side without instant detection. A guard was also placed on each floor of the house on the inside, although it had been most thoroughly searched, in advance, in every corner. It seemed as if the Prince of the Power of the Air alone, approaching through his own peculiar principality, could obtain entrance unobserved. And so they rested on their arms.

In the mean time, the winter's sun made haste to put an end to the short day, and the time arrived for the great sleighing-party to rendezvous in the North Square. Captain Hazlehurst's graceful little sleigh, contrasting curiously with his stout cob, was at the door, and he was speedily drawn up in front of Mr.

Forrester's mansion, awaiting the pleasure of its fair
mistress. She soon appeared, breathing a fresh summer upon the cheek of winter, and yet looking like
his youngest daughter, so befurred and betippeted,
and becloaked was she. Still, through all, you could
see the graceful outline of her shape, while her happy
face glowed through her world of habiliments, like
the sun through evening clouds. The moon would
perhaps be a more appropriate, but the sun is a more
splendid, simile : so let it stand. She was soon by the
side of Hazlehurst, and they were rapidly careering
away toward the North Square. A very few minutes brought them to the rendezvous, where they found
a large company of the *élite* of the garrison and the
townspeople, preparing for a merry scamper round
the town. There were large sleighs drawn by two,
and some by four, horses, containing parties, which
like the family party of the Vicar of Wakefield, if
they did not have a great deal of wit, they had a great
deal of laughing, which answered the purpose just as
well. There were not wanting modest single sleighs,
like that conveying our hero and heroine, which, if
not as well adapted for frolic as their larger companions, were better calculated for sentiment and for
flirtation. After the usual time had been wasted in
waiting for loiterers, and adjusting where everyone
should go, the procession set forward in due order;
the *quadrigæ* taking the lead, and the more unpretending vehicles following in due succession.

Aha! what a merry jingling of bells, and ringing of

laughter, resounded through the streets of Boston as the horses dashed through them, making the frozen earth resound with their tread! It was a sound of merriment that jarred gratingly upon the ears of many an unwilling listener, separated by the siege from beloved hearts, and suffering, perhaps, from cold in the depth of that dreadful winter, or with hunger, within the sound of the revelry of their oppressors. To many an ear the sweet bells seemed "jangled, out of tune, and harsh." But what was that to the revellers? What cared they for the pining of rebel hearts? Away, away! Up Hanover Street, down Queen Street, through the succession of streets now all amalgamated into Washington Street, up to the lines on the Neck! How the crackling snow glitters in the light of the full moon! What a volcanic effect do the rebel watchfires give to the lovely hills in the distance! You can hear the very hum of the camp, so near are you to it; and you have the pleasing uncertainty as to how soon a battery of cannon may open upon you, or a shell be sent to convey to you the compliments of those who are knocking at your gates. But what of that? Away, away! Back again to the Common, round it, and then dash down to the line of wharves that enclose the harbor, look out over the frozen sea, and then round again across those desolate fields which are now all populous streets or crowded marts. Oh, it was a merry drive! What though the hardships of a seven-years' war, ghastly wounds, and grizzly death, awaited some of the revellers, and

the bitterness of disappointed hope and of interminable exile was the appointed lot of others? They
knew it not. That glittering night was theirs — and
who has more?

There are worse places for a flirtation or a *tête-à-
tête*, let me tell you, than a sleighing-party, especially
where you have a sleigh to yourselves, the noise and
the bustle isolates you so completely. And then
the bear-skins roll you up together so comically,
that positively you sometimes mistake your neighbor's hand for your own. It 's very odd, but so it is.
Poets may talk as much as they please about summer
moons; but I have known quite as much mischief
done under winter moons. And, if I had a daughter,
I would quite as soon trust her with a " detrimental"
in a summer grove, beside a murmuring stream, with
the very best moon that was ever manufactured hang-
ing over their heads, as I would in a snug sleigh,
behind a good horse, making good time over a ringing road, in a cold, clear, sparkling night.

> "Now, ponder well, ye parents dear,"

and lay these, my words of wisdom, to heart.

Clara and Hazlehurst, you may be sure, did not fail
to improve their opportunities; and the evening's
drive furnished a very satisfactory epilogue to the
morning's drama. After a brief interval of silence, as
they rushed up King Street, Clara turned to Hazlehurst, and said laughingly to him, —

"But, Charles, you have not told me yet what
Captain Honeywood had to say to you; for, of course,

he must have been to call on his tenant by this time."

"Ah, my dear Clara, I am satisfied that he was a piratical old dog. I have but too good reason to think ill of him."

"Indeed! And how so, pray? Has he laid you under contribution already? Perhaps he intends collecting his rent in advance."

"If that were all," answered Charles, "I should care little about it. But I am afraid that the old villain is more of a rebel than a pirate. I fear he bears more of a grudge against the King than against me."

"That is natural enough, you know," replied Clara, "for it was his Majesty's predecessor who put him to so much inconvenience for his little mistakes in the matter of ownership. But you mean something, Charles — now tell me all about it."

"The all is soon told," said he. "The crafty old sea-dog has helped himself to the very thing that it is most important, for the sake of the service and for my own sake, should have been kept out of his hands — and I suppose I may have to pay for his villany."

"Good God, Charles!" exclaimed Clara, turning pale with affright. "What *do* you mean? What has happened?"

"Nothing, my love," he responded, "excepting that he has carried off the orderly-book of the regiment, which may convey intelligence to the rebels that will bring them buzzing about our ears, if they have the sense to make use of it."

"But you — how will it affect *you?*" inquired Clara, evidently thinking more of her lover than of her liege lord. "You said that it was bad for your own sake that this book had fallen into his hands."

"Indeed I hardly know myself exactly," he answered; "but I am quite certain that it can do me no good. And what a court-martial may think of it, they only can tell."

"A court-martial!" exclaimed Clara in consternation. "Dear Charles, what have you done for which you can be court-martialed? Pray tell me that you are only in jest."

"I wish I were in jest, my dearest Clara," said he in reply; "but it is no joke, I assure you. The orderly-book was in my custody, as the adjutant of the regiment. I left it on my table when I went to the assembly last night, and when I came back it was gone."

"Gone!" repeated Clara, echoing his words.

"Gone, my dear," he repeated. "And how or whither, the thief, and the devil that helped him, only knows. And when the loss is reported at headquarters, I have reason to fear that I shall be held responsible for it, and it may prove a serious business."

"But what can they do to you, dearest Charles?" almost gasped poor Clara. "It certainly was not your fault that it was taken."

"I cannot think it was," he answered, "after all the precautions I had taken. But one cannot tell

15

the Royal Tavern. The scene was not a very magnificent one, to be sure; but the company was as gay as if it had been a royal palace. The mulled wine was beyond praise. The floor of the large parlor was swept, and a noble fire diffused light and heat through the room. They had not a regimental band, as they had the night before; but the fiddle of a musical negro belonging to the house was sufficient to set them all dancing and flirting. And what could his Majesty's own band itself do more? At a proper time an excellent supper was served in the dining-room,—none of your perpendicular abominations, but a good, regular, sit-down supper, all hot from the spit, and served, if not with metropolitan magnificence, yet at least with provincial plenty. Ample justice was done to the viands; and the port wine and the everlasting punch were not neglected. After the sacred rage of hunger was appeased, the company returned to the great parlor, and resumed their gayeties, which were protracted until a late hour. Such were some of the schemes to which the beleaguered inhabitants of the town resorted to speed away some of their weary hours. And very good schemes, they were, in my opinion.

I do not know how it was, but the garrison gossips, of whom Hazlehurst had warned Clara, remarked that he was not as devoted to her as usual. From this they augured, with the sagacity of their tribe, that he was inclined to be off from the flirtation. Now *I* formed a directly opposite opinion from the circumstance. I am too old a bird to be *chaffed* in that way. I know, however, that the young lovers compared notes of what they heard and overheard on the subject, as they drove home, and that they were entirely satisfied with the success of the evening. What could have made them dissatisfied with it?

On arriving at his quarters, Hazlehurst found everything ready, but no ghost as yet. Dr. Holcombe, who much preferred a comfortable arm-chair, a pipe, and a tankard of punch, over against a rousing fire, to all the sleighing-parties that ever manufactured pleasure out of cold and discomfort, had volunteered to mount guard for the first evening in Hazlehurst's room. He protested, however, that all had been quiet, and not so much of a ghost stirring as would make the candles burn blue. He and Hazlehurst sat up till near morning, and then lay down alternately for an hour or two—but all was still. "Not a mouse stirring." They had their labor for their pains that night. Still they were not discouraged in their campaign against the powers of darkness by this withdrawal of the enemy. They still believed that they would have a brush with him yet. In this faith they renewed their arrangements for the next day, carefully managing them so cautiously that there should be no ground of suspicion given to the world around that there was anything extraordinary going on.

The allies met after breakfast to talk over the matter, and to decide whose turn should be the next to face the enemy. Major Ferguson, in right of seniority of rank, received the privilege. The men who were on guard during the night were examined; but they maintained that there was nothing that could be construed into a suspicious circumstance that had fallen under their observation. Renewed charges of secrecy were given and exchanged, not only for fear of the ghost's getting wind of the conspiracy against him, but lest the laugh at the mess-table might be turned against them. Lord Percy was curious to hear the result of the night's campaign, when the adjutant waited upon him for orders, and gave his approval of the steps taken, and encouraged them to proceed.

Another day, and yet another, passed away. Ferguson and Lyndsay had successively taken the field against the ghost; but none would come when they did call for him. Old Jamaica was the only spirit that was raised, and tobacco-smoke was the only intangible essence that infested them. What was to be done now? It was plain that the ghost was more than a match for them. They believed that they might be his masters in the field; but he certainly had the advantage of them in the strategy which avoids the presence of a superior enemy. They felt, in the slightest degree in the world, like fools, that they should have lost their natural rest for three nights, and expended a degree of skill and energy sufficient to have raised the siege, and all for nothing. Friday night was come. The morrow was the fatal Saturday, when the orderly-book must be found, or the loss reported at headquarters. The confederates sat rather gloomily over their wine at Ferguson's lodgings, — for Ferguson was a married man, and did not live at mess, — and considered with themselves what was to be done next.

"You have not won your supper at the Dragon yet, Doctor," said Ferguson. "The ghost does not seem to regard you with any more favor than the rest of us."

"The Ides of March are not past yet, my friend," observed the Doctor. "I shall have a double chance, as I shall keep watch the last night of the siege, as well as the first. You cannot tell what this night may bring forth."

"So you are not discouraged, I am glad to find," said Hazlehurst, "and still hold to your intention for the night. But don't you intend to go to Miss Forrester's this evening? I know you are invited, and your watch can begin after the party ends."

"Not I, indeed," responded the son of Galen, — "not I, indeed! I am not quite boy enough for that. It is all well enough for you youngsters, who have no turn for rational pursuits; but a pipe and a tankard for me, against all the gatherings together of flirting boys and girls, and gambling papas and mammas, that were ever held. I shall repair to my post early in the evening, and maintain it unseduced and unterrified."

"And faith! I believe that I will bear you company, Doctor," said Ferguson. "My wife has not

got over the cold she got at that cursed sleighing-party, and intends going to bed, instead of the party."

"Do so, by all means," replied Holcombe, "and I dare say, that, besides having a rational time together, we shall have a good account to give of the ghost by the time these boys are ready to come home. Only, I suppose, if we see the ghost both at the same time, you will expect to go snacks in the supper?"

"To be sure, I shall," said the Major, laughing. "We will be partners in the battle and in the spoils."

The party soon after dispersed, and went their several ways; and it will not surprise my readers to learn that Hazlehurst's way led him to Clara Forrester's. He just looked in to see if he could be of any service. He found the fair Clara in some little perturbation.

"What goes wrong, my love?" he inquired. "Has the Governor sent an excuse, or has *la belle* Wilton turned sulky, and refused to come?"

"Worse than either, I assure you, Charles," she replied. "I could spare a dozen governors and beauties better than black Domingo, who has selected this particular occasion to fall sick, and to throw me back on the mercies of James, who is hardly equal, as you know, to such an emergency."

"That is unlucky, indeed," said Hazlehurst. "But my John is quite at your service, such as he is; and he is certainly competent to the ministerial, if not to the legislative, duties of such an occasion."

"Thank you!" she answered. "He will be of great use, and I gladly accept your offer. But what will the Doctor and Major Ferguson do, without him to attend them, since you say that they are determined not to smile upon me?"

"Oh, never fear for them!" replied Hazlehurst. "John shall brew them a double supply of punch, and leave their supper ready laid for them, and they can wait upon themselves fast enough: they are too old campaigners to be disconcerted by a trifle."

"They shall be better treated than they deserve, then, for not coming to me," said she; "for I will send poor old Peter over to them with their supper, and with a bowl of the punch I have been superintending myself for the evening. So you will be good enough to let me have John as soon as you can spare him."

"He shall be at your command directly," he replied, — "as soon as he can put himself in proper trim. Peter will answer all the purpose for the Doctor and Ferguson."

After a few more passages between the lovers, which I do not think particularly concern my readers, Hazlehurst took his leave of his ladye-love, and proceeded to his quarters. I beg that no unkind imputations may be laid upon my Clara in consequence of her holding this festivity on the eve of the important Saturday; for the arrangements had been made for it before she knew anything of Hazlehurst's troubles. And as they were still a secret, and as she had as yet no acknowledged interest in them, if they were public, there was obviously nothing to be done but to go on. But the dear girl had suffered great distress and anxiety about it, especially as the week drew to an end without any tidings of the missing volume. But she had to put a good face upon the matter, and go through her hospitable duties with the best grace she could.

In those days the hour for the assembling of company was a very different one from that which now brings a party together. Before seven o'clock the rooms were filled. I cannot stop now to describe (though description is my *forte*) the beauty and splendor of the scene. We have nothing in these days, excepting the awkward imitation of a fancy ball, that approaches the glories of the days of brocades and scarlet coats, of gold lace and gold buttons, of diamond buckles, and steel-hilted rapiers that looked like diamonds, of powder, and high-heeled shoes. Ah! those were the good times, when you knew a gentleman by his coat, and were not obliged to cipher him out by his conduct or his conversation.

The company were received by Mr. and Miss Forrester, with all the ceremony of the old time. I have not introduced Mr. Forrester to the reader as yet, simply for the want of time. As he made no objection to Hazlehurst's proposals, when they were laid before him, only declining to ratify the engagement formally until the consent of Sir Ralph had been received, and as I, therefore, could make no use of him in the only way fathers can be successfully managed, — as cruel tyrants trampling on the young affections of their daughters, — I have had no occasion to mention him. He would have been well worth your knowledge, however, as a favorable specimen of the old pre-revolutionary New England gentleman. But I have no time left for you to cultivate his acquaintance. The fact is I want three volumes to make use of my materials. Maga is very good; but, like Chanticleer in the fable, "she is not enough." All that was eminent in rank or station (civil or military), all that was brilliant in beauty, and attractive in manners, that the besieged town could command, was gathered together on that gay evening. Youth and folly, old age and cards, were in happy proximity. And whatever there might be of *love* about the former conjunction, there was certainly nothing of it in the latter. Mrs. Battle herself never despised playing cards for *love* more heartily than the former generation of Boston dowagers. Gaming was in those days almost as much a necessity of life as drinking. At the proper time, when supper was announced, his Excellency led the procession, bearing aloft the fair hand of his lovely hostess, and not tucking it under his arm like a walking-stick or a wet umbrella. The tables were loaded with the choicest viands and the rarest wines, " and all went merry as a marriage-bell."

While these festive proceedings were going on in the next house, Dr. Holcombe and Major Ferguson were whiling away the hours as best they might, in such talk as the garrison and the mess afforded. The punch-tankard stood between them upon a little table, and filled up many pauses in their conversation. As they lazily puffed out the smoke from their mouths, they thought with satisfaction of the wisdom of their choice. The distant hum of the party, and the music, only enhanced their solitary satisfaction. At length, a tap was heard at the door, which, opening, admitted the sable form of poor Peter, to whom we introduced our reader in the second chapter. He entered the room with a dogged and almost an unconscious air of stupidity, bearing a basket in either hand, from one of which he produced some elegant extracts from the great supper, and from the other a fresh flagon of the most delicious punch that they had ever dreamed of, and, besides, two bottles of the celebrated old Forrester Madeira, which had "put a girdle round the earth" in its travels, and knew more years than I dare mention.

It is hardly necessary to say, that as soon as Peter had disposed of these edibles and potables upon the table, and retired, the friends drew up to it, and commenced an assault upon its contents which did infinite honor to their military education. The flagon was in constant requisition, and was pronounced nectar worthy of the Hebe who had dispensed it. Then, after their supper was finished, they uncorked the wine, and, drawing up to the fire, set in for serious drinking. They were seasoned vessels; but I am sorry to say, that in due time the liquor began to make inroads upon their brains, and to set their tongues in perpetual motion. They told excellent stories, only forgetting the point; but this, as they both talked at once, was of the less consequence. The Doctor grew professional, and the Major musical. The one described operations, and the other broke down in the midst of songs, all of which he sung to the tune of "Water parted from the Sea." Their eyes began to glaze, and their tongues to trip. They were not at all surprised at seeing duplicates of all the objects in the room, nor at finding themselves stopping short in the midst of stammering sentences. In short, I grieve to relate it, they were getting very drunk.

"I say, Doctor," stammered the Major, " won't you take another glass — of — ghost ? "

"D—n the — ghost ! " hiccoughed the Doctor. "I do be-believe, Ferguson, you 're dr-drunk ! I should like to see the gh-ghost that would face me n-now."

" Suppose — you — see, Doctor — whether the door 's — drunk ! " said the Major. "It looks d—d tottering to me."

The Doctor laid his course for the door, and, after a few judicious tacks, succeeded in making it. It was slightly ajar: so he shut and locked it, apostrophizing the ghost as he meandered back to his chair.

" D—n you ! You 'll have to c-come through the k-keyhole, to-night, m-my friend — if you c-come at all."

Having with great generalship recovered his seat,

they attempted to resume their "rational enjoyment" and improving conversation. But nature was too strong for them, and it was not many minutes before they were both fast asleep in their chairs. I am sorry to say that such scenes were not so rare, or so discreditable, in those three-bottle days, as they have happily since become; and the sight of two middle-aged gentlemen drunk on either side of a fireplace would have been no astonishing sight seventy years ago.

How long it was after this point of their adventures, I cannot exactly tell, but it was not long, before the men who were keeping guard were alarmed by a loud and most startling noise in the haunted chamber. They all incontinently rushed to the door, and heard within the sounds of a clamorous struggle. The ghost was evidently caught at last. But it was also plain that he was fighting for his life. He was game to the last, clearly. He was apparently almost a match for his two adversaries; for loud cries resounded through the house.

"Here he is, d—n him!" "I've got him!" "By ——, he's choking me!" "Murder, murder!" "Help, help!" "Where are you, you scoundrels?" All attended by a running accompaniment of furniture-breaking and chairs tumbling into chaotic heaps. The men tried in vain to open the door, when Hazlehurst rushed up stairs in hot haste, having been summoned, by his own direction, at the first alarm.

"Where are your muskets, men?" he cried in strong excitement. "The bloody rebels are murdering them! Dash open the door with the butt-ends!"

Seizing a musket, he suited the action to the word, and the door was soon broken down, though not without difficulty, as doors were then. The scene was frightful. The furniture was overturned; the lights were out; and lying on the floor, either mortally wounded, or exhausted by a fruitless struggle, lay the watchmen of the night.

"Where is the villain?" cried Hazlehurst, rushing into the room.

"Here's the d——d scoundrel!" cried the Doctor, laying hold of the Major.

"This is the infernal rascal!" bellowed the Major, seizing the unhappy Holcombe by the throat.

And, as they shook each other, they vainly endeavored to rise from among the wreck of things that surrounded them.

It needed no conjuror to tell how the matter stood. Hazlehurst sunk into a chair, which, fortunately, had survived the fray, and made the whole house ring with interminable peals of laughter. His followers could not resist the contagion, which was made the more irresistible by the drunken gravity of the two heroes, who sat like so many tipsy Mariuses amid the ruins of another Carthage. You would have thought that a legion of laughing imps had taken possession of the mansion, and were consecrating it to their service.

As soon as Hazlehurst could command his voice, he gave directions to the men to separate the unlucky ghost-seers, and to carry them carefully to bed. Then, taking a candle, he surveyed the prospect before him. The emptied flagons and broken bottles sufficiently accounted for the scene he had just witnessed. He glanced his eye upon the table. His color changed. He started forward. By Heaven! THERE LAY THE ORDERLY-BOOK !

. . . .

Two or three years had passed away, and a happy family party were assembled around a Christmas fire at Hazlewood, the seat of the Hazlehursts. Vigorous age and blooming infancy clustered around the hearth: in the centre of the circle were Charles Hazlehurst and his lovely Clara. He had consented, reluctantly, to retire from the army, that he might sustain the declining years of his parents. He had brought his wife with him, and there they sat, as happy and beloved a pair as ever lived and loved.

The evening had been sped away with games and gambols. At last the sports were over, and the party, closing round the firebrands, yielded to the inspiration of the hour, and vied with each other in tales of *diablerie*. At last, Charles is asked to narrate his adventure. He told it well, and was rewarded by alternating deep-drawn breaths of interest and by peals of laughter. But the mystery still remained unsolved. While they were all offering their several explanations, Hazlehurst exclaimed, —

"I would pay down a handsome reward to any-one who would tell me where that book was during those four days!"

"And would you grant an amnesty," asked Clara, "to all concerned, if you could know it?"

"That I would, with all my heart; for the excellence of the joke, now that no mischief came of it, redeems its roguishness."

"Then I can easily satisfy you, my dear," resumed his wife. "It was all the time in my dressing-table drawer."

There was a moment of silent astonishment, and then Hazlehurst exclaimed, —

"In your drawer? Why, were you the ghost, Clara?"

"Not exactly," she replied. "But I had an Afrite that did my will quite as well as any ghost could do."

"What *do* you mean, my love?" inquired her husband. "You are surely jesting. What Afrite do you mean?"

"You remember poor Peter?"

He nodded assent.

"Well, he was the ghost, and none but he. I never meant to tell the story; but it is too good a joke to be kept to one's self."

"But how? What had you to do with it?"

"Remember your proclamation of amnesty, and I will tell you. You know that he was the servant of the Vaughans" —

"No," interrupted Charles, "I knew no such thing

16

— only that he belonged to a family that had left the town."

"True," she resumed. "I remember that I kept back that particular, for fear of exciting your suspicion. But their servant he was, and treated with merited kindness for the service done his master; which resulted in disordering his poor brain. After he came to live at my father's, he never seemed to feel at home, but would often wander away at night. I suspected that his resort was to his old master's house, and that it was his prowling about it that gave it its bad name. But, as the officers who first occupied it were not especially pleasant neighbors, I did not interfere with his amusements. But when you came, my dear" —

"You took me under your protection, and I thank you," said Charles, laughing.

"Certainly I did," she continued; "but I thought he might just try your courage for one night. I had him watched out of the house by my maid, and, from the glee in which he returned, I had no doubt of his entire success. That was the first night."

"But pray tell me," asked her husband, "how he performed the feat, if you happen to know. He must have had wings, though I never saw them."

"That I can," she replied. "Poor Peter was a native African, and was as lithe and agile as a monkey, though you would not think so to look at him. He could go up the side of a house by the spout, or the slightest inequalities, like a cat. When you heard him walking over your head, and went up to look for him, he swung himself out of the window, shutting it cunningly after him, and, sliding down the spout, was in a second at the window of your closet. It was but the work of a moment to do what you found done, and of another moment to escape as he entered. It was a sort of spite he felt against intruders in that house."

"But how came he by my orderly-book?" inquired Charles.

"That I must claim as my unwilling glory," answered Clara. "I cross-examined Peter privately on the subject of his night's adventures, and strictly forbade his repeating his visits without my knowledge. I must confess, however, to a strong desire to mystify you a little further, especially as I had learned from my maid, who was a flame of your orderly, of your precautions. I accordingly told Peter that he might visit your room once more, disturbing nothing, and only bringing away a single book from the table. When I found what it was, I was frightened enough, and, when I learned how much mischief I was near doing, you know I was half distracted."

"I remember it well, and put it all down to my own account."

"And so you should, to be sure, Charles. It was all on your account. I was relieved by finding that the mischief could be repaired if the book were returned in time. So I devised several ways of getting it back to you, which I abandoned, for fear of detection. My party, however, on Friday night, gave me the opportunity, you recollect, of spiriting away your servant, and getting poor Peter within your lines of intrenchment. By watching his opportunity, he climbed unperceived to your closet, where he ensconced himself, biding his time. I had told him to restore it as nearly as he could to the place whence he took it, for fear of mistakes. In due time, the snoring of your watchful friends told him that the season of action was come. He stole into the room, deposited the book on the table, blew out the lights, knocked the two sleepers' heads together, and retired, covered with glory. The rest you know as well as I. This," continued Clara, " is the revelation of the only secret I ever kept from you. It was the first : it shall be the last."

" Well," said Hazlehurst, as the party rose to retire for the night, " there is an end of my only ghost-story. But this is not the first time that THE DEVIL has had the credit of a piece of mischief which was, in truth, only due to A WOMAN."

LEWIS HERBERT.

LEWIS HERBERT;

AN INCIDENT OF NEW ENGLAND SLAVERY.

"WORDS are things," said Mirabeau, and very troublesome things men have sometimes found them. Abstract propositions are now and then as dangerous as edged tools. The "rhetorical flourish" of the Declaration of Independence has produced effects of which the honest men who uttered it never dreamed. It produced an explosion in France, which shook all the thrones of Europe, and unsettled the deepest foundations of old establishments. It has overthrown the domestic institutions of the British West Indies, and is even now threatening our own with destruction. There is no telling where its ravages will be stayed. Indeed, a new idea is at any time a very dangerous thing to be allowed to go at large in a quiet community. If a man has hold of one, he must take care how he lets it go. If he cannot knock it on the head, let him make a cage for it in his own breast, where it may serve to divert himself and his particular friends occasionally; but let him beware how he turns it loose upon society. It will be almost sure to worry himself first of all, and then to play the very deuce in the neighborhood. And the mischief is, that, when a new idea is once on foot, it is next to impossible to catch it or destroy it. And this, notwithstanding the respectable part of society has an instinctive antipathy to the anomalous monster, and does all it can to prevent its mischiefs and to despatch it, and that, generally, without much regard to the punctilios of the chase. The world is sadly infested at this moment with these vermin. A man cannot be at peace in his study, his pulpit, his business, his sect, his party, or his possessions, for them. They respect not the old philosophies and theologies; they dabble in physic and in law; they buzz about in churches and capitols; they interfere between men and their spiritual and temporal masters; like harpies, they carry away the very meat and wine from our tables; they demand a reconstruction of society; they even come betwixt us and our very bank-stock and money-bags. I wonder that the well-disposed part of mankind do not make a grand *battue* for the extermination of these pests of the species. We shall never have a quiet world again until they do.

Our ancestors of the times that tried men's souls had their own experience of the impracticable nature of new ideas. The discussions which ushered in the great " rhetorical flourish " of the Fourth of July, " that all men were created free and equal," were not held in a corner, and would not always be limited to a fit audience. The slaves, as they stood behind their masters' chairs (for be it known to our Southern brethren, that their favorite system, though ever a patriarchal, was not always a peculiar one), or mingled in the excited crowds in the streets, could not help hearing statements of general principles, which, though notoriously a stupid generation, they contrived to generalize sufficiently to make them include themselves. A practical consequence of these new ideas of human rights was, that many slaves made free with so much of their masters' property as was comprised within the circumference of their own skins, and, dispensing with the parental care under which they had grown up, rashly undertook the charge of themselves. Among this thoughtless and ungrateful class was Lewis, the slave of a wealthy and distinguished New England gentleman, whose real name I shall disguise under that of Herbert. Lewis was born in the house of Mr. Herbert, and had grown to manhood in his service. He had no reason to complain of harsh treatment, or of inattention to his bodily necessities. He had passed the middle period of life, and was not many years younger than his master, who ever treated him with much consideration and indulgence. In the realms of the kitchen he ruled with absolute sway, — one of those despots of whom most families whose traditions reach so far back have heard the fame and the deeds. Mr. Herbert scarcely dared to bring a friend home to dine with him, without consulting the convenience of

Lewis; and as to a dinner-party, the master of the house knew himself to be but second in command on such a field-day. Over the larder, the kitchen, the wine-cellar, the plate-chest, and the china-closet, he reigned undisputed sovereigu.

Notwithstanding his ample rule and high prerogatives (and Lewis magnified his office), he was never quite satisfied that he had his due. He heard the word "slave" used as the most iguominious epithet that could be applied to human infamy, and he learned to hate it. He heard the blessings of liberty extolled as the birthright of all mankind, and he wished to know what they were. He did not see (poor slave that he was) why he should endure a condition which so many great men seemed to regard with such abhorreuce, or why he had not as good a right to that freedom of which they discoursed so eloquently, as they had. I must do Mr. Herbert, however, the justice to say, that it was not from his lips, or in his house, that Lewis imbibed these extravagant ideas. He was (God bless him!) a stanch Tory, and held all these levelling doctrines in utter abhorrence. But the air was tainted with them, and it is not to be wondered at that poor Lewis should have been infected, especially as his temperament and condition predisposed him to receive the contagion. He was so severely afflicted, that he resolved to leave the home where he had been born and bred up, and where he enjoyed all the substantial goods of life, in pursuit of that phantom, Liberty, — that *ignis fatuus* which has often led men such a dance, and at last left them in the mire. Accordingly, one fine night, he left his master's house, with a heavy heart and many tears; for the love of the African race for their homes and old familiar haunts amounts to a passion. With many a bitter regret at leaving his old master and his young mistress, and with many a sigh at all he left behind, he fared forth in search of what great men have deemed but a name, — of freedom and self-mastery. Whether his experience confirmed or confuted this philosophy, I am not able to say. All I know is, that he never returned to his master's house, though he well knew that he would receive a joyful welcome, and full restitution to all his former dignities. Mr. Herbert, though grieved and hurt at the departure of Lewis, took no measures to recover his services, but suffered him to seek a better condition if he could find it.

.   .   .   .

Several years had passed away since the flight of Lewis, and no tidings had been heard of him. The cloud which had been so long gathering, now brooded in blackness over the land, ready to burst upon it in a storm of desolation. Indeed, the first red drops, the forerunners of the coming tempest, had already fallen at Lexington, and men were awaiting the general crash with hearts of mingled hope and fear. The siege of Boston was forming gradually; and the timid of either party were endeavoring to escape to it or from it, according as their political principles led them to welcome or to abhor the protection of the British crown. Mr. Herbert was a loyalist, — the most loyal of the loyal. His faith in the omnipotence of the British Parliament was worthy of a crown lawyer. He believed that the struggle would soon be over, and its only result would be to establish King George III. more firmly than ever upon his throne and in the hearts of his people. He had retired several years before to his country-seat, about ten miles from Boston; and his advancing age and increasing infirmities indisposed him to a hasty removal to a beleaguered capital. Though he had held office under the crown, still he was not especially obnoxious to the popular side, and he hoped that he might be permitted to remain a quiet spectator of the struggle, unmolested by either party. He thought that an elderly man and his young daughter could not be regarded as very dangerous obstacles to the progress of a revolution. He hoped that age and innocence might be safe from popular violence. But, good easy man, he had been brought up under the old ideas. Had he lived at this time, he would have known better.

It was a blustering evening about the beginning of May (not the May of the poets, but the May of New England), in the year of grace 1775. Mr. Herbert and his daughter, his only child, were seated together in the parlor (for in those days drawing-rooms were not) of his pleasant country-house. The shutters were closed, and the heavy crimson curtains drawn, concealing the deep recesses for the windows and the inviting window-seats, now, alas! seen no more below. The light of the noble wood fire (always a necessary attendant on a New England May, and that season was what Horace Walpole would have called a *hard* spring), roaring up the ample chimney, its jambs adorned with Dutch tiles, and its mantel-piece with carving in wood, of which Grinling Gibbons need not have been ashamed, flashed comfortably back from the panelled walls, pleasantly overpowering the rays of the wax candles on the table. Every panel of the wall supported a full-length portrait of some of the ancestral Herberts, from the pencil of the Smiberts and the Blackburns of the early provincial days; while upon two of them the magic art of Copley had impressed an immortal moment of the cheerful age and of the brilliant youth of the pair before us. Change but the brocaded dressing-gown and crimson velvet slippers of the old man for his claret-colored dress-coat with gold buttons, and gold-buckled shoes, and divest his head of the black velvet skull-cap turned up with white silk, and you could scarcely tell which was the picture, and which the original. And under the green riding-habit, heavily laced with gold, and the riding-cap, with its black ostrich-plume, you could not fail to discern the form and features of the beautiful Emily Herbert. Curiously carved, high-backed arm-chairs; cabinets that would have driven a modern collector mad; tables of every variety of shape, some grasping a huge ball in a single clawed foot, while others sustained themselves upon an unaccountable confusion of legs; and other strange furnitures, whereof modern upholstery knows not the names, were duly arranged in their proper places about the ample apartment. The survivors must blush at the confusion in which they now awake and find themselves, after their half-century of sleep, in modern drawing-rooms. Books there were good store, and in the corner, by the door, a globe, brought from the library for some special consultation. The father and his fair child sat by the fire, beside a small table, upon which stood the supper-tray. The repast was slight; but the display of plate was such as would be thought unbefitting the occasion in these days. But in that world, before fancy stocks, — when cities under water, and railways to the Dismal Swamp, were unimagined things, — much capital, comparatively, was invested in plate. And these marks of wealth, reported by the British officers who were feasted in Boston on their return from the conquest of Canada, are said to have been a main temptation to the ministry to seek to repair their necessities by the taxation of the Colonies. Tall decanters blushed with the glowing vintages of Madeira and Portugal, and beside them an exquisitely delicate bowl of curious china sent up the fumes of that punch which was our fathers' "earliest visitation, and their last at even."

The old man sat looking wistfully into the fire, while his daughter, leaning her cheek upon her hand, gazed anxiously upon his face; for those were days that made fair young brows look sad and thoughtful before. their time. The clock in the hall had just struck ten when they were roused from their contemplations by the sudden opening of the door. They hastily looked round, and, to their surprise, the long-lost Lewis stood before them. Time had somewhat altered him ; and his whole air and bearing was changed from what it was of old : but he it was. "So you have returned at last," began Mr. Herbert ; but he was hastily interrupted by Lewis. " Sir," he exclaimed in an earnest tone, "you must instantly leave this house. You have not a moment to lose."—"Leave my house! at this hour! Why, pray ? "—" Because the mob is coming, vowing your destruction and that of all that belongs to you." —"The mob ! and for what ?"—"They say that you have been the cause of all their troubles ; that they have discovered letters and what not—but make haste, sir. They are close at hand. If you will listen, you can hear them even now." He hastily opened the window, and a confused murmur of voices was heard, approaching nearer and nearer. Mr. Herbert, who had started to his feet at the first address of his slave, now sunk despondingly back again in his arm-chair. " I cannot go," said he. " Save my child, and leave me to my fate."—"For God's sake," exclaimed Lewis, "rouse yourself. They will murder you. They swear that you are worse than Hutchinson, and that they will have your heart's blood."

The old man shook his head. "Leave me," said he faintly, "and save her."—"Dearest father, do you think I will leave you?" cried Miss Herbert, passionately embracing him. "If you will stay, I will stay with you. But will you suffer your only child to see you murdered before her eyes, and then to be exposed to the fury of a rebel mob?" This expostulation seemed to revive him in some degree; and the resolution beaming from his daughter's eyes gave him new strength and courage. There was indeed no time to lose. The shouts and imprecations of the excited populace were now too distinctly audible, as they approached the rear of the house. Mr. Herbert was almost carried out of the house, through the hall-door, between his daughter and his slave. The house was about a quarter of a mile distant from the high-road. There were no artificial grounds around it. The thick grass grew up to the door, and the natural lawn was irregularly dotted with aboriginal elms and oaks which the axe of the pioneer had spared. At some distance on the left, the lawn was skirted by a young growth of forest-trees. To this point Lewis first directed the steps of his charge; and under its shelter they approached the road before the mob had reached the house. There he paused for a moment, to allow his companions to take breath, and to permit the stragglers who were coming in from the country around to leave the road free. They looked towards the house. Lights were seen flashing at every window. The mob were in search of them.

They could hear distinctly their curses of disappointment and rage. Presently the windows were dashed through, and the furniture thrown furiously out upon the lawn. The very quiet room, where, a quarter of an hour before, all had been peace and stillness, was stripped of all its treasures to heap high the bonfire which was to crown the orgies of the night. The mob had soon broken into the wine-cellar; and this circumstance, and the prospect of the " festal blaze," it is probable, was the safety of the fugitives, by delaying the pursuit. Presently the bonfire began to crackle and blaze; and the shouts became more and more ferocious under the combined influence of liquor and mischief.

Foolish tourists in America complain that we have no amusements in this country. I wish they could have been at Walnut Hill that night. But they are a perverse generation. Have they never heard of our merry times of old, — sacking Governor Hutchinson's house, and tarring and feathering obnoxious officials, and the grand old tea-party of '73 ? And then our rare sport in burning convents, and halls dedicated to freedom, and dragging insolent varlets about the streets, who dared to say that the Declaration of Independence meant anything, and shooting them down at the doors of their printing-offices ! They might at least have remembered the fun we have had in hoaxing " the English epicures " into investing their solid hoards in a very rotten commodity of ours, called public faith, worth about as much

17

as a dicer's oath, or the bought smile of a prostitute. And our repudiation, too ! If that be not an excellent jest, I should like to know what is. I say nothing of the royal pastimes of burning men alive by a slow fire, of hunting negroes with bloodhounds and rifles, of whipping women to death, and selling one's own children by the pound ; for these are the recreations of our betters, the guarded prerogative of the privileged classes. This kind of game is strictly preserved, and secured for the amusement of our masters, as the chase was in old time confined to the corresponding class in Europe. Like them, too, our lords claim the privilege of pursuing their game over the soil of their vassals. But, though shut out from these diversions of our superiors, we can still share with them the stirring excitement of the mob, the delicate pleasantry of repudiation, and the delicious irony of lynch law. Why, what would these cavillers have ? No amusements, indeed!

The blazing bonfire soon attracted all the loiterers in the road, and Lewis seized the opportunity to cross it, with his companions, into the fields beyond. He knew that the main roads in every direction would be soon thronged by yet greater numbers, attracted by the blaze ; and he pushed across the fields towards the seashore, about two miles off, as the most probable way of concealment or escape. They hurried along, as fast as the infirmities of Mr. Herbert would permit, over the uneven surface of the land ; and slow enough it seemed to his companions. The night was more like one in November than in May, and the chilly wind drifted the clouds in black masses over the waning moon. They accomplished in safety about half the distance, and found themselves in a lane leading to the coast. Here Mr. Herbert declared that it was impossible for him to proceed. It was in vain that his daughter and Lewis endeavored to re-assure him, and drag him forward. He sunk despondingly upon the ground. At that moment a single horseman rode up. He stopped to see what was the matter. The cloud passed from the moon for an instant, and he saw at a glance how it was. "So the old rascal has got away," said he with an oath; "but I'll soon bring those that will settle his business." He was just putting spurs to his horse, when Lewis, seeing the emergency of the case, seized his bridle fast. It was but the work of a moment. The horseman was dragged from his seat, and thrown upon the side of the lane, and Lewis had lifted Mr. Herbert into the saddle. Leading the horse, and entreating Miss Herbert to assist in steadying her father upon his back, he hurried onward as fast as he dared. This was the more necessary, as they heard the dismounted cavalier, as soon as he could recover his breath and his senses, making towards the light, roaring for assistance. It seemed as though they never would reach the end of the lane. Mr. Herbert swayed upon the saddle like a drunken man, and it was with difficulty that they kept him from falling. Before they had gained the shore,

they knew that their pursuers had been put upon
the right scent. They were nearing them fast, when
the fugitives at last came out upon the sands. The
hurried footsteps, shouts, execrations, and dancing
lights of the mob, seemed fearfully near. What
were they to do? Fortunately, Lewis espied a
gentleman's boat-house, built over a little creek
hard by. "I must make free with Colonel Vernon's
boat," exclaimed he, and, suiting the action to the
word, he demolished the padlock on the door with a
huge stone. By an equally summary process he
freed the boat from its moorings, and pushed it out
of its covert. It seemed to be too late, for the rioters
were almost upon them. He dashed through the
waves, and, taking Mr. Herbert in his arms, deposited
him in the forward part of the boat, and then, in like
manner placing Miss Herbert at the helm, with a
hurried instruction how to hold it, grasped the oars.
A second's delay or misadventure had been fatal; for
the crowd were already upon the beach, exulting
over their prey. But a single stroke of the oars
placed them beyond their reach. Maddened with
drink and rage, the pursuers rushed into the sea
with yells and imprecations, in hopes to seize the
boat. A shower of stones rained upon the fugitives.
But, luckily, the rioters had no fire-arms, and a
sweep or two more of the oars placed them beyond
danger and annoyance. The bay upon which they
were launched was so completely land-locked, that
it was more like an inland lake than the wide Atlan-

tic. They were soon careering over the gentle billows, leaving the confused noise of the baffled mob far behind them, and they forgot for the moment, in the sweet sense of present security, what they had suffered and lost.

As soon as the first tumults of joy were over, Lewis explained his agency in the matter. It seems, that, after he left Mr. Herbert's house, he had gone to Portsmouth, in New Hampshire, where he lived until he happened to hear that his old master had removed permanently into the country. He then returned to Boston, not long before, and went into the service of a distinguished patriot. He had left the town previously to the siege, with this gentleman's family. It was in this situation that he heard of the popular excitement against his old master, as a traitor to the country (whether just or not, we have not time now to inquire), and of the determination of the populace to wreak their vengeance upon him. By pretending to join them, he had been able to get enough in advance of them to defeat their plans, as we have seen. While thus explaining, the boat rounded the point of Long Island, and was instantly challenged from his Majesty's frigate " Arethusa," which lay at anchor in the channel. Explanations were soon given. The fugitives were cordially welcomed to the hospitalities of the ship for the night, and the next morning they were safely landed in Boston.

   .   .   .   .

Long years passed away. The struggle was over. The seven years of apprenticeship were at an end; and the American Colonies, erected into the United States, had set up the trade of government on their own account. The expectations of the English ministry were disappointed, and the hopes of the loyalists crushed forever. The treaty of Paris had crowned the work: and the rebellion was transmuted, by the magic of success, into the Revolution. Many hearts rejoiced at the prosperous issue; some, because they glowed with patriotic fires; some, because they saw a new and untried career of ambition opened before them; some, because the final seal was set upon the confiscations and forfeitures of the troublous times, and confirmed their titles to other people's estates. But there were, too, sorrowful spirits and breaking hearts, wearing out sad years of exile in a foreign land, upon whose ears the distant rejoicings sounded like the death-knell of their hopes. To such we turn.

One of the gloomiest days of a London November was drawing towards its close. The sun vainly endeavored to pierce the thick fog that buried the city in an untimely night. The street-lamps were lighted, though it was not yet sunset; and the windows of the shops and houses shot forth uncertain glimmerings into the darkness. A single candle sufficed to light up a humble room on the fourth floor of a dilapidated house in an obscure part of the city. It had not much to reveal. A ragged carpet strove to hide the middle of the floor; a few common chairs (no two alike), a deal table, and a rough bedstead, all bearing the tokens of poverty and the pawnbroker's shop, filled up the disposable space of the chamber. A handful of coals upon the grate seemed to be endeavoring to excite themselves into a blaze, sending out into the room an occasional puff of smoke as an earnest of their good intentions. The room was scrupulously clean, but in all other respects bore the marks of extreme poverty. Upon the bed reclined an old man, propped by pillows, apparently in the last stage of life. By his side sat a woman of perhaps thirty, but upon whose countenance care and sorrow had done the work of many years. The unnatural brightness of her eye, the hectic spot on her cheek, and the frequent though stifled cough, showed that she was not much longer for the world than her aged companion. "Emily, my love," said Mr. Herbert, for he it was, "what was that knocking that just awoke me?"—"It was nothing, sir," replied his daughter, "but Mrs. Hobbs, coming after her rent. You remember that the doctor's fee last week, when you were so ill, swallowed up that week's rent, so that we are now a fortnight in arrears. But I pacified her by promising she should be paid as soon as Lewis arrives. You know it is Saturday night."—"Ah! she awoke me from a most delicious dream. I thought I stood, as I often do in dreams, upon the lawn at Walnut Hill. The shadows of the old trees fell, sharply defined, on the grass; beyond, the Neponset reflected the trees on his banks, as he used to do; the Blue Hill was on my right hand, the old woods on my left, and the ocean gleamed in the distance. As I stood there, it seemed to me as if all that I have ever known during my long life passed in friendly procession before me. First my parents, and brothers and sisters, then my school-fellows and college-companions, and so on, as long as I had a friend left. It seemed as if they were gathered to some great festival, of which I was the central attraction. How I rejoiced in the sight of their beloved countenances!" — "You have at least one friend left, sir," interposed his daughter. "True, my dear, and one worth hundreds that have called themselves so. What would my proud ancestors have said, what should I have said in my pride of life, 'had it been foretold that I and my child would one day be dependent for our daily bread on the bounty of a negro!" — "Dear Lewis!" said Miss Herbert, "he has saved our lives many times. What should we have done without him?" — "What, indeed!" rejoined her father. "When the compensation allowed for my losses by the government was absorbed by my old English debts, and when, that not sufficing, my very pension was sold, we must have starved, or come upon the parish, but for him. God will reward him." A light tap was heard at the door, which was gently opened, and Lewis entered, his face beaming with satisfaction, for it had been a prosperous week with him. Years had grizzled his hair, and slightly bent his frame; but "his age was like a lusty winter, frosty, but kindly." He wore the dress of the waiter of a tavern, in which capacity he had for many years supported himself and his *protegés*. On his arm he bore a covered basket containing provisions, which he had just been purchasing. He cheerfully advanced to Miss Herbert, and gave her money for her clamorous landlady and other expenses. He then busied himself in putting the room to rights, and in performing various services about the sick-bed. There was a cheerful alacrity about him which showed that his labors were indeed those of love. There was nothing of servility about the marked respect which he paid to Mr. and Miss Herbert. His good-breeding was learnt in no *coterie* or court; but it could not have been surpassed by the most accomplished graduate of either; for he bestowed the greatest of benefactions without seeming conscious that they were such, and saved the pride of his beneficiaries while he supplied their necessities. He was fully aware of the obligations under which he had laid the helpless pair before him, and they knew it; but they both felt as if his relation to them was that of a father or a brother. Misery is a great leveller of the distinctions men have made between themselves and their fellow-men. But there was nothing in the deportment of Lewis that ever reminded his former master and mistress of their obligations to him.

At last, he said that it was time to go, as there

was a great supper at the Angel that night. As he
turned to leave the room, Mr. Herbert detained him.
"Lewis," said he, "I feel as if my time was short,
and I have a word or two to say to you." Lewis
put down his hat, and approached the bedside. "My
friend," Mr. Herbert resumed, "my child and I owe
you many lives. You saved us from a mob in
America, and from starvation here." Lewis made a
deprecating gesture; and his countenance indicated
so much distress, that Mr. Herbert proceeded, "I
am not going to thank you, my friend, for that I cannot do, — God will thank you, — but to ask you to
continue to be the friend of my child when I am
dead." Lewis looked half reproachfully at his old
master, as if hurt at the implication that such a
request was necessary, and then turned his eyes
upon Miss Herbert. They filled with tears as they
rested upon her; for he saw, though her father did
not, how short a time she was destined to remain
behind him. He could not speak; but he took Miss
Herbert's hand and kissed it. Lord Chesterfield could
not have done it more expressively. Mr. Herbert was
made easy on that point. "Now tell me," he resumed,
"whether you have made any inquiries as to my old
loyalist friends at the other end of the town: do
they suspect where I am?" — "I have good reason
to know," replied Lewis, "that they believe you
returned long since to America, and have no suspicion of your being still in London." — "That is
well," rejoined Mr. Herbert: "let the secret be still

kept, that the world " (his little loyalist world) "may never know of the latter days of Philip Herbert." He extended his hand to his benefactor, and, sinking back upon his pillow, closed his eyes. Lewis, in strong emotion, stole from the room. He returned about midnight, and, as soon as he looked upon the face of the sick man, he saw that he was dying. Miss Herbert had suspected as much, and was anxiously awaiting his arrival. They exchanged looks: no words were needed. Lewis took his station on the other side of the bed, and they remained all night watching the face of the dying man. Towards morning, he opened his eyes, and turning them first upon his friend, and then upon his child, with that look which only a dying man can give, he closed them again forever.

.   .   .   .

I need not prolong my tale. More than half a century has passed away since all its actors disappeared, like drops of rain in the ocean. They sleep together in one of the hideous churchyards of London, and are forgotten. Of the colonial glories of the Herberts, of the miseries of their exile, of the heroic self-devotion of Lewis, not a trace is left, except this imperfect tradition. Heroic his conduct surely deserves to be called ; for what is heroism but intelligent self-devotion to an unselfish end, self-sacrifice for the advantage of others ? And when those for whom the sacrifices of years were made had inflicted upon him who made them the greatest wrong man can do to man, when self-devotion was thus the companion of godlike forgiveness, surely it was a height of virtue to which the annals of the race can furnish but few parallels. For Lewis was no besotted slave, whom favors or blows had so imbruted that he could not discern his own rights, so that he blindly followed his master, in the belief that he was entitled to his lifelong service. He had shown his sense of the degradation and injustice of his servile estate by leaving the persons and the scenes he loved, for freedom, though in a worse condition, and refusing to return again until misfortune had overshadowed them. That he did not grudge his services, he showed by his cheerful gift of them to those he loved, when they were his own to give.

Perhaps there may be some who will deem it strange that the Herberts should have consented to be thus the dependents of a negro once their slave. Such should be very careful of their censures, for they may reach farther than they think. Was it more disgraceful to the Herberts to live in London upon the earnings of a negro, freely offered for the love he bore them, than it is to grave judges, learned divines, and honorable women, to live upon the earnings of negroes in Charleston or Baltimore, extorted by the fear or the application of torture? Which is the meaner and more ignominious livelihood of the two? The same practical results are worked out on many a broad plantation and in many a splendid city mansion, that we have seen produced in an obscure garret in London ; only the motive-power that creates them is the scourge or the branding-iron, instead of generous affection. There are many men of eminent station, and who boast loudly of the sensitiveness of their honor, who eat dirtier bread every day of their lives than did the Herberts during their last and evil days.

There may be others who cannot understand why Lewis, when he was so ready to give his services for nothing in the days of his master's distress, should have deserted him in the days of his prosperity, when his fidelity might have met with some reward. If there be any who cannot perceive the difference between the free gifts of love and the extorted tribute of involuntary servitude, I have no time left to point it out. I can only say, that, if it were an error, it was one which he shared with the noblest natures and the most generous spirits. The divine instinct of liberty, to which he yielded, and which is even now urging hundreds of fugitives towards the polar star, is that which has shed the purest glory upon the page of history, and given to poetry its truest inspiration. Its manifestations, however coarse or barbarous they may have been, ever have appealed with resistless power to the universal human heart. It was this principle that wreathed with myrtle the sword of Harmodius, and has invested with immortal memories the steel of Brutus and the shaft of Tell. It was this that sent Hampden reeling in his saddle, a dying man, from Chalgrave field; that taught Milton

"To scorn delights, and live laborious days;"

and that made Vane and Sidney lay down their heads upon the block, as if it were some beloved bosom wooing them to repose. To those who feel that freedom is the only element in which the soul can grow and expand, and who can appreciate the virtues which are its genial growth, in however humble a breast or obscure a lot, I cheerfully commend the memory and the example of LEWIS HERBERT.

TWO NIGHTS IN ST. DOMINGO.

TWO NIGHTS IN ST. DOMINGO;

"AN OWER TRUE TALE."

IT was a gay night at the Habitation du Plessis, that of the 22d of August, 1791. The evening breeze, fresh from the cool fields of the ocean, had breathed a new elasticity into hearts that had been all day fainting beneath the vertical sun of a tropical midsummer. The first rustle of its wings, as it stirred the trees that imbosomed the mansion, had summoned the scattered guests from their various inventions for speeding the weary day, and assembled them in the great hall that occupied the whole depth and height of the central building. The lofty doors were flung open, and the tall windows on either side of them expanded their slender valves from the floor to the ceiling to welcome the healing gale. The small party, consisting of some half-dozen besides the master and mistress of the house, were dispersed over the spacious apartment, in various attitudes and different employments. A card-table engrossed the souls of the elder and more sedate division of the company. A younger group was clustered around the harp of the beautiful

18

Mademoiselle de Mirecourt, the sole heiress of this noble estate and its thousand slaves. And, when her song had ceased, the gay Abbé de Valnais showed by the brilliancy of his sallies and the piquancy of his *bons mots*, that he had left neither his wit nor his good spirits behind him at Paris, when he fled from it with the first emigration.

While the hall rung with the gay voices and merry laughter of this mercurial circle, Mr. Vincent, a young American newly arrived in the island, and but that day at the Habitation, stood by himself beneath the broad veranda, and looked out upon a scene of such beauty as he had never before gazed upon. Beneath him lay the plain of the Cape, sleeping in the mellow light of a moon that might well put to shame most of the suns of his colder skies, skirted by shadowy mountains, standing around it like guardian giants, and terminated in the far distance by the ocean, that gleamed in the moonlight like a sea of molten silver. All around him was a wilderness of trees and shrubs, new to his Northern eye. The multitudinous sounds of a tropical night fell strangely, but not unharmoniously, on his ear; while the air that played about his temples came loaded with perfumes such as might have breathed from "the spicy shores of Araby the blest."

He turned his eyes to the scene within, and it was scarcely less a scene of enchantment to one who had sprung up to early manhood on the rocky shores of New England. The lofty and beautifully proportioned

hall, filled with all the appliances and means of tropical luxury, — somewhat too massive and gorgeous in
its furniture, perhaps, to please a severe eye, and better suited to the meridian of Paris than of St. Domingo,
but all splendid with gilding and carved work, in the
rich though somewhat questionable taste of the later
days of the French monarchy, — seemed as if it might
be the palace of Armida rising in the midst of her
enchanted gardens. Out of the hall opened a noble
library, rich with the spoils of all past time. Next
to it, the billiard-room invited the lovers of such pastime. On the opposite sides, the saloons, or, as they
would now be called, the drawing-rooms, their walls
glittering with gilding, and flashing with mirrors, and
furnished as only French upholsterers then knew how,
seemed as if some magician had transported the saloons of Paris many a league across the ocean, from
the banks of the Seine to this distant isle. Adjoining
them was the dining-room, furnished with equal richness, though in a more quiet style; the splendid sideboard groaning beneath the ancestral plate of many a
generation, and its walls hung with choice cabinet
pictures, chiefly of festive and joyous scenes, suggestive of wine and mirth. But at this torrid season
the hall, from its greater height and airiness, was the
chosen scene of the reunions of the household. As
the young American turned from the scene of beauty
without to that of splendor within, he thought only of
the happiness which must be the attendant of such
boundless wealth : his mind dwelt as little at that

moment on the misery and wrong upon which all this splendor was upreared, and on the ruin which the upheaving of those foundations was about to work, as it did upon the volcanic fires that lay beneath the exhaustless soil and superb vegetation that surrounded him, and which might in a moment make the whole paradise a waste.

And the Marquis de Mirecourt himself, as he laid down his cards, and joined the rest of the party, when supper was announced, for a moment forgot, as he gave himself up to the enchantment of the scene, that he was an exile from that Paris he so dearly loved. Though surrounded with every luxury that the most unbounded wealth could furnish, in the most delicious of climates, and in the midst of the divinest of scenery, he still sighed in secret for the narrow streets, formal gardens, and crowded saloons of the metropolis of the senses. He had left France amid the very first mutterings of the Revolutionary storm, and, leaving his paternal chateau in Dauphiné to the mercy of his white slaves, whose hour had at last come, he betook himself to the estate in St. Domingo, which he had received by marriage with a young Creole heiress, whom he espoused from the convent, whither she had been sent for her education.

On this night, however, his heart was glad within him ; for he was surrounded by kindred spirits, — men of high birth, of aristocratic habits, of refined tastes — such as had been the companions of his happier days. The supper-table was laid in the centre of the hall. In all its appointments it would have done no discredit to the most historical of the houses of the age of *petits soupers.* Candelabras of massive silver poured down a flood of light upon the repast; tall shades of the clearest crystal guarding the wax candles from the welcome gale. The most exquisite of French dishes (for M. de Mirecourt had not been so improvident as to leave his *chef de cuisine* behind him), served upon solid plate, gave place at their due time to the most delicious of the tropical fruits, glowing in the beautiful porcelain of Sèvres, — a gift of royalty when royalty was something more than a name. The richest and rarest of wines, cooled to a charm, were marshalled in that festive procession, which the experience of successive generations of *gourmets* had established as their due order of precedence. The delicate chablis ushered in the feast; the frolic champagne, and the freshness of the fragrant Rhine-wine, enlivened its solemn march as it moved onward; while

> "The gay, serene, good-natured Burgundy"

threw a sunset glow over its brilliant conclusion. A slave in the rich livery of the De Mirecourts stood behind every chair, in seeming, an automaton of ebony, moved only by the will of him whom he was appointed to serve. A white Major Domo, in plain clothes, stood by the temporary sideboard to anticipate the slightest wish, and to prevent the labor of its utterance. Nothing that wealth could summon from the four quarters of the globe, to heighten or add a poignancy to luxury, was absent from that splendid banquet.

And the circle for which it was furnished forth was not unworthy of the magic feast. Besides the Marquis and his beautiful daughter, there was Madame de Mirecourt, a beauty somewhat past her prime, who had superinduced an affectation of French vivacity upon her native Creole apathy and indolence. Here was the Abbé de Valnais, of whom honorable mention has already been made, and the Chevalier de Tillemont, who had served with distinction in America under Rochambeau, and now commanded one of the regiments at Cape François, with the Cross of St. Louis suspended from his button-hole. A cadet of a noble family in France, who was attached to the general government of the island, at that time swayed by M. de Blanchelande; a wealthy planter and his Parisian wife, who were on a short visit at Plessis ; and the American Vincent, to whom the knowledge of these particulars is due — made up the rest of the party. All were in the highest spirits. The national festivity of spirits, relieved for the time from the anxieties caused by the progress of the Revolution at home, and the sympathetic excitement of the colonial extremities of the French monarchy, which had checked its genial current, gushed forth with the joyousness of a fountain leaping from its cavern. Exile and impoverishment, and blighted prospects, and disappointed hopes, and homesick yearnings, were all forgotten. The magic of the present hour triumphed over them all. The troubles in France and in St. Domingo would soon be over, and the old régime virtually restored. The fierce populace of Paris, and their humble rivals in the Provinces and Colonies, would soon be reduced to their natural position, — under the feet of the *noblesse*. It was as absurd to suppose that the *sans-culottes* at home could permanently lord it over their birthright masters, as it would be to suppose the negro slaves capable of maintaining an ascendency over their natural lords. A sudden tempest had disturbed the elements of society; but, as soon as it was blown over, things would find their natural level again.

Ah! there were gay visions seen through that convivial atmosphere that night. The Abbé beheld in the brilliant distance a mitre, perhaps a cardinal's hat; and there were some dim images that looked like Mazarin and Richelieu. A marshal's bâton danced before the eyes of the chevalier. The Marquis saw himself restored to all his baronial rights and enormous rents; while the opera, the Comédie Française, the masquerades and balls of dear Paris, once more seemed within the reach of Madame de Mirecourt and her daughter. As to the rich planter, he saw armies of negroes, and mountains of sugar, which were to help him to a speedy return to France, and perhaps to a patent of nobility. The young American, I fear, had no more gorgeous or chivalric imaginings than of heavy commissions, great profits,

cent per cent, the largest house in Boston, and the
neatest villa in its neighborhood.

It was a night, too, to be remembered for itself,
divested of the tragic interest with which a few hours
invested it. The absurdities and awkwardnesses of
the new men who had taken the place of the old
nobility in the direction of affairs, and the comic
situations into which their ignorance of the conven-
tions of society betrayed them, afforded fertile themes
for the gay wit and playful raillery of the Abbé, and
for the bitter sarcasms of the Marquis. The politics
of the theatre and of the ballet were discussed with a
seriousness which those of the Revolution could not
command.   Literature, and the quarrels and private history of the world of letters, were suggestive
themes to men who had sat at the tables of D'Hol-
bach and De Geoffrin and Du Deffand, and who
remembered Voltaire and Rousseau and D'Alem-
bert and Diderot.   Scandal, too, lent its wings to
hasten on the hours, and the Queen of the Antilles
witnessed that night the death of many a Parisian
reputation. The crowning satisfaction, however, of
their Epicurean philosophy, to which they often re-
curred with new glee, was their happy removal from
the disturbed heart of the kingdom to a spot whence
they could watch its mighty pulsations in safety and
peace. Here, at least, they might live without danger from the slavish mass, which must, in all civilized countries, form the groundwork of society. The
quarrels which had distracted the Colony had arisen

from the struggles of the superior classes alone for the mastery. All classes looked with equal contempt and certainty upon the submissive deportment of the slaves, whose toil supplied them with their wealth. Strong in this security, they enjoyed a " Lucretian pleasure " in standing in safety upon the shore, and seeing the barks of others buffeted about by the tempest, or sink foundering in the billows. M. de Mirecourt felt and said that he could not feel as if all were lost, even if he never recovered his confiscated estates in France, so long as a thousand negroes extorted from the soil of Plessis half a million of livres every year, and emptied them into his coffers. With such an income, life might be endured for a time, even in that banishment. All were blest in the consciousness of present security and the confident expectation of future good. Gay wit, light laughter, and rosy hopes, all helped to chase the hours of that genial night.

But the most genial of nights must have an end at last, and the most perfect of suppers cannot endure forever. At length the party separated, at an hour when the Southern Cross, quenching its radiance in the Atlantic waves, told that the morning was at hand of a day ever memorable in the history of mankind. They all dispersed " in measureless content," weary with mirth, and tired with revelry, little dreaming that sleep would be that night, for the last time, a visitant to the princely Habitation du Plessis. All retired, and all slept, except the American Vincent.

The excitement of a scene so new to him drove sleep from his eyes, and after attempting for an hour or two to banish from his mind the beaming faces, gay voices, and ringing laughter of the last few hours, he rose, and in his *robe de chambre* walked forth upon the terrace on which the house was built. The moon had set, and a world of new constellations glittered gloriously above his head in a firmament of the blackest blue. The thousand voices of a tropical night still maintained their eternal concert. The vast masses of vegetation which covered the mountain-sides, and which were to be dimly descried through the night in the nearer distance, seemed to be clothed with the very blackness of darkness, gilded, indeed, by the flashing light of innumerable fireflies. It was a scene of peace and coolness which soon quieted Vincent's excited brain.

As he turned to seek his apartment again, he heard the conch sound in the distance, summoning the field slaves to their daily toil. He knew then that sunrise was near, and he waited to look upon its glories. He had not gazed into the night long, before the sun vaulted, as it were, from the eastern waves, "and that moment all was light." The darkness fled away, like a fiend before the rebuke of an angel, and all the landscape was bathed in the rejoicing beams. From the height on which he stood, the vast plantations of the plain of the Cape seemed like fairy gardens. No portion of the soil was left neglected. The soft green of the canefields and of the Guineagrass beautifully contrasted with the darker hues of the coffee-plantations, and of the overarching trees that sheltered them from the scorching heat, looking like graceful columns supporting a canopy of verdure. The mountains, feathering to the top with their forests of enormous trees, reared themselves in a thousand shapes of beauty, while endless varieties of light and shade played over their surface. In the far distance might be discerned the smoke, curling upwards from the city of the Cape; and farther yet, the amethyst and emerald sea, with here and there a white sail gliding over its surface, like blessed spirits floating over a lake in Paradise. And presently the long lines of slaves were seen winding their way to their appointed task, each division driven by an overseer, a long-lashed whip under his arm, with which he would ever and anon urge his lagging herd to a brisker pace. The almost naked forms of the negroes as they dispersed themselves over the canefields, and the loose white linen dress and overshadowing hat of the overseers, beheld from that distance, and in the midst of that tropical landscape, seemed to a stranger's eye like a scene from the Arabian Nights. As Vincent gazed upon it, he felt no forebodings of a coming woe. There were no signs in the air of that lovely day, that told of the dread Nemesis that brooded over the fated island to avenge the hoarded wrongs of bloody centuries. No earthquake heralded the downfall of the white race. No tornado shadowed forth the approaching tempest.

All was bright and fair and calm on that last morning of slavery.

.   .   .   .

There was to be a state dinner-party at Plessis on the 23d of August. Several of the neighboring planters had been invited to meet the distinguished guests who enjoyed its hospitality. This is a serious matter anywhere and at any time, but especially beneath an August sun, between the tropics. The guests had retired to their apartments to endure the tortures of a Parisian toilet within twenty degrees of the equator. Madame de Mirecourt sat listlessly in her dressing-room, bewailing in that sacred retreat the ungenerous hostility of the climate to *rouge*, while its inroads upon the complexion made such foreign aid the more important, when the door opened, and Stéphanie, her own woman, hastily entered the apartment. Madame de Mirecourt wondered, as much as her apathetic habits would admit of such an emotion, at her unsummoned appearance; but then Stéphanie was her foster-sister, and had lived with her in France, and in a humble way shared her education, and might be permitted liberties which could not pass unpunished in any other slave. The surprise of the mistress was increased, when the slave cautiously opened all the doors that led out of the room, as if to ascertain that no one was listening, and then placed herself before her.

"What does all this mean, Stéphanie?" drawled

out Madame de Mirecourt, "My indulgence has bounds — and Le Fronde has a whip!"

"It means," replied Stéphanie in a low voice, "that the time has come when the accursed Le Fronde's whip will be broken, and when he will taste some of his own infernal cruelties himself, and know how sweet they are."

"You forget yourself, Stéphanie," replied her mistress. "You have been brought up too tenderly. You have heard of the proverb that speaks of the insolence of an unwhipped slave?"

"It is to that tenderness of which you speak, madame," replied Stéphanie, "that foolish tenderness, that you will owe your life, if indeed it can yet be saved. It is an unwhipped slave that would save you and yours a faint taste of those horrors which your race has so long heaped upon mine."

"Just Heaven!" exclaimed the Marchioness, startled out of her apathy. "What is it you mean?"

"I mean," solemnly answered Stéphanie, "that Heaven *is* just; that the day of my people's deliverance is come; that this night the whole plain of the Cape will be filled with fire and blood, — a slight atonement for centuries of outrage! The insurrection, thank God! is so well matured that failure is impossible. And now it is my folly to wish to save you for your selfish kindness to me. And yet" —

"O God! my daughter!" exclaimed the agonized mother; for there was that in the tone and looks of

Stéphanie which forbade her to question the truth of her words. "Oh, save her! save her!"

"Command yourself, madame," replied the slave, "and you may both be saved; but it will depend entirely on your control of yourself."

"O Stéphanie, Stéphanie!" exclaimed the humbled mistress, throwing herself at the feet of her slave, and embracing her knees in an agony of despair. "Remember all you owe to me! Recollect my kindness, my indulgence, from the day when we had but one mother!"

"Yes," answered Stéphanie bitterly—"yes, I remember that you treated me like a petted lap-dog or a tame paroquet. And yet I do owe you more than you imagine; for, had it not been for the lessons you permitted me to receive in the Convent of St. Agnes, this holy insurrection could never have been so secretly and yet so surely planned as to be certainly triumphant. But rise, madame: that is a posture never again to be assumed by one mortal to another in St. Domingo."

"Not till you have promised me to defeat this dreadful rebellion," cried Madame de Mirecourt, still clinging to Stéphanie. "You shall have your freedom; you shall have wealth such as none of your caste ever dreamed of possessing; you shall be honored forever as the savior of the white race, if you will but delay it till troops can be brought hither from the Cape."

"My freedom!" replied Stéphanie scornfully. "I

thank you, madame; but I mean to take that myself
without the leave of any earthly being. As to delaying the sacrifice, it is not in my power to do it; but,
if it were, not all the wealth of France would induce
me to defer it a moment when it is ready to be
offered."

"Then I will do it myself," exclaimed the Marchioness, starting to her feet, and making a move-
ment towards the door.

"Stay, madame," said Stéphanie calmly, and de-
taining her mistress with a grasp not to be resisted.
"You will but hasten the catastrophe by such madness. The first peal of the alarm-bell, — the first
shriek that will tell that all is known, — and in five
minutes twenty knives will be in the heart of every
white man on the estate, and in a quarter of an hour
the flames of Plessis will tell to the whole plain that
the hour is come. As to the women," she continued,
partly unsheathing a knife concealed in her bosom,
"I shall take care, in such case, to save you and
mademoiselle from the terrible vengeance which I
fear the husbands, fathers, and brothers of the out-
raged slave-women *will* wreak on the wives, daughters, and sisters of their tyrants."

"O God!" exclaimed the distracted Marchioness,
sinking, half-fainting, upon a couch, "what is to be
done?"

"Leave that to me, madame," said Stéphanie: "your
part is to appear below as if all were well. After you
are dressed, I shall see M. le Marquis, and concert my

plan with him. Remember that all depends on your playing your part well, so that no suspicion may be awakened in the minds of the slaves behind your chairs. For I need not say that suspicion would be instant death. And now, madame, to your toilet."

And never since Stéphanie had performed those offices about the person of her mistress did she discharge them more accurately than on that last day of her servitude. Madame de Mirecourt, half-stunned, and feeling the power of a strong mind over a weaker one, yielded herself implicitly to the hands of her slave, and promised to obey her directions in all points. She wore her diamonds, at the instance of Stéphanie, and concealed other valuable jewels about her person.

"These would have been mine," said Stéphanie. "But no matter: you will need them more than I in the strange land whither you must go." Madame de Mirecourt shuddered at the idea of poverty and exile; but nearer and worse dangers soon drove it from her mind. Heavens! What a toilet was that!

.   .   .   .

It was a princely banquet that graced the great dining-room at Plessis that day, but as dreadful to some of those that sat around the board as was the Egyptian feast to the novice, when the falling rose-wreath disclosed to him the grim features of his skeleton companion. M. de Mirecourt had managed to inform all the gentlemen of his household guests of their danger, and of his plan of escape.

The circumstances with which Stéphanie had confirmed her story had put the matter beyond a doubt. Nothing remained for them but to save their lives by flight, according to the plan she pointed out. And there they sat in full dress around the splendid table, with this dreadful secret weighing upon their hearts, playing the part of gay revellers! Ah, it was a ghastly feast! How changed their hearts since the merry hours of last night's revel! The ancient story, of the sword suspended by a single hair over the head of the parasite, as he reclined at a regal banquet such as was spread for his tyrant, did but shadow forth the horrors of that night! Oh, those interminable courses! It seemed as if they would never come to an end. How "palled the tasteless meats and joyless wines!" And then those insufferable guests of the day, who knew nothing of the fearful truth — how they did prose! They ate and drank as if they knew that it was their last dinner, and were resolved to make the most of it. They discussed the viands and wines as if an accurate acquaintance with their virtues was the necessary passport to paradise. And then they talked of their crops and their slaves, the annual loss by overworking and necessary correction, and all the economics of whipping and starving and maiming — and this to men who knew that the slave behind every chair had a cane-knife, sharpened on both sides, in his bosom! Human nature, even French human nature, could not have endured it much longer.

19

At last — and it *was* an at last — the guests made a move to depart, murmuring something of the lateness of the hour and the distance they had to go, hoping to be pressed to stay with hospitable urgency.

" Must you go, indeed ! " exclaimed the Marquis, assuming an air of half-tipsy jollity. " Then we will all escort you a mile or two on your way, and drink a parting bottle by the roadside, in the moonlight."

The proposition was hailed by all, in the secret and out of it, as a most whimsical and admirable frolic. The coaches were ordered round; and the Chevalier de Tillemont directed his horse to be saddled, as better fitting his knightly character. When the carriages came round, that of the Marquis took the lead, and was followed by two others of the planter guests. As they were entering them, Vincent protested against being enclosed in any such prison upon wheels, and declared his intention of mounting the box, so that he might see the country to the more advantage. As the moon had not yet risen, and it was almost pitch dark, this was hailed as an excellent jest; and the Abbé also, in the same vein, insisted upon mounting the box of the carriage that came next. M. de Tillemont rode alongside of the third.

In this order they proceeded until they came near the place where the two planters would turn off from the road to Cape François. Here, at a signal from the Chevalier, Vincent pointed a pistol at the head of the coachman by whose side he sat, and threatened him with instant death unless he suffered himself to be pinioned peaceably. The Abbé, at the same moment, threw his arms round those of his neighbor, and confined them until he could be secured; while the Chevalier, mounted on a charger which obeyed the least touch of the foot or slightest word, with a pistol in either hand, took charge of the third coachman and of all the footmen, and with the help of the attaché, and of the gentleman who had been a visitor at Plessis, succeeded in binding them all on the ground before they well knew what had happened to them. He then briefly stated the exigency of the case to the planters who were not in the secret, and who were scarcely less astonished at the treatment their slaves had received than they were themselves. They were not convinced, however, of the danger. Their contempt of the blacks supplied whatever might be wanting in personal or moral courage, and they persisted in proceeding to their own homes. There was no time for expostulation: so, after their slaves had been disarmed, they were set at liberty, and proceeded with their masters across the plain. It is needless to say that those masters never saw the light of another sun.

The rest of the party crowded into M. de Mirecourt's carriage, which Vincent undertook to drive, with the exception of the Chevalier, who, with a passing farewell, put spurs to his horse, and galloped off at the top of his speed along the rough road as it wound around the side of the mountain ; the sparkles from his horse's hoofs marking his course long after he himself was lost in the darkness. Vincent was no experienced whip, and was entirely unacquainted with the road ; so that their progress seemed slow to their excited fears. Thus they proceeded through the dark night, when of a sudden a ruddy glow shot through the air. They turned their heads, and far away, where it was notched into the mountain's side, they saw Plessis one sheet of flame. It was a beautiful though a fearful sight; but it was one that told the Marquis that he was a beggar.

They were now emerging from the mountain-side upon the plain. They had been hitherto unmolested; but the number of estates they would have to pass rendered the next two leagues of their journey full of danger. This was soon made more clear to them ; for, as if they had waited for the signal-fire to be kindled on the height of Plessis, the whole plain, and the sides of the skirting mountains, were lighted up with a hundred conflagrations. In the glare of this fearful illumination they drove on for a mile or two farther, when they came to an estate the mansion of which was but a bowshot from the road. It was just wrapped in flames, — the negroes could be seen dancing in mad mirth around it, — while fearful shrieks, such as Vincent remembered to have heard ushering in the day at the Cape, and even at Plessis, though now issuing from other lips, were heard above the roar of the fire and the shouts of the insurgent

slaves. It was soon plain that they were perceived,
and their errand suspected. They were loudly ordered to stop; and, when this command was disre-
garded, a company of thirty or forty negroes set out
in full pursuit. It was a pastime that had the charm
of novelty to the pursuers. They had some of them
been the quarry of the slave-hunt; but they had none
of them ever engaged before as the hunters in the
chase of the white man. Vincent had nothing left
for it but speed. He lashed the horses with all his
strength, and gave them the rein. They dashed onward with furious speed, and he hoped soon to leave
his pursuers far behind. But unluckily, when in full
career, sweeping away over the plain, one of the
horses fell, and, though he almost instantly recovered
himself, the accident gave a fearful advantage to the
pursuers.

Before Vincent could put up his steeds to their full
speed again, it was clear that the enemy were gaining
upon him. Their yells sound nearer and nearer; the
light of their torches flashes brighter and brighter
from behind; their footsteps fall more and more nu-
merously upon his ear. The taste they have had of
the white man's blood that night has only maddened,
not satisfied, their thirst. They are even now upon
him. Some seize the spokes of the wheels to hold
them back. Others rush to the horses, and attempt
to hamstring them, and to cut the traces. Vincent
has no longer any control over them as they plunge
and rear in pain and terror. He gives up all for lost;

and well he may, for a more formidable band never set about a work of death. Some bore in their hands huge brands from the burning house, which they waved over their heads ; some brandished their cane-knives in their hands; and others had them fastened to long poles. Some were armed with axes, and some with huge iron bars. Some were almost naked ; and others were fantastically dressed in the rich damasks and brocades of their masters and mistresses. Almost all had blood on their hands or on their garments. They seemed like fiends who had been for a long time subjected to the will of a magi-. cian, but who had at length surmounted the charm, and were enjoying the delight of torturing their tormentor.

They gathered around the coach, and their cry was for blood. Vincent exhorted the gentlemen within the carriage to sell their lives as dearly as they might. They were only armed with the short rapier, which at that time formed an indispensable part of full dress : he had, besides, a pair of pistols. With these, he attempted to keep the insurgents at bay, but with brief success. Uttering a charm which they believed a specific against gunshot wounds, they rush upon him, clambering in crowds upon the coach-box. Others force open the doors of the carriage, and are about to drag out the occupants. All seems to be over when a rushing sound is heard in the distance.

What is it? The assailants pause for a moment to listen. It is surely the tread of horses' feet. It

sweeps on nearer and nearer. Can it be possible ?
Yes, it is indeed the gallant De Tillemont, at the
head of a detachment of his regiment, coming to
their aid at their utmost need. They advance at
their fullest speed,—their carbines are unslung,—
they pour a sharp though scattering fire upon the
insurgents, and then charge upon them with the sabre.
The negroes had not then learnt that they were a
match for the regular troops of France, and they
slowly and reluctantly retired, and left their prey.

This was indeed a deliverance out of the very jaws
of death. But there was no time for congratulations
or compliments. They did not know but that a multitude to which their force might be unequal would
intercept their return. Troop horses hastily supplied
the place of those that the insurgents had wounded,
and in the shortest possible time they were on their
rapid way to the city. Years of sensation were
crowded into that hour. It was worth the experience of many a long life to have shared that brief but
fearful journey from Plessis to the Cape. They met,
however, with no further opposition, and entered the
city just as the bell of the cathedral tolled twelve.

　　·　　　·　　　·　　　·　　　·　　　·　　　·

They were safe for the night; but Vincent was
sure that the insurrection would soon sweep over the
city. He had a vessel in the harbor, under his control, and he determined to make use of her for his
escape. He offered a passage to all his late companions in peril. None accepted it but M. and Madame

de Mirecourt, and their daughter. The rest all felt
safe under the protecting arm of France. But many
months had not elapsed, before they had all of them
fatal reason to regret their confidence. The very
next day, Vincent and his late hosts set sail for
America; and within a fortnight of the day when
M. de Mirecourt rejoiced in the possession of a thousand slaves and half a million of rent, he stood upon
the shores of New York without a resource save the
jewels which Stéphanie the slave had secreted about
the person of her mistress. For a while after his
return to Boston, Vincent heard of them often as
favorites in the fashionable circles of New York; but
at last they disappeared, and all his researches after
them were in vain. Whether they returned to France,
and there perished in the Days of Terror, or whether,
after their stock was exhausted, they carried their
poverty to some distant part of America, where,
under a different name, they could without shame
support themselves by manual labor, is yet uncertain;
and it is not likely that it will now ever be known.
The latter fate was most probably theirs. It was a
common one in those days of change. Many of the
proudest of the historical names of France fled to
this country at the time of the emigration, and, after
shining a while in this new firmament, set forever,
and were seen no more below. Many an emigrant
sunk a marquis, a viscount, or a chevalier in one city,
and rose a cook, a confectioner, or a hair-dresser in
another. In that obscurity did many of the noblest

names of France go out, and leave no trace behind. Had Sterne made a sentimental journey to this country fifty years ago, he might have seen stranger sights than a Chevalier de St. Louis selling pies in the streets of Versailles. If such were the fate of the Marquis de Mirecourt and his family, we may at least hope that they were happier, as they were certainly more innocent and useful, in their humble occupations, than when they rioted in luxuries wrested from the unwilling hands of a thousand slaves.

.   .   .   .   .   .

Such was the story which Mr. Vincent would tell on a winter's evening to his children and his friends. It has a moral, which is not limited by the scene nor the actors of this little drama. It exemplifies the operation of eternal and universal laws. It shows that the day of account will surely come wherever there is wrong or crime. Who knows what country may afford the next example of this awful retribution! Nemesis never sleeps. Though she is long-suffering, she forgets nothing, and overlooks nothing. When men have filled their cup with blood and cruelties and unutterable abominations, to its brim, it is that very cup that she commends to their own lips. There is but one Power of might enough to wrest it from her inexorable hand, and that Power is REPENTANCE.

PHŒBE MALLORY.

PHŒBE MALLORY; THE LAST OF THE SLAVES.

> " But when returned the youth ? The youth no more
> Returned exulting to his native shore ;
> But forty years were past, and then there came
> A worn-out man, with withered limbs and lame,
> His mind oppressed with woes, and bent with age his frame."
>
> CRABBE.

I WAS once a great pedestrian, and have performed feats in my time which should entitle me to a respectable standing, if not an exalted rank, in the sporting world. I used to think little of forty miles a day, and have "made" my six miles within the hour. But all that is over.

> " It is not now as it hath been of yore."

Walking for its own sake, like virtue on the same terms, is but too apt to be an enthusiasm of youth. I have not, indeed, entirely subsided into the opinion which a gentleman, recently deceased, who successively distinguished himself in the gay world, at the bar, and in the pulpit, once pronounced *ex cathedra*, in my hearing, — that " legs are given to man only to enable him to hold on to a horse;" but still a sober ten miles satisfies me now. It will be well for me if this be the only good habit of my youth from which I have fallen away.

During my days of pedestrious grace I resided in Boston, and my walks made me tolerably familiar with the beautiful country that environs it for ten miles on every side; itself being ever the crowning charm of the landscape. It is a great advantage Boston possesses over most other cities, that one can almost immediately exchange the bustle of the streets for some of the most lovely and rural scenes in the world. An hour's drive, or an afternoon's walk, transports you, as it were, into the heart of the country. The winding country-roads and green lanes, hedged with barberry-bushes, might beguile you to believe that you were a hundred miles from a great city, were you not continually tempted to turn and see how gracefully, at airy distance, she seems to sit upon her three hills, and lord it over the prospect.

One fine autumn afternoon about ten years ago, when I had been

> " Wasting in woodpaths the luxurious day,"

I found myself on the summit of one of a chain of hills, looking towards the city. And what a prospect lay before me! On my right were hills covered with woods clothed in the gorgeous hues of autumn, looking like troops of "shining ones" just alighted on some mission of mercy; in the middle distance, tufted groves, village spires, farmhouses, meadows dotted with cattle, and a brimming river sparkling in the slanting rays of the sun; in the distance the city, relieved against the Blue Hills; and on the left the noblest burst of ocean, — Nahant breaking the expanse, with Egg Rock beyond, and then stretching leagues and leagues away, till it had put a girdle round the earth. It was a noble prospect.

After I had feasted my eyes and heart on these glorious apparitions, I was recalled to a sense of the things of earth by the reflection which was forced upon me, that I had had no dinner. I accordingly marked from my hill-top, where all the country lay mapped out at my feet, the course I would pursue on my return home. Descending the precipitous face of the hill, I plunged into

> "An alley green,
> With many a bosky bourne from side to side,"

which led me, though somewhat deviously, in the direction of the city. After I had followed its windings for some miles, I began to wax thirsty, and, to say sooth, a little weary to boot. So I looked about me as I walked, for some hospitable door at which, though no saint, I might ask for a cup of cold water.

I pique myself on my skill in the physiognomy of houses, and it is not at every door, any more than of every man, that I would ask a favor. Accordingly I passed by several houses of some pretensions, but which had to my eye an ill-favored and ill-conditioned expression, and passed onward till I came to one that I thought might answer my purpose. It had not much to recommend it in its exterior. It was a cottage of the very humblest description, the walls of bare boards, blackened with age; but yet there was something about it that made my heart warm towards it. It stood a little withdrawn from the road, and the grass grew green up to the broad flag-stone, half sunk into the earth, which served for its door-stone. There was no litter or dirt about the door; the windows were all whole; and there was a general air of neatness about it which showed that the poverty of the inhabitant was at least not sordid.

It had a promising look, and I knocked at the door. It was opened, after a short interval, by an " old, old " woman, as black as jet, slightly bent by age, and lean-ing upon a staff. Though not expecting to see a person of color, I was pleased to find, that, as far as I could judge from her appearance, I had not been de-ceived by the lineaments of her habitation. Her dress was of the coarsest materials; but the snowy whiteness of her cap and handkerchief, and the scrupulous clean-liness of her checked gown, proved the presence of that virtue which is said, on high authority, to be akin to godliness. She received me with the kindliness and good-nature which mark her race, and, upon making my necessities known, she cordially invited me to walk in. This I did, nothing loath; and, while my hostess was selecting the best of her three mugs for my service, I seated myself, at her pressing instance, in one of her two flag-bottomed chairs, and took a survey of the premises.

They were rough and bare enough, God knows, but still were not without that air of comfort which thorough neatness and good order can give to the humblest dwelling. Her house could boast of but one apartment; but that was sufficient for her purposes. A bed, two chairs, an invalided table, and a pine chest made up the sum of her furniture. The walls could boast of no decoration except a print, over the head of the bed, of the capture of André, in which the cow-boy militiamen were looking most truculently virtuous as André tempted their Roman firmness with a watch of the size of a small warming-pan. The floor was well scrubbed and sanded; and some peat embers smouldered upon the hearth. After I had slaked my thirst with some delicious water, of which she was justly proud, — all cold and sparkling from the open well, ministered unto by the picturesque puritanic well-pole, — she resumed her chair and her knitting; and as I rested myself I entered into conversation with her.

She seemed pleased with the interest I felt in her affairs, and simply and frankly told me all she had to tell about herself and her way of life. She had lived on that spot for many years, and had mainly depended upon her skill as a laundress for her subsistence. As she had grown old, however, and the infirmities of age began to press heavily upon her, she confined herself

20

to the nicer branches of her profession; for the exercise of which the ladies of the neighborhood supplied her with ample materials. Whatever deficiency there might be in her means of comfort, after she had done her best to provide them, was cheerfully made up to her by the kindness of her neighbors; for, to do them justice, neglect of the poor, black or white, at their own doors, is not one of the vices of the people of New England. She seemed to be very well satisfied with her share of the good things of this life, and evinced a degree of unaffected contentment which is not always seen to accompany a much higher degree of prosperity. I was greatly interested in her character and history, and never walked in that direction again without calling to see her. In the course of my acquaintance with her, I learned at different times the simple incidents of her story, which I am about to relate. They seemed to me, when I heard them, to be worth the telling; but I am by no means sure that anybody else will be of the same opinion. Such as they are, however, you have them here.

   .   .   .   .   .   .

Phœbe was born somewhere about the middle of the last century, in the family of the Honorable James Mallory, for many years one of his Majesty's Council for the Province of Massachusetts Bay. He used to live in that fine old house with the Corinthian pilasters, and the magnificent lime-trees in the courtyard, which stood on your left hand as you went down King Street towards Long Wharf. It vanished years ago, and gave place to one of the granite temples of Mammon which have long since thrust from their neighborhood all human habitation. There was Phœbe born. Her father and mother were both of them native Africans, who had lived out all their life of servitude under the roof of Mr. Mallory. They were fortunate in falling into such good hands. The few New England slaves were mostly owned by the wealthy families, and were chiefly employed as house-servants, and their treatment was at least as good as that of the same class in any country. But, Phœbe said, nothing could prevent her father from remembering the day, when, as he was hunting the hippopotamus in the sacred river that flowed by his hut, just as he leaped from his iron-wood canoe to draw the monster ashore by the line fastened to his spear, a party of a hostile tribe rushed from among the reeds, and hurried him to the seacoast, fifty miles away, and there sold him to a Bristol trader. To be sure, he had obtained civilization and Christianity by his involuntary emigration; but — as the one appeared to his half-savage mind to consist in wearing clothes, and cleaning another man's shoes; and the other in sleeping on his knees through family prayers, and in being obliged to listen, from the gallery of the Old South Church, for several hours every Sunday, to sermons which he could never have comprehended, delivered in a tongue he very imperfectly understood — he must not be blamed as ungrateful, if he thought them but inadequate compensations for the exchange

he had made of the sunny skies and golden sands of
Africa for the leaden firmament and rocky coast of
New England.

Phœbe was more fortunate than her parents in
being "native, and to the manner born;" so that
her lot was much more tolerable than theirs. She
was kindly treated, and taught to read and write.
She felt all the strong attachment of the African
race to the house in which she was born and to the
family which had brought her up. To the end of
her days she believed that there was never a house
that equalled in magnificence that of Mr. Mallory
in King Street. There was never anything half so
graceful and dignified as the manners of Mr. Mallory
himself, or half so beautiful and accomplished as the
daughters, or so handsome and good-natured as
the sons, of his house. Many were the Old-World
stories she told me of the loves and the feuds of
that generation, — of their joys and their griefs,
of their festivities and their funerals. A petted
slave, brought up from infancy in one of the foremost families of a small community such as Boston
was then, she became a perfect incarnation of all
the gossip and scandal of that little world. And
some very choice bits of both I extracted from her,
I assure you. She certainly had no artistic skill in
her narrations, and yet there was a life in the very
simplicity with which she related facts, which painted
them vividly to the mind's eye; and I think I have
a clearer notion of the way in which people lived in

Boston eighty years since, from them than from more generally recognized authorities.

Her admiration, however, was not entirely monopolized by the higher powers of the family. There was a certain Ambrose, who had also been born in the house a few years before Phœbe, and had been brought up along with her, who claimed his share. They had played together as children, and worked together when they grew older, and it will not surprise the experienced reader to hear that they fell in love with each other as soon as they were old enough to take the infection. Ambrose was a fine, well-made, athletic young fellow, shrewd and capable, and of the most imperturbable good-humor. His skill in music was such that he was often summoned to the parlor, with his violin, to excite the dance when his young masters and mistresses had their friends with them. Both Ambrose and Phœbe were great favorites with the whole family, — old and young, bond and free, — and their loves were looked upon by all with complacent eyes. They formed a little underplot in the domestic drama, which was not unamusing or uninteresting to the actors or actresses in similar scenes above stairs. Their true love flowed smoothly on, and it seemed as if no obstacles could be interposed to disturb its course. It was a conceded thing that at some convenient season Ambrose and Phœbe were to be married.

While the affairs of the humble lovers were in this prosperous train, great events were at the door. The signs which prognosticate a coming storm were frequent and menacing. Voices were heard in the air, telling of disaster and woe to come. Portents were seen in the political firmament,

> " With fear of change
> Perplexing monarchs."

It was obvious to all discerning persons who were willing to see, that great changes were at hand. Mr. Mallory was a Tory, as might be expected from his official station and position in society. Like many others of his way of thinking, he exaggerated the power of the British king to suppress disaffection, and undervalued the powers of resistance of the colonists. Though he had never permitted himself to doubt that the fever-fit of the Province would soon pass away, still his position was sufficiently disagreeable while it lasted. He had made himself obnoxious to the popular party, and his situation was at times worse than disagreeable : it was absolutely unsafe. Phœbe described to me the night when the mob, flushed by the impunity which had attended their previous excesses, came trooping down King Street to execute summary justice on the Tory Mallory. Their approach was so sudden, that the family had barely time to escape as they were, through the garden, leaving the candles burning, and the work-boxes and books open on the table, as they fled.

Mr. Mallory's house would probably have shared

the fate of Governor Hutchinson's, had it not been
for a singular and unexpected diversion. When the
mob was gathering in the street in front of the house,
and preparing for the assault, the hall-door opened
suddenly ; and Ambrose, like a new Orpheus, issued
from it with his violin in his hand. He immediately
struck up a lively air, and the effect was magical.
The many-headed monster was in a better humor than
usual that night. Whether it was that the edge of
its appetite was in some degree taken off by the sop
it had already had, or whether it was that the patriotic punch (which has never yet had its due as one
of the main promoters of the Revolution) had not
yet more than half done its work, still the mood of
the mob was changed at once from mischief to fun.
This unexpected apparition moved their mirth ; and
Ambrose, taking advantage of their humor, performed
such antic tricks in the moonlight as threw them into
inextinguishable fits of laughter. With all the ca-
price of a mob, they themselves soon began to dance
to his music ; and not all the influence of their leaders
could bring them up again to the point of mischief—

"So Orpheus fiddled, and so danced the brutes."

This danger over, the arrival of the British regiments prevented any apprehension of its renewal.
But the situation of the Mallorys was gloomy and
uncomfortable enough. The gayeties which the arrival of the forces produced in the loyal circles were
no compensation for the breaking-up of old friend-

ships, and for the doubt and uncertainty that hung over their future. At last the provincial resistance began to assume a more threatening form. The siege clasped the town around with its iron arms. The beautiful hills which encompass the town were now changed into mimic volcanoes, belching forth fire and smoke and death against it. All who could and dared fled from its borders. Mr. Mallory's political offences were too flagrant to allow him any choice. He was obliged to abide by the result of the conflict where he was. To be sure, neither he nor his children would ever admit, even to themselves, the probability of the rebels being ultimately successful ; but then there could not but be painful misgivings as to what might befall before the insurrection was finally quelled. It was a dismal winter, indeed, as Phœbe told its private history. Not all the balls and assemblies and private theatricals that were devised to while away the weary hours could dispel the sense of pain and apprehension which their situation excited in the breasts of the loyalists.

It was not long before the forebodings of their prophetic hearts were fulfilled. The dreary winter wore away and the dreary spring began. The intentions of the commander-in-chief were kept strictly secret; but there were plenty of surmises abroad as to what they were. But that Boston, open as it was to the sea, of which England was the mistress, would be occupied by the British forces until the rebellion was suppressed, was a thing that had settled down into a recognized certainty. It could not enter into a loyal heart to conceive that the royal troops could be dislodged from the capital of New England by the rabble rout that surrounded them. But at last the fatal news fell upon their ears like a clap of thunder, that the town was to be evacuated, and abandoned to the besiegers. What distress and despair of those who had placed themselves and all they had under the protection of the British sceptre, and who found it powerless in their utmost need! All remonstrance on their part was in vain. General Howe was inflexible, for he knew that his post was no longer tenable; but he assured the distressed loyalists of all possible assistance in removing their persons and effects beyond the reach of the exasperated rebels.

Phœbe described to me with lifelike effect, for it was what she had the most to do with, the confusion of the few days that elapsed between the announcement of the intended evacuation and the embarkation. The grief of the Mallorys at leaving the home of their childhood, perhaps forever, and the uncertainty which hung over their future fate, was disturbed by the necessity of deciding which of their effects they should take with them. A limited amount of freight was all that could be possibly assigned to each refugee, and it was hard to decide, among all the objects which habit had rendered necessary, or association dear, which should be chosen, and which abandoned. All was hurry and bustle and distress. They were obliged to select such

articles as contained the most value in the compact-
est form, and to leave the rest behind. Their clothes,
plate, jewels, and such other valuables as they could
compress into the smallest possible space, were all
that they could take with them. But all the old
companion furniture, speaking to them of ancestry
and of happier days, the family pictures, the trifles
which affection magnified into things of moment,
because they were seen through the atmosphere of
love and friendship which surrounded them, all, all
had to be left behind them.

It was a dreadful night, that of the 17th of March,
1776 — the last that they were to spend in the home
of their fathers. Early the next morning they were
to embark on board the transports, to go they knew
not whither. The young ladies, deprived of their
usual employments, and their recent mournful occupation being over, as the trunks and packing-cases
were already on board, wandered about the house,
from room to room, like ghosts haunting scenes once
loved, reluctant to look their last upon those beloved
walls. The gentlemen of the family were busy in
making what arrangements they could to secure the
wrecks of their property. It was long past midnight before they retired to rest, if rest they could,
for the last time under that old-accustomed roof.
They had not been long retired, however, when they
were aroused again by a clamorous knocking at the
door, and the intelligence that they must repair at
once on board ship, if they would not be left behind.

The rebels had taken up a position on Nook's Hill, which rendered it necessary to evacuate the town at an earlier hour than the one first appointed. The confusion may be imagined. The carriage was at length at the door, and performed its last service in conveying the family to the wharf, before it passed into the hands of the patriotic gentlemen who had purchased it at a fourth of its value. They found, with some difficulty, the transport assigned to them, and, embarking, awaited the signal of departure.

While they were thus expecting their sailing-orders, one of the young ladies discovered, that, in her hurry, she had left her watch behind her. It had a value beyond its intrinsic worth, as having belonged to her mother. Her distress was great, and the question arose whether there was time to send for it. The captain of the transport gave it as his opinion that there would be ample time. Then who was to be the messenger? Ambrose could not be spared from some essential service in the arrangement of the luggage: so Phœbe alone remained to perform the errand. She was accordingly despatched, with strict injunctions to make a speedy return. It was a raw blustering March morning, and, as Phœbe threaded the narrow streets, the light snow was blown in fitful gusts in her face. She made a somewhat wide circuit to avoid the principal streets, which were now full of soldiers; the inhabitants being under orders to keep within doors until a certain hour. She had some difficulty, too, in procuring the house-key from the neighbor who had charge of it; and when at last she obtained entrance, it was still dark, and she had to strike a light in order to commence her search. Everything seemed to conspire to delay her return to the ship. And, after she had procured a candle, the object of her search was not to be found. She looked for it in every place where it should and where it should not be, but without success. This consumed many precious moments. At last she abandoned the matter in despair, thinking that her young mistress must have the watch about her after all, or else it had been dropped on the way to the ship. After securing the house again, she made what haste she could to the wharf. But what was her amazement and despair at seeing no sign remaining of the good ship on board of which all her treasures were embarked!

She could not at first believe her eyes, and she stood for some time in mute astonishment. But before long her mind received a distinct impression of the dreadful truth, and she made the air resound with her shrieks and lamentations. She flew distractedly up and down the wharf, imploring to be taken on board some of the transports destined for the same port; but no one had any leisure to attend to her. It was in the height of the hurry of the embarkation, and ship after ship was dropping down with the tide, and making what haste they might to Nantasket Roads. Almost immediately after Phœbe had left the ship, orders came down directing her to get under way directly, and she was already out of sight. She remained on the wharf in a state but little removed from distraction, renewing her entreaties to all she met for assistance in regaining her master's party. But all the reply she received was curses, and orders to mind her own business and to get out of the way. Exhausted at length by her exertions, and finding there was no hope for her, she returned in agony of mind to the deserted house in King Street. There, in solitude and despair, flung upon her face on the nearest sofa, she lay for hours, weeping as one that refused to be comforted. The merry peals of the bells, and the distant sound of military music, might have told her that General Washington and his victorious army were making their triumphal entry into the town; but she neither heard nor heeded them. Her heart and her eyes were following the stout ship which was bearing away from her, probably forever, the friends of her childhood and the lover of her youth.

In this state she continued for four and twenty successive hours. But, after the first paroxysm of grief and despair had exhausted itself, Phœbe was not of a nature to abandon herself to fruitless repinings. It was fortunate for her that it was necessary to take some immediate measures for her own support; for the poor girl was now in a singularly unfortunate predicament. She absolutely belonged to nobody. The imperfect legislation of those primitive days had not provided for such a case of destitution. Had she had the luck to live in these times, in the Southern States, such an anomaly could not have occurred. There, the abeyance of the abandoned property in herself would have been terminated in favor of the fortunate finder; or at worst it would have resulted to the State. But in those days, before political economy, she was suffered to escheat to herself. And so she had nobody to take care of her. Thanks, however, to the thorough breeding she had received in Mr. Mallory's house, she was able to command at once her choice of the best services in the town; and she was soon as comfortably situated as she could be under her unhappy circumstances.

The long years of the war, of course, cut off all definite intelligence of the Mallorys and of Ambrose. And the longer years of the peace which followed it brought little more satisfactory information about them. All that was certain was, that Mr. Mallory had been provided for by an appointment in Antigua, and it was taken for granted that he had proceeded thither with his family. The humble Ambrose, of course, had no share in these imperfect advices, and Phœbe was left to guess at his fate as best she might. The Mallorys left no relatives behind them in the Province, and all interest in them or their affairs soon died away. There was but one humble heart in which they occupied all the room that was not before engrossed by Ambrose their slave.

Meanwhile more than thirty years rolled away since the emigration. Phœbe was become a prosperous woman. She had been for some years retired from service, and had invested her earnings in a small confectioner's shop, which was well frequented by those who respected the excellence of her character and of her pastry. She had never married, though not unsought, but still remained constant to the memory of Ambrose; though she had for many years abandoned all hope of ever seeing or hearing of him again.

One afternoon, as she was sitting sewing behind her counter, a man entered her shop. His dress was sordid and travel-stained, and he walked with difficulty, supported by a rough stick. He stood with his back to the light, so that Phœbe could not see his features distinctly. He stood, and gazed long and earnestly in her face. She grew alarmed, and asked his business. In the act of replying, he shifted his position, so that the setting sun shone full upon him. She started from her seat, shrieked, and fell senseless upon the floor.

"I dropped," to use her own words, "as if I was shot." It was Ambrose himself, come in the flesh to claim her at last. Happily, joy is not a mortal disease, or Phœbe might not have survived to tell me her story. Water was at hand, and she soon opened her eyes upon the face of him whom she had loved so long and well. It was changed indeed. Years of slavery had not passed over his head without leaving furrows on the brow, and wrinkles on the cheek. But still it was *his* face, and that was all she asked. Time and ill usage had grizzled his hair, and bent his broad shoulders; but to her eyes he was still young, for she saw him with the eyes of her heart.

It would be hard to say whether pleasure or pain predominated in that first interview. But it was not long before they knew that they were happy. Phœbe took Ambrose to her house, fed, clothed, and nursed him, and finally married him. And though their union was late, and did not continue long, it was as happy a marriage as ever knit two hearts in one.

The story of Ambrose, when he was able to tell it, was simple and common enough. He had followed his master from Halifax to London, and from London to Antigua. There Mr. Mallory died. The young ladies married, and returned to England; and the sons took to bad courses, and died not long after their father. Ambrose was taken in execution for a debt of the last of them, and sold to a Jamaica planter. In Jamaica he suffered for many years the horrors of sugar-making, aggravated by the contrast of the easy service of his previous life. A few months before, he was sent to Kingston with a load of sugar, and, finding a vessel on the point of sailing for New York, he concealed himself on board, and succeeded in effecting his escape. Arrived in New York, he begged his way to Boston, being detained on the road by a fever, caused by the sudden change of climate, and arrived footsore, weary, and sick at heart, little expecting the happiness that awaited him.

Before long, Ambrose grew weary of the town, and, as his health had never been good since his return home, Phœbe sold her shop, and bought the cottage in which I found her. Here they supported themselves comfortably enough for the few years that Ambrose lived. But the hard winters of New England were too much for the constitution of one so long accustomed to the climate of the tropics. He died of a consumption, lovingly watched over and tenderly mourned by his faithful Phœbe.

Such is a plain narrative of the incidents of her life, which I gathered from Phœbe Mallory in the course of my acquaintance with her. I think that they might have been invested with a good deal of romantic interest, had they fallen into the right hands. But such as I have I give unto you.

Phœbe always averred that she was the last surviving slave in the State; and, as I could not contradict her, I was willing to believe that it was so. I confess it increased my interest in her, and made me look upon her in some sort as an historical character. And I could not but think of the day when the last American slave will excite a feeling in the breast of some future inquirer somewhat analogous to that created by the sight of the last mouldering fragment of the Bastille. May that day soon arrive!

Several years ago I removed from the city, and lost sight of poor Phœbe. Not long since, having a leisure day in town, I felt strongly moved to go and see if she were yet alive. Yielding to the impulse, I took the well-remembered road that led by her hut. But it had vanished away, and in its place stood a fine Gothic cottage with an Egyptian entablature at one end supported by four fluted Doric pillars. I knew at the first glance that it would be of no avail to inquire after my old friend at such a structure as this. So I continued my stroll till I came to the village, about two miles off. There I inquired of the first man I happened to meet, whether he knew anything of the fate of Phœbe Mallory. I was in luck in my man; for he chanced to be none other than good master Sexton himself. With the cheerful solemnity which marks his calling, he informed me that she had died about three years before, and was buried in the churchyard over against which we stood. I asked him to show me her grave, which he did with professional alacrity. It is the third grave beyond the elm-tree, on your right hand as you enter the gate, next the wall.

I could not but feel a sense of satisfaction, mingled with regret at the loss of my good old friend, to think that the last relic of Massachusetts slavery lay buried beneath my feet. I felt proud of my native State for what she had done as a State to mark her aversion to slavery; and I hoped that the time was not far distant when she would brush aside the cobweb ties which prevent her from telling the hunter of men in yet more emphatic tones that her fields are no hunting-grounds for him.

I have no taste for monumental memorials, as a
general thing. At least, I see no fitness in attempting to preserve the memory of mediocrity or obscurity by monuments whose very permanence is a
satire on the forgotten names they bear. But I have
no quarrel with the feeling which prompts men to
mark with marble the ground where the truly great
repose, or to record the resting-place of humbler
merit when it is fairly invested with some just historic interest. Of this latter class I esteem the grave
of Phœbe Mallory. And I shall think it neither
absurd nor extravagant, if, within a few months, a
plain white marble slab should be found marking the
spot where she lies, with an inscription somewhat to
this effect : —

" HERE RESTS FROM HER LABORS,

BENEATH THE FREE SOIL OF MASSACHUSETTS,

Phœbe Mallory,

THE LAST SURVIVOR OF HER SLAVES."

OLD HOUSES.

OLD HOUSES.

I LOVE an old house. Even though its walls, battered and decayed, speak of nothing but poverty and toil, still there is something touching in the thought of the tide of human passions and human affections which have flowed through it; of the happy marriages, the joyous childhood, the cheerful age, which it has sheltered; of the many spirits which it has beheld beginning the strife of being, which, after enduring the labor and heat of the longest of life's days, have gone to their eternal home, of whose existence not a single trace remains in any mind on earth. It is not necessary that the many centuries which are required in older countries to invest the habitations of man with the venerable dignity of old age should have swept over its threshold and its hearthstone to sanctify to my heart one of those quaint constructions which I love to people anew with the beings of a vanished generation. All I ask is, that it should speak to me of the past, of the forgotten.

It is my delight to take my solitary walk through those streets of our city which have suffered least

from the levelling hand of modern improvement.
I eschew, as I would an infected district, that mush-
room growth of human habitations which has climbed
the airy heights of West Boston, and filled up its
pleasant valleys, where in my boyhood I used to play,
with a profane load of brick and mortar.   But where
Washington Street extends its tortuous length, and
where the North End displays her labyrinthine maze
of narrow lanes and alleys, — now, alas ! with a pitiful ambition, all erected into streets, as every petty
prince must nowadays, forsooth, be a king, — there,
to the mind of a true lover of bygone days, the spirit
of the past broods as sensibly as over the most ancient metropolis of Europe.   What matters it to him,
that the din of busy life is in his ears, that he is jostled
at every turn by eager traffickers, and that his escape
with life from the thundering throng of drays and
stage-coaches is a standing miracle ?   He hears not
the uproar ; the bustle disturbs not him ; his eyes are
with his heart, in the good old days when schoolboys
played unmolested in what are now the busiest thor-
oughfares.   Visions of fine old men, in a costume
worthy of the dignity of men, and gorgeous dames
worthy of the men they loved, float before his mental
sight.   He walks in the midst of a generation which
now lives on earth only on the canvas of Copley,
where their brocades and satins still rustle, and their
faces still beam with the bloom of immortality.   The
old walls around him are still vocal with the mirth
and gladness of households which many a sorrow has

chastened, with the frolic laugh of children who have long since reached — faint pilgrims! — the utmost boundary of human existence, and gladly laid down the load of life in the still chambers of the tomb. Friendly faces look kindly upon him from the casements; sweet though solemn voices tell him of the days gone by, and remind him that the century that will comprise the lives of all his contemporaries is hastening on rapid wings to join the ages before the flood, and that the hour will soon be here when the memory of him and his will be swallowed up in the advancing tide of coming ages, as a drop of rain melts into the ocean. The roofs under which our fathers lived and died are full of instruction: they teach us a lesson, mournful, yet pleasant to the soul, of the brevity of human life and the uncertainty of human hopes.

This edifice before us is but of yesterday, as it were; and yet who laid the corner-stone? Who counted the cost, and thought he was undertaking a work of mighty moment? Where are the hands that reared the pile, and brought daily bread to their children from their daily toil? Where is she who first established within its boundaries the gentle sway of domestic government? Perhaps she passed over its threshold a smiling, tearful bride, casting a lingering look behind at the happy home she had left, yet regarding the one before her with the hopeful confidence of a woman's heart. Where are the troops of friends which flocked to its portals with cheerful looks and hearty congratulations ? Where are the children, in whose promise and success hearts were garnered up ? They have all departed from the earth. To us they are as if they had never been. One after another their funeral processions have blackened the streets. For each, in succession, have human hearts refused to be comforted, and for a season thought that the sun would never shine on them again as it used to do, until time and care and fresh griefs plucked from the bosom the sorrow which seemed to be rooted there forever. One by one the actors who played their parts on this little stage have withdrawn from the scene, and the curtain long since dropped, when the last lagging veteran retired, and the drama was ended.

But although I love an old house in itself, for its own sake, and independently of any specific associations, yet in a special manner do I delight in the dwellings of my old familiar friends, whose faces are familiar to my eye, whose characters are dear to my heart, whose various fates are as present to me as my own personal history. Mistake me not. I do not mean any of the round-hatted, frock-coated, breeches-less generation which now encumber the streets. I care but little for this stereotyped edition of humanity, all bound alike, and not differing much in the nature and value of their contents, like the washy concoctions of some knowledge-diffusing society.

No, no! I refer to times when "Nature's copy"

wore a dress which spoke to you of the meaning it contained, as in some solemn library the tomes

"Which Aldus printed, or Du Sueil has bound,"

tell you, even before you open them, of the classic mind within.

Too few, alas! of these abodes, consecrated by the memory of departed worth, have escaped the ruthless hands of the money-lovers of this age, who regard one of my dear old houses as only so much improvable real estate, and who think of nothing, when they gaze on its time-honored walls, but how much the old materials will bring. The good old class of " garden-houses," in which it is recorded that Milton always chose to live, is now almost as entirely extinct here as in London itself.

How well do I remember one of these, in which some of my happiest days and merriest nights were spent! It stood with its end to the street, overshadowed by a magnificent elm of aboriginal growth, which made strange and solemn music in my boyish ears when the autumn winds called forth its hidden harmonies at midnight. Entering the gate, you proceeded on a flagged walk, having the house close to you on your left, and on your right the courtyard, filled with " flowers of all hues," and fragrant shrubs, each forming the mathematical centre of an exact circle cut in the velvet greensward. When within the front-door, you had on your left hand the best parlor, opened only on high solemnities, and which used to excite in my young mind a mysterious feeling of mingled curiosity and awe whenever I stole a glance at its darkened interior, with its curiously carved mahogany chairs black as ebony with age, its blue damask curtains, the rare piece of tapestry which served as a carpet — all reflected in the tall mirror, with its crown and sceptred top, between the windows. I remember it used to put me in mind of the fatal blue chamber in Bluebeard. I am not sure now that there was not something supernatural about it.

But it was the parlor opposite that was the very quintessence of snugness and comfort, worth half a hundred fantastic boudoirs and modern drawing-rooms bedizened with French finery. On your right hand as you entered were two windows opening upon the courtyard above commemorated, with their convenient window-seats — an accommodation which I sadly miss — with their appropriate green velvet cushions, a little the worse for wear. On the opposite side of the room to the windows was a glass door opening into the garden, — a pleasant sight to see, with its rectangular box-lined gravel walks, its abundant vegetables, its luxuriant fruit-trees, its vine trained over the stable-wall. As you returned to the house through the garden-door, you had on your right the door of a closet with a window looking into the garden, which was entitled the study, having been appropriated to that purpose by the deceased master of the house. This recess possessed substantial charms to my infant imagination as the perennial fountain of cakes and apples, which my good aunt — of whom presently — conducted in a never-failing stream to the never-satisfied mouth of an urchin of six years old. I thought they grew there by some spontaneous process of reproduction.

A little farther on, nearer to the study-door than the one by which we entered, was the fireplace, fit shrine for the Penates of such a household; its ample circumference adorned with Dutch tiles, where stout shepherdesses in hoops and high-heeled shoes gave sidelong looks of love to kneeling swains in cocked hats and trunk-hose; while their dogs and sheep had grown so much alike from long intimacy as to be scarcely distinguishable. How I loved those little glimpses into pastoral life! I have one of them now, which I rescued from the wreck of matter when the house came down. Within the ample jaws of the chimney, which might have swallowed up at a mouthful a century of patent grates, crackled and roared the merry wood fire, — fed with massy logs which it would take two men to lift, as men are now, — casting its cheerful light as evening drew in on the panelled walls, bringing out the curious *"egg-and-anchor"* carvings, which were my special pride and wonder, and flashing back from the mirror globe which depended from the beam which divided the comfortable low ceiling into two unequal parts. And let me not forget the mantelpiece, adorned with grotesque heads in wood, and clusters of fruit and flowers, of which Grinling Gibbons himself need not have been ashamed. And then the Turkey carpet, covering the breadth, but not the length, of the room; and the books, — the "Spectator's" short face in his title-page, the original "Tatler," the first editions of Pope. But time would fail me were I to record all the well-remembered contents of that dear old room, — the sofa or settee, of narrow capacity, looking as if three single chairs had been rolled into one; the card-table, with its corners for candles, and its pools for fish scooped out of the verdant champain of green broad-cloth. But enough: let us now approach the divinity whose penetralia we have entered, and who well befits such a shrine.

In an elbow-chair at the right of the fireplace, sat my excellent aunt, Mrs. Margaret Champion, widow of the Honorable John Champion, long one of his Majesty's Council for this Province. When I first remember her, she had passed her seventieth year, and she lived in a green old age till near a hundred winters had passed over her head. What a picture of serene and beautiful old age! Her placid countenance, which a cheerful piety and constitutional philosophy had kept almost unwrinkled; her large black eyes, in which the fires of youth were not yet wholly extinguished; the benevolent smile which was seldom absent from her lips — spoke of a frame on which Time had laid a gentle hand, and of a mind at ease. When I knew her, the profane importunities of the fairer part of her relatives had obtained a reluctant consent to abandon the gently swelling hoop and lowering crape cushion in which she once rejoiced. But you could never have seen how she became her decent white lace cap, her flowing black lace *shade*, her rich silks for common wear, and her stiff brocades for high solemnities, and not have known that she was a gentlewoman born.

I attribute a good deal of my love of other days to the short winter afternoons and long winter evenings which I sometimes spent alone with her. I say *sometimes*, for she was not one of the instances of neglected old age; but her society was courted by young as well as old.

"The general favorite as the general friend."

My aunt Champion was born not long after the commencement of the last century, and remembered Governor Dudley. The succeeding inhabitants of the old Province House were familiar to her recollection, from Colonel Shute down to Sir Francis Bernard. She was a staunch Tory, God bless her! and loved the king to her dying day, and thought that no greater men ever lived, at least on this continent, than his Majesty's representatives in the Province. How well would she touch off the characters of the successive Excellencies who in turn did penance in the unthankful office of provincial governor! With what skill (though all unconscious of any) would she individualize them, and bring them body and soul before your eyes!—Shute, with his military bluntness

and frank sincerity, relieved by a little of the sub-
acidity of temper which distinguished Mr. Shandy,
and rather too much aptitude to go off at half-cock;
Burnet, mild and gentlemanlike, fond of pleasure and
of elegant letters, and intended by nature and education for a wider and more brilliant sphere, and whose
gentle nature was not made of stubborn stuff enough
to bear up against the perpetual dropping of the
petty vexations which he encountered in his official
duties, and the dislike with which his genial propen-
sities were regarded by the sterner religionists of the
day. I think that he was my aunt's favorite; but
then his reign was contemporary with her own, and
she looked upon him and his court with the eyes of
eighteen. Then came Belcher, plain, serious, dignified, whose appearance and conversation indicated a
sound judgment and a cultivated mind, but whose
character, though acceptable to the colonists as one
of themselves, and of interests identical with their
own, did not find equal favor with his predecessor in
the eyes of a lively young woman who loved to hear
of the court of Anne and George, and of the brilliant
constellation of wits which shed its selectest influences in that period of Burnet's life when he was the
chosen companion of Addison, Pope, Steele, and Con-
greve. Next appeared the elegant, versatile Shirley,
intelligent, graceful, full of nice tact, which stood
him in good stead in his public as well as private life.
He was the only one of the colonial governors who
so laid the course of the ship of state as to avail

himself both of the tide of royal favor and of the shifting gales of the popular breath, and to keep the helm for nearly eighteen years. His was a glorious reign too.

During his supremacy, Louisburg fell, — an event ever memorable in New England history. With what interest would my good aunt describe the intense anxiety which filled every heart while the fate of the expedition was uncertain! and then the transports of joy with which the news of its complete and almost unhoped for success was received, the sermons, the illuminations, the oxen roasted whole, the oceans of punch, the broached hogsheads of wine; for in those days temperance societies were not. Mrs. Champion looked upon this victory as totally eclipsing all the military glories of the Revolutionary War, and indeed it was not surpassed by any single action of that great struggle: as for Sir William Pepperell, why, General Washington was a fool to him.

Then came Pownal, gay, hearty, jovial, whose brilliant balls and gay dinners almost made my dear aunt forgive his leaning to the popular side. His festivity of temper and the gay coterie with which he had surrounded himself made her sorry, I am sure, though she would never admit it, when he was removed to make way for the less accommodating nature of Sir Francis Bernard, whose saturnine temperament and impracticable temper made him a suitable lever in the hands of an infatuated ministry to

22

detach entirely and forever the American Continent from the British Empire.

Then how many tales she had to tell of pre-revolutionary festivities, of the old aristocratic families, too many of which are now extinct, or scattered by the Revolutionary storm over foreign lands! And again : there were sadder stories of later days, — the bitter scenes which preceded the flight of the Tories from their native land, when they stood, a small phalanx, surrounded by a host of the bitterest foes, filled with a jealousy and hatred even surpassing that of warring brothers ; and when, the cruelest of all, the flame of discord raged in almost every family, destroying all the charities of domestic life, and alienating fathers from sons, and daughters from mothers. And then, when the confident hope which they had entertained, of the power of the British Government to protect them, at last failed them ; when the report —at first disbelieved, and more dreadful than the rebel cannon — was confirmed, that the town was to be evacuated ; what consternation filled all their hearts! To stay would be to encounter the rage of the rebels flushed with victory : to fly, perhaps forever, from all the scenes they loved best, would be to leave their estates to certain confiscation, and to reduce themselves to a miserable dependence on the precarious bounty of the British king. What agonies of indecision, what years of suffering, were crowded into those few hours ! what heart-breakings, when the most obnoxious resolved on flight! what leave-takings of parents and children, of brothers and sisters, of husbands and wives! what partings —

> "Such as press
> The life from out young hearts."

of the beloved and the betrothed!—some, alas! never to meet again, and others not till years of sorrow and of hope deferred had changed their countenances, and perhaps chilled their hearts.

Then she would tell melancholy tales of how the condition of the refugees was changed from that palmy state which their better days had known, of the neglect they encountered, of the poverty they endured; some of them long lingering out a sordid existence in obscure parts of London on the pittance which their royal master allowed them, buried in the utter solitude of a great city; some ending their days in the King's Bench; the most fortunate passing the rest of their lives in an honorable exile, in some petty official station in the pestilential climate of a sugar island.

I do not know whether it is from the sympathy which naturally springs from the contemplation of great reverses in private life, when we are far enough removed from the distorting passions of contemporaries, or whether it is that I caught the infection of my good aunt's enthusiasm, still, though I reverence the fathers of our liberty, and am on principle of the Revolutionary side, I must confess that I do love the Tories. I am glad that I was not old enough at that time to take an active part on either side of the divisions that then rent society asunder — for I am afraid that I should have been a Whig.

Mrs. Champion herself was bound to the soil by too many ties of offspring and kindred to be able to break away. And happy for her it was, or perhaps she would have died of a broken, homesick heart, like her sister, or perished beneath the sun of Jamaica, like her two brothers, instead of attaining a happy old age, attended with all that should accompany it, honored even by those who abhorred her loyalty.

The mention of my dear old aunt has led me far away from my theme; but it is hard to check the procession of images which her name conjures up to my imagination. Let us return to the present day, and contemplate one or two of the yet surviving localities of her happier hours, and mourn over those that have vanished.

The old Province House — for about a century the centre of that world which was comprehended within the bounds of Massachusetts Bay — still stands; but how shorn of its beams! After passing through a variety of evil fortunes, it is now an eating-house; and those apartments which a century ago beheld the assembled wisdom, wit, and beauty of the Province, and witnessed the elegant hospitality of the foremost man of all that little world, now see nothing but greasy citizens, impatient for their dinner, or clamorous for their grog. It still bears some traces of its better days in the iron railings, the freestone steps, and some of the ornaments of its front. It has the air of some ancient gentleman, who, after spending his youth and manhood in a sphere suited to his rank, is reduced in his old age to some unworthy, perhaps menial, condition: whatever may be his employment, and however dilapidated his dress, you feel that he is not in his right place. The old Indian, too, still bends his bow above its roof, and not without his legend, which used to tell my wondering boyhood that at midnight, just as the clock struck twelve, the bowstring twanged, and the shaft sped away into unknown worlds, — whither, I neither asked nor cared. I troubled not my head with sceptical inquiries into mysteries which are the province of unseen powers. Its ample courtyard, which had beheld many a military and many a civil pomp, has been long since filled up with a staring row of vulgar modern brick houses, presuming, like some upstarts newly rich, to turn their backs upon their betters. An envious screen! And yet I do not know but that it is now more pleasing to the genius of the place to have its wreck of former greatness thus shielded from the common gaze. I think it may save the stout old walls some blushes.

Reader, be pleased to exercise at my bidding that wonder-working power which we all possess, and sweep away that mass of brick and mortar, replant the noble trees, and restore the fine old pile to its pristine splendor. Conjure up the men and boys of a hundred years ago, and, as you love me, forget not the women. It is a lovely day in June. All the world is abroad. The country seems to be super-induced upon the town. It must be some special holiday. It is, indeed, the greatest of the year, always saving and excepting Commencement. It is the feast of the ANCIENT AND HONORABLE ARTILLERY COMPANY, the most ancient military institution in the United States, and which was regarded at its creation with a jealous eye by our prudent ancestors, forewarned by the example " of the Prætorian Band among the Romans and the Knights-Templars in Europe." There they are, drawn up martially before the gate, ready to take up the escort. Their presence has just been intimated to the Governor. The door opens, and, surrounded by a splendid cortège, his Excellency appears. Observe his collarless scarlet coat, richly laced with gold, his embroidered white satin waistcoat, his scarlet breeches, white silk stockings, high quartered shoes and gold buckles, and neglect not to remark the cut steel handle of his dress-sword. Mark with what an old-school grace he takes up his cocked hat, and advances bowingly forwards in acknowledgment of the lowered pikes, presented firelocks, and rolling drums of the citizen soldiers, and the hearty shouts of the gazing crowd. Would that time would serve us to follow the procession to the Old Brick, and listen to a sermon containing matter enough to furnish forth a century of the delicate discourses of our times ! Thence we might repair to the well-spread board; and, when those rites have been duly solemnized, we might accompany them to the Common, and witness, with a generation long vanished, the ceremonies of the pomp and circumstance of which we have now but a type. And then the brilliant evening, when his Excellency threw open his doors to a polished and elegant circle unsurpassed at any subsequent period! But something too much of this.

It is about four years since I took a melancholy walk to the North End, to take a last farewell of one of the few historical houses which then survived. I mean the mansion of Governor Hutchinson, a man whose name will by degrees lose much of the odium with which the unfortunate view which he took of the interests of his country has invested it, and whose faults will be thought, perhaps, by posterity, to have been expiated by his misfortunes. When I arrived, the hand of destruction was already there. The house was disembowelled, the windows gone, and the whole scene presented an air of desolation which would have transported a less vivid imagination than mine to the morning — seventy years since — which succeeded the night, disgraceful in our annals, when a brutal and inebriated mob made a ruin of the finest house in the Province, and, what was worse, destroyed collections for the loss of which our history must ever mourn. The political magicians of that day, who foresaw the tempest which was brewing, and thought that they could so direct the storm as to produce only the good

effects of a wholesome agitation of the political atmosphere, found, too late, that in fostering the mob-spirit
they had evoked a devil which they could neither
control nor lay, and which, once raised, seems like to
become the master of their descendants. It will be
many years before we shall see another house at all
comparable to this one of the last age, either in its
architectural excellence, or the substantial elegance of
its internal economy.

From the ruins of this edifice and those of one
other adjoining house of one of the old Tory families
— which well deserves a separate essay for its description — have sprung a crop of SIXTEEN fine new brick
houses, all stark alike, as if they had been run in the
same mould, meaningless, soulless masses of matter.
How heavily must their weight lie upon his soul who
effected the change! I would not have such a load
on my conscience for the world.

Another venerable monument of a former generation has since bowed its head in the dust, and given
place also to a crowd of upstart heirs, who perk their
commonplace, vulgar visages in your face as if they
were of better worth than the noble ancestral stock
from which they sprung. It was the residence of Sir
William Phipps. That " fair brick house in the Green
Lane of North Boston," which, before the tide of his
affairs had turned, he prophetically boasted to his un-
believing spouse that he would one day possess, is forever gone ; and the fine old height, from which it once
proudly surveyed the country round, is the abode of a

brick-and-mortar monster, compared with which the gerrymander was grace and proportion itself. This stately house, to which the adventurous boy had looked forward as the summit of human hopes when he was keeping sheep at Casco Bay, or wielding the adze and the hammer in one of the shipyards of Boston, was completed after his extraordinary enterprise had been crowned with remarkable success, when the hand of majesty had laid the honor of knighthood on his shoulder, and the poor journeyman mechanic had returned to his native land invested with its highest dignity. It is well that corporations have no souls, or I fear that the one which delivered up this last stronghold of the past into the hands of the Philistines would stand in fearful peril of utter perdition.

There is, however, still standing an abode of less aristocratic pretensions, but of more illustrious associations, than those just celebrated. It is the house in which Benjamin Franklin spent his early years. It makes the corner of Hanover and Union Streets on your right hand as you go towards the North End from Court Street, and may be distinguished by a ball protruding as a sign, with the date 1698. I have somewhere seen a letter from Doctor Franklin, in which he says that he was born in this house; but accurate antiquarians who have carefully investigated the subject are of opinion that his father did not remove to this house till after the Doctor's birth; which they assert took place in a house (now, of course, demolished) which stood on the site of Barker's furniture warehouse in Milk Street, a little lower down than the Old South Church, on the other side. However this may be, whether Milk Street or Hanover Street may boast of having witnessed the entrance of the great philosopher on the scene which he so long adorned, still we may be sure that those unpretending walls beheld the first dawning of his infant intellect, and were associated with his earliest recollections. It was from that door that the self-complacent urchin issued with his pocket full of coppers on that famous holiday morning when he exchanged all his treasure for the ever-memorable whistle, and with it bought the experience, which, comprised within the compass of a proverb, he has added to the stock of the world's wisdom. It was in that cellar, that, in his early economy of time, he shocked his worthy progenitor by proposing to have grace said in the lump over the whole barrel of beef which he was putting down, instead of over each piece in detail as it came to the table. Here, too, it was, that his father, patriarch-like, sat at his table surrounded by thirteen grown-up children; of which numerous race I believe there is not a single descendant extant, certainly not of the name. It was to this home, too, that young Franklin returned, after his successful elopement to Philadelphia, with a fine coat upon his back, and money in his pocket — the admiration of his parents and the envy of his brethren. If walls had tongues as well as ears, what histories might not these unfold! Reader, if you are worthy to look upon this hallowed scene, make haste, delay not your pilgrimage till to-morrow, nor even till after dinner; for, even while I write, its fate may be sealed and its destruction begun. In other countries the roofs which have sheltered less eminent men than Benjamin Franklin are preserved with filial reverence, and visited with pilgrim devotion. It should be so here.

Both time and patience would fail me if I were to recount at large the other deeds of destruction which have been worked out within a few years past. The mansion-house of the Faneuils, with its princely courtyard and old French palace-like front, with the grotesque heads grinning from the tops of the windows; the house of the Vassalls, the headquarters of Lord Percy during the siege, and afterwards the abode of Mrs. Hayley, the sister of John Wilkes, with its hanging-gardens terraced to the summit of one of the original peaks of old Trimountain ; the hospitable home of the Bowdoins, eloquent of the past — they are all vanished. The very soil on which they stood is removed, and cast into the sea.

I have lived long, and seen many changes. The friends of my early years are mostly cold, either in death or in estrangement. The grand-daughters of my early loves now reign in their stead. The world is governed by a generation yet unborn when my career of active life began. I have seen heresies in politics and in religion usurp the rightful supremacy of the good old orthodox platform. I have witnessed the decline of hoops, the desuetude of powder, the

almost total extinction of breeches. The last of the
cocked hats, too, has set forever, and is, like the lost
Pleiad, " seen no more below." I have beheld divinest punch driven forth from the society of polite
man, and forced to take refuge in the grogshops.
Even Madeira's generous juice have I seen elbowed
aside by pretending coxcombs from the south of
France and the Rhine. But stay! I take back the
disparaging epithet. One is too apt to undervalue the
merits of newer friends when they interfere with the
modest claims of long-tried and well-known worth.
I will not be unjust to the newer excellence of

> " The gay, serene, good-natured Burgundy,
> And the fresh fragrant vintage of the Rhine ; "

but surely, surely for the solid, serious drinking that
man came into the world to do, Madeira is the only
satisfying good.

All these changes, however, have stolen so gradually upon me, that my natural and acquired disinclination to change has not been rudely shocked.
The times have changed, and I have changed with
them. But the violence that is done to my steadfast
nature by the sudden and total demolition of my old
companion walls, the very scenes of my youthful
pleasures, is mitigated by no gradual and stealthy
approach. The pickaxe enters into my soul. The
difficult tug which in the death-grapple can hardly
bring the sturdy old walls to the ground, too roughly
tears the web of remembered joys. I rejoice to think

that I shall not remain long enough behind to behold the utter extinction of all of my old familiar friends. This roof, at least, under which I write, and which has sheltered more than four generations of my ancestors, will remain to be the abode of my age. It cannot yield to Vandal force until I have exchanged its friendly shelter for "the house appointed for all living."

DINAH ROLLINS.

DINAH ROLLINS.

ALL the world knows that the blessings of the patriarchal system were not always monopolized by our Southern brethren. New England, also, once rejoiced in its benign influences. Although the fathers of New England did not exactly make "slavery the corner-stone of their republican institutions" (for the science of political ethics was then in its infancy), still they were not so fanatical as wholly to reject it from the fabric of their new State. The scarcity of laborers in those early days reconciled some of them to a system, which, when first proposed, they rejected with abhorrence; and the obvious convenience of having their work done without having to pay for it might well help to silence any fantastic scruples as to the justice of the arrangement. Others, again, in whom the religious principle predominated over the economical, thought they discerned the finger of Providence indicating the spiritual things which were to be imparted to the involuntary immigrants in exchange for their carnal things; and they hailed every fresh importation of African heathens as so much raw material to be worked up into American Christians, and thus, before the inception of the foreign or domestic missionary enterprises, united the benefits of the former plan with the conveniences of the latter. The privilege of extending the advantages of modern civilization and Christianity to these savage and Pagan strangers, whose experience of both during the middle passage would favorably prepare them for their reception, reconciled these good men to any apparent hardship in the mode of bringing their neophytes within the sphere of their influences. The happy project of reshipping them or their descendants to their native country, after they had been fully saturated with the blessings of that of their adoption, had not then been developed, or the philanthropy of their benefactors would have received a new impulse from the beatific vision of these new apostles carrying back the civilization and religion they had learned during their sojourn in this favored land to that of their birth ; which, if truly reported to their savage countrymen as preached and practised by the vast majority of ministers and people of almost every denomination, could not fail of awakening in their breasts a holy emulation, and of inducing an instant renunciation of their favorite barbarisms of fighting, killing, and enslaving one another. Notwithstanding this disadvantage, our good ancestors satisfied their consciences as well as they were able, in one way or another, and submitted to be served without wages with the best grace they could. In justice to their memories, however, it should be said that New England slavery was the very mildest form of involuntary servitude. The nature of the agricultural and mechanical productions of that day, the difficult communication and comparatively infrequent intercourse between the different Colonies, and the severe morality which marked the character of that peculiar people, prevented the overworking of the slaves, the separation of families and disruption of natural ties, and that toleration, if not compulsion, of the grossest vice and licentiousness which form the most hideous features of the system as it exists at the present day in this country. Tradition relates that the old slaves often ruled with almost absolute sway over the farmhouses in which they had passed their lives, while by the wealthier families they were frequently indulged more like spoiled children than favorite domestics. Many circumstances might be related to show that the value of " this peculiar species of property " was very different in those days and these ; or else that our fathers were not the wise men in their generation that they are reputed to have been. I will only mention the advertisements which are not unfrequently found in the curious little newspapers of the times, to this effect: "To be given away, a likely negro child of five years old; apply to the printer." Now, among the many modern slave advertisements which I have consulted, whether in the columns of Southern newspapers themselves, or when transferred to the collections of the curious in such matters, as affording the most indisputable, unimpeachable evidence of the true character of the system (unless, indeed, it be true, as was once suggested to me by an elderly gentleman of respectable appearance in a stage-coach, that they are inserted in the Southern papers by the abolitionists, for the purpose of making an impression at the North), it never has been my fortune to light upon an advertisement of this description. Now, as generosity is well known to be the inseparable companion of chivalry, it cannot be supposed that the absence of such advertisements is owing to any lack of a giving spirit. It must be accounted for either by modesty, which shrinks from such a parade of liberal designs, or by a change in the value of the gift, which makes such a proclamation unnecessary in order to find one willing to accept it. The reader must settle this point for himself while I proceed to my *historiette.*

It was in that world before wages, but towards the close of those happy days of primitive simplicity, that our heroine made her first appearance upon this disjointed scene of things. She was "born," about seventy years since, "in the house" of Judge Rollins of Somersworth, N.H., — a circumstance, which, we learn from high authority, brought her as effectually within the protection of the scriptural sanctions of slavery as if she had been "bought with

his money."[1]   If her master happened to be troubled
with any silly scruples about his relation to poor
Dinah and his other slaves, it is a thousand pities
that he lived too soon to enjoy the ghostly consolations just quoted, and others equally cogent and to
the point; as, for example, the positions recently
maintained by a reverend divine (Rev. R. Fuller of
Beaufort, S.C.), that "the domestic relations here
existing" are authorized by God, not condemned
by Jesus Christ, and "expressly authorized" by the
Holy Ghost; and that consequently their condem-
nation by abolitionists is "a direct insult to the
Unchangeable and Holy One of heaven."[2]   In default of such comforters, however, Judge Rollins and
his family appear to have quieted their conscien-
tious scruples, if they had any, by treating their
slaves in the kindest manner. As long as any of
the family survived, Dinah remained an affectionate
inmate of their household. At length, however, the
Rollins family became extinct, as was the case with
many others of the old New Hampshire families,
which helped to transmute the most aristocratic of the
Colonies into the most democratic of the States ; and
poor Dinah was left without anybody to take care of
her. The reader will perhaps conclude from this,

[1] See the passage on this subject in the work on Moral Philosophy by the Rev. Jasper Adams, D.D., president of the college in
Charleston, S.C.

[2] See his Letter to the Rev. Elon Galusha, in the Recorder and
Watchman.

her unhappy predicament, that she either immediately took to begging, if not to stealing, or else
transported her poverty to another State, or at best
came upon the parish. No such consequences ensued, although we are credibly assured that such
must be the inevitable effects of emancipation. She
migrated no farther than Portsmouth, where she obtained an honest livelihood by serving as hostler in
a livery-stable.

I apprehend that a less authentic historian than
myself, priding himself on the dignity, rather than
the truth of his narrative, might be tempted to soften
this circumstance, if not to suppress it entirely; for
in the course of a pretty extensive and careful circle
of studies, including most of the Annuals and Souve-
nirs of the last dozen years, and other kindred
branches of literature, I do not remember to have read
of a single heroine, whatever might have been the
extremity or the variety of her distress, who was
reduced to rub down horses, and sweep out stables,
for her support. I am apprehensive, too, lest my
Dinah should seem to some masters in our Israel to
have been "impatient of her proper sphere," and
to have "stepped forth to assume the duties of the
man" in her choice of a field of labor; and that she
may even come within the range of the fulminations
of the Pastoral Letter of the Massachusetts General
Association of Congregational Ministers, and be exposed to be likened unto "a vine, whose strength
and beauty is to lean upon the trellis-work, and half

conceal its clusters," but which "thinks to assume the independence and overshadowing nature of the elm." I am concerned, also, lest a distinguished gentleman who stands in the first rank, if not in the first place, of our Republic of Letters, and who has lately discoursed eloquently to an elegant audience on the sphere of woman, or some of his admirers (should this little story fall under the observation of any of them), may condemn her as deficient in that perfect propriety and feminine delicacy, which form the chief ornaments of the sex. My business, however, is to relate facts, and not to extenuate them, and I must leave poor Dinah to the mercy of all censors, whether clerical or laic, who may choose to sit in judgment upon her. I must, in justice, however, state, that, great as may have been her deviation in this particular from the gentle elegancies and graceful proprieties of perfect womanhood, it was not owing to anything unfeminine in her education. I am not sure that she is even possessed of those elements of reading and writing, which, according to Dogberry, "come by nature;" and I think that I can assure the fastidious reader that she is perfectly innocent of the knowledge of the classics, of metaphysics, of the higher mathematics, and, in general, of all the eminently masculine branches of learning.

Whatever may be the opinion of the learned, or of posterity, as to the abstract fitness of Dinah's position in the livery-stable, there she was when the

circumstance occurred which I have thought worthy
of recital.   While she was thus engaged in the
charge of steeds, an occupation for which I forgot in
the proper place to say she had the example of the
Homeric princesses and of the dames of chivalry,
she was one day accosted by a white woman who
had once lived at service with her, and who told a
piteous tale.   She had spent a long life in menial
service, and after having drudged for many years,
and endured the caprices and exactions of many
masters, she was now in her old age, and when dis-
abled from labor by infirmity, thrown destitute upon
the world.   No resource seemed left her but the
alms-house, for which she entertained the dread
so common to honest poverty, and which seems to
argue some vice in the system, which cannot be entirely subdued, even when it is administered in the
most humane and enlightened manner.   It was a
common tale, and of every-day distress, such as would
excite but little attention at the corners of the streets ;
but it went straight to the good heart of Dinah.
Here was an old friend in want, and what could she
do for her?   When the heart is opened to receive a
friend in distress, the door does not long remain
closed.   If the heart is large enough, the house
is seldom found too small.   Accordingly, Dinah
soon remembered that her habitation, though small
enough for one, was still large enough for two.   And
as for the increased expenses of her establishment
—why, she must work the harder to meet them,

that was all. Her plan was soon arranged in her mind, and as speedily reduced to practice. She took her old companion to her humble home, and has ever since (it is now several years) shared it and all that it contains with her. So little did she think that she had done anything out of the common way, that it was a long time before her remarkable action became known. Since then she has been an object of interest and of good offices to many benevolent individuals. What has seemed most extraordinary to those who have observed her proceedings has been the natural delicacy and good breeding which has taught her so to dispense her bounty to her helpless charge as to take from it the appearance of an obligation. This, no doubt, arises from the circumstance, that she does not think of herself as conferring one; and having the things, benevolence and forgetfulness of self, it is but natural that she should possess the politeness which is but their visible sign. If she had ever read Cicero (which, as I have already observed, I do not think probable), she might cite in support of her philosophy the wise saying of Socrates, which he quotes: "Whatever you would seem, be." I will mention one instance of her delicacy in her treatment of her guest, which will perhaps be more highly appreciated by some of my readers than by others. "Knowing," as she said, "that white folks don't like to have colored folks live with them," and having but one room for their joint accommodation, she divided it into two parts by means of a line hung with old clothes, that she might give her guest a separate apartment in deference to her supposed prejudices. Her conduct in every respect towards her unfortunate friend, I am assured by those who are well acquainted with the facts, might serve as a model of disinterested kindness to persons of much higher pretensions and greater advantages.

I was told this story during a visit which I lately made to the beautiful town of Portsmouth, and I conceived a strong desire to see the scene and the heroine of it. It was the annual Thanksgiving of New Hampshire, and I was invited, though a stranger, to join an affectionate and accomplished family circle on that domestic festival. The rain poured in torrents; but we heeded it not, for " our sunshine was within." Notwithstanding these inducements, both within doors and without, to stay where I was, I stole away after dinner, from the hospitable table, and proceeded with an old college acquaintance, one of the clergy-men of the town, to the abode of Dinah Rollins. She was not at home when we first arrived at her door, but soon made her appearance from a neighboring alley. And now shall I describe her ? A more pru-dent historian would leave his readers to imagine how she looked; but I feel it due to them and to Dinah to portray her appearance. She certainly was a very different person from the heroines of the gen-erality of the " hot-pressed darlings," which are annually furnished forth by " the trade " to friend-ship and love, as gifts for Christmas and New Year.

She would find herself brought acquainted with strange company in the "Book of Beauty" or the "Flowers of Loveliness." Her face was of the intensest black, and her features of the strongest African cast; but still there was an expression of goodness and benevolence pervading her countenance, which, if it did not amount to positive beauty, at least made amends for the want of it. She was between four and five feet high, very broadly and strongly built. She wore a man's hat upon her head; a cloth cape, like that of a man's great-coat, coming down to her waist, over her shoulders.

She received us kindly, and invited us into her house, or rather room, which presented a different aspect, to be sure, from the scene of elegant hospitality I had just left. The room contained a few rude articles of furniture and a stove. The plastering had parted from the laths of the ceiling; so that the sawdust of the mechanic's shop overhead would shower down at times upon the floor. Within the enclosure of counterpanes and old clothes we found "the old lady," as Dinah always calls her, who has been bedridden for a long time, being eighty-four years old, and so deaf as to be absolutely impervious to sound. She seemed, however, sensible of the kindness of our intention in coming to see her. The devotion of Dinah to her, and her absolute unconsciousness that she was doing anything remarkable, was perfectly beautiful. She did not seem to know but that such a scene was acting in every house in Portsmouth.

In a sort of shed behind her room she showed us a hog of huge proportions, which she was raising for winter supply, and also her harvest of Indian corn, which she had garnered there; for, the infirmities of her old friend requiring more time than her office of mistress of the horse could spare, she had resigned it, and turned her attention to other more manageable modes of getting a subsistence, among which was farming on a small scale. She cultivated to good purpose, as I should judge from her crop, a small piece of land belonging to the town ; and to the honor of the town be it told that it refuses to take any rent of her, thus affording an exception to the general rule that corporations have no souls. She showed us these stores with an honest pride, and evinced none of the shame, or indeed of the consciousness, of poverty.

I do not know but some scrupulous persons may be disposed to find fault with Dinah's *protegé* for being willing to be a burden upon her scanty revenue. Possibly some admirer of the Caucasian race may think it especially unworthy of a daughter of that superior family to receive her support from one of African descent. I would entreat such a one to desist from his speculations at once, lest he should find himself tampering with "delicate subjects," or, peradventure, meddling with what is none of his business. I would, however, in justice to my old friend at Portsmouth, say that she is kept in countenance by multitudes of reverend divines, learned

judges, and honorable women in the Southern States who are provided with board and lodging, and supplied with pocket-money, by negroes. Nay, more; that not a few of the most eloquent advocates of the rights of man, and the boldest opposers of monopolies, in both branches of the national Legislature, and some, at least, of those who from the chair of state have uttered forth the oracles of democracy, are or have been dependent for their daily bread and necessary clothing upon the earnings of colored men and women. So I conceive that Dinah's friend is borne out by the example of these illustrious paupers, and is not to be called in question by any one as to her means of subsistence. Moreover, it should be remembered that her support is given her cheerfully and voluntarily, which, it is said, is not always the case in the other instances I have cited; so that it appears the difference is in her favor in the particular in which the cases are not parallel. I did not hear, indeed, of any attempt on her part to flog, brand, or even sell her benefactress, upon any temptation of pique or profit. But we must make allowances for the disadvantages of her former condition and for the defects of her early education.

What I saw and heard at this visit seemed to imply that slaves may be able to take care of themselves, and to dispense with the providence of a master, without danger of starvation or beggary. I also gathered from it that they were competent, not only to take care of themselves, but of white people too, even though they might not stand to them in the relation of proprietor.   Moreover, I perceived that goodness of heart and refinement of feeling are not limited by color, or conferred by education.   I discovered, too, that the truest riches may be possessed by the poorest person, and that there are nobler acts of munificence than those chronicled in religious newspapers.   Grateful for these lessons, I took a kind farewell of her who had imparted them, and heartily bade God bless her; and if ever I am tempted to take a gloomy view of life, or to despair of the improvement of the race, I shall refresh my spirit by reverting to my interview with DINAH ROLLINS.

University Press: John Wilson & Son, Cambridge.

www.ingramcontent.com/pod-product-compliance
Lightning Source LLC
Chambersburg PA
CBHW051215120726
47905CB00004B/1131